By Katherine Sturtevant

At the Sign of the Star
A True and Faithful Narrative
The Brothers Story

The
Brothers
Story

Katherine Sturtevant

The Brothers Story

FARRAR, STRAUS AND GIROUX
NEW YORK

www.fsgteen.com

Library of Congress Cataloging-in-Publication Data
Sturtevant, Katherine.
    The brothers story / Katherine Sturtevant.— 1st ed.
        p.   cm.
    Summary: In the late seventeenth century, fifteen-year-old Kit, driven to desperation
by the starvation of one brother and mistreatment of his own simple-minded twin, realizes
his dream of becoming an apprentice in London but feels drawn by duty to return home
to Essex.
    ISBN: 978-0-374-30992-3
    [1. Lond███████████████████████████████████████in—History—
Charles II, ███████████████████████████████████████tion.
5. Brothers—Fiction.   6. Twi███████████████████████es—Fiction.]
I. Title.

PZ7.S94127 Bro 2009
[Fic]—dc22

                                                              2008035513

For Joe, who is a good brother

The Brothers Story

1

THE MOMENT I woke that morning I knowed that the firewood was at a end, for the cottage was painful cold. I sat up and began to rub my feet with my hands, but my sitting pulled the blanket from my twin, Christy, who shared it with me, and he sat hisself up as well.

"Awful cold, Kit," he said to me.

"Ye think so?" I answered him.

"My feet ache terrible."

"Rub 'em, same as I'm doing, see?"

He set to rubbing, but his ouching soon woke Mam and Michael, who was huddled together neath the other blanket. We had all fell asleep on our pallets near to the fireside the night before.

Mam stared into the ash and said, "The wood's gone, an't it?"

Her hair was tangled, and her mouth was lacking a good many teeth, and she sounded scared. She was scared most of the time these days, except when her fear bubbled over like a pot does, and turned her to angry hissing.

"It's gone," I agreed as I pushed my stockinged feet into my shoes.

Little Michael set into whimpering, and Mam wrapped her arms around him to give him warmth.

"Well, what's to be done?" she asked me, and her voice was sharp.

I'd have liked to turn the question on her, for she was the parent; I was just fifteen. But who else was she to ask? Dad was dead, and Michael was three years old, and Christy was simple. It was Mam and me together who kept things going.

"I'm thinking on it," I answered her. "But I'd think better with something in my belly. An't there some porridge left from last night?"

There was. It was more colder than clay and had about the same feel to it, but anyways it wasn't raw. I had to make myself eat it, and I made Christy eat it, too.

"I an't hungry," he said, puckering his face up at the nasty stuff.

"Eat it, ye dolt. Food helps to keep the chill out."

So he ate his share of porridge, and Mam did, but we could not make Michael touch his. "Nasty!" he said, and began to cry.

But I pulled him onto my shoulders for a piggyback ride, and soon he was laughing his shrill, hoarse laugh and near pulling my hair out.

Mam stayed fretful. "He must eat!" she said. "And we must have wood to burn, else we'll die, every one of us, here by this cold, cursed hearth!"

"An't there anything we can put to pawn?" I asked as I slid Michael off my back. I looked round the room, but I wasn't thinking of the things I saw—the tabletop on its trestles, the benches and stools and such—but of the nicer things we had when Dad was alive and worked steady on the land. Things was different then. He meant for me to rise in life. He taught me to keep a tally with a piece of chalk upon a wooden table, and later I was bought a hornbook and sent to a woman to learn my letters and my numbers. I got them so quick, and did so well with my primer, that she told my father I was uncommon apt, and said I ought to be sent to a master to learn true reading, and to study writing, sums, and Latin. But before it could happen my dad was took off by the same fever what killed my sister, Jane, and after that our fortunes turned. Just Mam and me was fit to work when there was work to be had, and of course someone must look after Christy and Michael. We sold the cow and the chickens, and put the nice things to pawn, but at last we had no choice but to go on the parish. Then the overseers gave us something for rent and food and firewood, but in wintertime it was only by begging and borrowing that we got by.

"Something to pawn! Of course there an't, ye dolt!" Mam said to me.

So I knowed the pot had boiled over.

"I'd like to pawn yer clothes, and his, too!" she kept on. "I'd pawn yer brains if ye had any. Ye're both about as useful to me as worms to a dog."

I clenched my jaw to keep from saying things a son must not. I couldn't abide it when she put Christy and me together that way. Anyone could see that he was simple and I was not, though 'twas the only difference between us. Our faces was just alike and we had even the same name, both called Christopher on the expectation that one of us would die—him, most likely. When he didn't, they called him Christy and me Kit to make a difference between us.

And it rankled me to hear her say I was not useful—me, who worked on the land whenever I could, and brung my pennies home to Mam like a son ought to do. I was the one who went to market and the one who fetched the ale, 'twas me who stood on the table that I might hang a bag of cheese or barley from the rafters where the rats could not get it, and me who gathered kindling enough to last us through the winter—only I'd not reckoned on it getting so cold. There was hardly any left: a handful of axe chips, some holly, and a piece of tree root. The dried moss we used for tinder was gone entirely.

That reminded me there was some justice in Mam's anger, but I could not keep myself from saying, "If I'm no use to ye here I could go to live in London."

"Oh, ye're always wishing for London," Mam answered me. "Essex an't good enough for ye, I reckon."

"I'm wishing for work is all! I'm wishing to put some fire in the chimney and some gloves on our hands and a decent meal in our bellies instead of a trickle of porridge night after night!"

"Well, ye're not in London, anyways."

After that we didn't speak for a piece. Mam went on murmuring to Michael, and Christy snuffled, and I sat shoulder to shoulder with him so's the blanket would reach around us. Praise God we was both thin as thread, though we was tall. I thought about all the boys I knowed who had gone to London; girls, too, sometimes. Martin Hinde and John Early and Margaret Cole had all gone within a twelvemonth, and Robert Reade and Tristram Kershaw and John Hoby before that. And they was only the ones from our village. Seemed like half of England was making its way to London Town, where there was work to be had, and passing me by to do it. I'd have gone, too, if not for Christy.

I tried to picture that great city filled with working boys: boys in livery and boys in aprons, carrying lanterns or carrying letters, swatting flies or sweeping up turds. Boys running to and fro making all things right for their masters. And prentices, too, up before dawn to help the brewers and bakers, and the tailors and goldsmiths, for that matter. I thought of them with envy, wondering could a boy like me ever rise so high. Nicholas Lawrence was prenticed to a cooper in Chelmsford, and it cost his parents five pounds for his premium. Five pounds. I didn't reckon I'd ever see so much money at one time.

"Ye an't going to go to London, are ye, Kit?" Christy asked me.

"What did I say last time ye asked me?"

"Nay."

"Well, it's still nay." I stood up. "I'm going to the tavern, is where I'm going, to see if anyone's hiring."

I thought Mam would argufy, for we both knowed no one would be hiring today. But instead she quit rubbing Michael's arms and kissing his curls and looked up at me—eager as a dog, but cunning as a cat.

"Aye, go, Kit," she said. "Take Christy with ye, and have another look round for firewood whilst ye're out. Maybe ye'll find a bit of brush or a branch what's been overlooked."

I stared. "Why, Mam, there an't a bit of unclaimed fuel for miles."

"We must have wood, else we'll perish. If there's none to be found, ye must get it another way."

I knowed what was coming, and I could feel obstinancy breaking out like a rash on my face.

"Ye must find us a little charity, Kit."

"We've already took as much as can be spared by our neighbors."

"'Tis the season for giving."

"And they've gave all they could."

"Not Mr. Dean."

It vexed me that she said his name, for she'd promised she'd not ask me to go to him again till a month was past. We'd took a goodly amount of charity from Mr. Dean, some of it as lately as Sunday last. He gave more than I asked for that day, and told me it must last us till the new year, and I promised him it would. But they was charging for firewood like it was Indian calico, and though it was lacking more than a week till Christmas we was without again.

"It an't right to ask Mr. Dean for more, after everything he's gave us."

"What's a few pennies to him, when he has firewood enough to burn down the countryside?"

That was the very way of thinking Mr. Dean disliked. *Do you mean always to be poor, Kit?* he asked me every time I saw him, and explained it was a man's habits kept him poor, and taught me about prudence and thrift and hard work and duty and living by the law no matter what. The preacher taught 'twas God who made one man poor and another rich, and said it was a sin to wish ourselves above our stations. But other times he talked like Mr. Dean, and said the poor was poor on account of their lazy and improvident ways. I did not see how both could be true, so I chose to believe Mr. Dean, who encouraged me, and taught me to do sums with a pencil.

"I'll not ask him for another penny," I said to her.

"Then stay with Michael, and I'll go."

I just stared, for she knowed as well as me that Mr. Dean wouldn't give her so much as a farthing. I was one thing: quick and clever and hardworking when I had a chance to be. But Mr. Dean thought Mam was one of the idle poor, what didn't deserve his help. 'Twas true she didn't spin or knit, for her hands pained her—or so she said. I own they never kept her from working in the Curtis kitchen when extra help was wanted, and eating some of what she cooked there. She'd been in service before she met my dad, and knowed how to cook a sturgeon or make a marrow-bone stew or seal a woodcock pie with so much butter it could be kept on a shelf for many months before eating. But of course a cook must live with the family she cooks for, and Mam lived with us. She might have been a alewife, like Tabitha Osborne, but she liked better to drink ale than to brew it.

"Ye know he'll give ye naught," I said at last.

"He'll give me naught if he knows it," Mam said. "But there's plenty of wood in his hedges for the taking."

"Mam, no! The law says ye may be whipped for such thieving."

"But justices are mostly merciful in winter."

"It an't come to that yet."

"If it an't come to charity and it an't come to stealing, what's it come to, then?"

And I knowed I must go begging after all.

"Curse this weather! If we lived in London it wouldn't have come to this, anyways!"

"Well, we don't," Mam said.

"I an't taking Christy. One of his shoes is broke."

I looked down at him, and he bent his head back and looked up with his mouth agape.

"It an't me makes him go," Mam said.

It was true. Everywhere I went, Christy came along after me. "He's yer shadow," Mr. Pearson at the smithy always said, and Mr. Lowry at the tavern said, "He follows ye like a dog." But they was wrong. A shadow never troubles a body, and a dog will be a friend, if ye let him, and neither one casts doubt upon ye. If I had to say what Christy was, I would say he was like my shame-fullest bodily part: a boil on my backside, some days, or my prick when it rose up at the sight of Kate Haddon's paps pushing at her bodice whilst she served at the tavern. He was that much a part of me.

"Can't I come, Kit?" Christy asked.

"Oh, come on, then, and do as ye're told or I'll leave ye in a ditch and come home without ye. Here, let me wrap yer hands, or those chilblains will never heal."

I looked carefully at the purple splotches on his fingers. He'd been scratching them, but they wasn't bleeding. I bound his hands with rags, and my own, too, for we'd none of us gloves to wear. It was as well for Christy to come with me when I begged,

I thought as I finished my task, for it reminded folks just how bad off we was, with both a child and a simpleton to feed.

"If ye can't find any firewood get some beer off someone and bring it home," Mam said. "It warms a person wonderful well."

But I turned my back on her and walked out into the winter.

2

CHRISTY FOLLOWED ME out the door and almost at once he tripped over a root. He grabbed my arm in the hope of keeping his feet, and we both went down onto that hard, cold ground.

"For God's sake don't snatch at me like that, ye fool!" I scolded once I was standing again. I pulled him up after me and added, "And walk more carefuller."

"I'll walk more carefuller, Kit."

He smiled one of his smiles—he had about a dozen, different ones for different uses; they was like words for him. This one was confident and promising, like he hadn't just gave us both a new set of bruises, or like the chill wasn't needling through him the way it was through me. Between us we was wearing every stitch we owned—more of it on me than on him. I wore my dad's old coat, which was everywhere spotted and patched. It was much used before it ever came to his hands; 'twas heavy with years of dirt and rank with the sweat of folks I'd never met. My breeches was of coarsest grogram—wool and mohair mixed—and was stiffened with gum; they was itchy and scratchy together.

"Where we going, Kit?"

"Going begging," I said.

"To Mr. Osborne's?"

"Now, why would ye think that?" It was clever in him, I thought, for there was three cottages on the road before the Osborne place, and I'd stopped at all of them plenty of times with my hand open. But they was like spots in the river what's been fished out, and I knowed for certain there wasn't another farthing to be got at any of them before Lent. Most likely Dick Osborne had been fished out, too, but it was a place to start.

"Because ye like him," Christy said, and I laughed, for it was true.

Dick was a packman, or peddler, as some say. Spring to autumn he walked round England with a pack on his back, and winters he came home and lived with his sister, Tabitha, who brewed ale—or knitted stockings, or spun thread—whatever she must to make shift.

I liked to look at Dick's ware, when he had some to show: muslin and fustian and blue linen what he sold by the yard; gloves and stockings; hoods and caps; needles and pins and sewing tape; and buttons made of bone. He carried a few pretty trifles what could be used for the giving of courtship gifts, such as bracelets and little looking glasses. Then there was the writing things: parchment, pens, knives, and wax; and the reading things: little books of tales, some godly and some merry, which he could read in a slow, halting way. Once he showed me a pack of playing cards, and another time a almanac what had a picture of all England in it. He pointed to the great towns: Oxford and Norwich and Bristol and of course London Town, and said he had been in them all. It was a wonder to me, for I had never been farther than the market in Chelmsford. I liked to listen to his stories, too, though they was sometimes dark to hear: the awful weight of his pack near breaking his body as he trudged the road with it, or how he was locked up in one town, and whipped in another.

This is how it was: he went up and down England trading his ware for shillings, and when his pack began to grow empty he took to trading his shillings for hair; that way he was not a mark for robbers as he came back to London. 'Twas English maids and wives what did the selling. Long, gleaming tresses they was, dark as a crow's feathers or fair as spun flax, and every color in between. In London he sold the hair to the peruke-makers, who turned it into wigs for gentlemen. He let me touch some once, a soft coil of hair the color of ripe horse chestnuts, the ones we used to play at conkers every autumn. I petted it with my finger and wondered would any maid ever let me pet such a glory while it yet lay warm upon her head.

Mr. Osborne and his sister was both at home—where else would they be in such weather? They welcomed me heartily, which didn't mean they'd give us money; it was just their way. The rooms in their cottage was ceiled, so that the hot air did not rise to the rafters as in ours. The moment we was through the door the heat began snaking over us, curling round our noses and petting us like we was cats. Dick pushed us right up to the fire so's we could warm ourselves, and Tabitha went off to the buttery. Soon she was back with a pewter mug of barley beer in each hand.

"I wish it was mulled wine, instead," she said with a smile as she passed me one.

"Thank ye, Mistress Osborne, this'll do wonderful well," I answered her. I'd have liked to know what mulled wine tasted like, or any kind of wine, but all the village said Tabitha Osborne was a fine maltster, and I was happy enough to take what she brung me.

Just then I saw Christy about to make ruination. "Don't sit on that, ye dolt, it'll break!" I cried out.

Christy straightened hisself and smiled his guilty smile.

"Oh, that pen's a sturdy one," Tabitha said. "No, Christy, the hens will bite ye if they can. Come, I've some barley beer for ye."

He gave up poking at the chickens through the wicker with his rag-bound hand, and came to get what she held out for him.

Dick settled back down in his oaken chair. He was a short man, but his shoulders was like hams and his chest like a barrel. He had dark, lank hair what was sprinkled with the scurf that fell from his scalp, and a brown, freckled, merry face.

"How is it at yer place, Kit?" he asked me.

I stood with my hat in my hands and made my face grave. "Not so good, Mr. Osborne."

"Food?"

"Plenty of barley, but no firewood to cook it over."

"This weather's a curse, an't it? The little I brung home to last the winter's being ate up so fast it's frightening."

Mistress Osborne shook her head. "It'll be gone before January's out, and I don't know what we'll do."

"We'll sell some of yer fine wool," her brother said to her.

She was working at her spinning wheel whilst we talked. It

was a wonder to me how the unruly fibers was twisted by that machine into usefulness and order. We had a spinning wheel once, but it was put to pawn after Jane died. I turned to look at Christy. He was leaving the hens in peace, and now studied the printed woodcuts pasted on the wall; he always loved to see 'em. They wasn't anything pretty, just people milking cows or drinking at a alehouse or selling sheep at a fair. Poor man's pictures. Dick sold them all round England, and put one of every kind he sold upon the wall of his own house. I liked to look at them as well, but only to aid me with my letters—Dick had read out the captions neath the pictures so many times that I'd learnt the words in 'em.

"Wish I could help ye, Kit," Dick said at last. "There's a man in Northumberland owes me eight shillings for muslin neckbands I sold him—if I had it now I'd share."

"If ye had it ye'd pay what ye owe Mr. Jackson, that linen-draper in Milk Street," his sister said. Her wheel clicked, and she quit working it, for she'd spun a full hank now.

"Why, not with him off in London and Kit right here beside me," Dick said with a wink, and we all laughed. Even Christy laughed, not knowing why. Maybe just for the good rich sound of it filling up the room.

I drained the last of my beer and got up to go.

But Christy said, "Ye going to give us a penny, Mr. Osborne?"

"Hush yerself, ye great dolt!" I said to him. "If ye can't be bothered to listen, then hold yer tongue and ask me after, haven't I told ye a thousand times?"

"I fear ye'll be telling him till Judgment Day," Dick said with a sorrowful look. "He's a trial, that's certain."

But Tabitha squeezed Christy's hand and said she would give him a penny if she had one to spare, and Christy smirked in my direction, like he'd got the better of me.

We left soon after, and the moment we stepped outside, the heat we'd took in was sucked clean off us, and the cold felt more colder than it did before we got there. We tramped down the road toward the tavern, me wondering who I'd best go to next. The squire never gave but on the Lord's Day, and then never more than a penny.

"Where we bound now, Kit?" Christy asked me.

"Searching for firewood," I told him.

He looked from one side of the road to the other as though he expected to see a fallen tree and a axe to cut it with.

"Look for something made of wood," I said. "Anything."

He put his mind to it. "Mr. Grayson's house is made of wood," he said, staring at it as we passed.

"We an't going to burn any houses in our little grate," I said. We trudged on.

"Mr. Potts has a wagon made of wood," he said after a while.

"Will he let us use it in the fireplace, Christy? What d'ye think?" I let my voice give away the answer, and he got a pleased-and-proud smile on his face.

"Mr. Potts an't going to let us burn his wagon for firewood," he said, shaking his head.

"We don't mostly burn houses and wagons in our grate, do we?"

"We *never* burn houses and wagons in the grate!"

Now we understood each other, and we went as far as the tavern on the strength of it, hoping to get a few pence from Mrs. Lowry, or anyways to warm ourselves by the fire.

The room was filled up with folks who had come to spare their own fuel, crowding near the hearth and drinking ale or wine and smoking their pipes and talking all at once, so there was a roar of words but not a sentence what could be understood. The air was thick and dark with smoke. For a moment I breathed it in and thought, Hell must be like this, and wanted to go there, so's never to be cold again.

I looked round for Kate Haddon, and finally saw her: she stood with a tray at a table near the fire. The man sitting there had his arm around her arse and I wished I was him. Once at Christmas revels Kate let me kiss her, and I think she would have let me touch her bosoms if I'd tried. But I dared not with Christy hanging by, for he hadn't wit enough to keep secrets.

"Why, Kit, are ye out in this cold?" Mrs. Lowry said to me, and I had to look away from Kate. "I hope ye an't come to ask for more money, after what I gave ye Thursday last? For I've naught to spare."

"Only searching for work, Mrs. Lowry. Or for firewood."

"Must have been Christy's idea, that," came a voice.

I knowed who said it before I looked, and changed my mind about wanting to go to hell, being deadly certain John Frith would be there, still dressed in the squire's gold-and-black livery. He was the boy in all the world I envied most, for he spent many weeks of the year with the squire in London, and when he came back told tales of it what aimed to make a body feel low for never having went there.

"We an't fool enough to sit by a cold grate and expect the firewood to fall down the chimney," I answered him as Mrs. Lowry moved on.

But he wasn't through with us. "My master gave ye a penny only Sunday—it an't gone already?"

"Ye're lucky everything is provided for ye," I said. "If ye had to pay for firewood from yer own pocket, ye'd be begging yerself."

"I reckon God knows who deserves good fortune," he said with a smirk.

If he liked to know who God favored he ought to have looked at hisself in a mirror, and then at us. John was short of stature with a crooked shoulder. Christy and me was tall and straight, and our shoulders was broad. John's face was scarred and spotted; we had only some scattered pimples what hid themselves in the red of our cheeks. But for all that he looked fine in his livery.

"How ye keeping, Christy?" John asked.

He never could leave my twin alone. Generally I took Christy off when I saw him coming, but the numbness in my fingers was just starting to go, and I had hope for my toes if we stayed a little longer. Christy must take his chances.

"Keeping fine," Christy said. He was using his slow, hopeful smile, the one what meant things might not be easy as beans but they couldn't be as bad as last time.

"Learned yer numbers yet?"

"I know my numbers, John."

"Leave him be, why can't ye?" I said. I was cross with John for tormenting my twin, but more crosser with Christy for smiling through his torment.

"I know my numbers, Kit," Christy said, sounding sure and glad, like he'd saw the stones across a brook and knowed he could get to the other side.

"Why, that's fine, Christy!" John clapped him on the shoulder. "Say 'em for me, there's a lad."

"One two three four five six seven eight nine ten."

"Beautiful! And after ten?"

Christy looked like one of the stones he was stepping on had begun to wobble under his foot.

"If ye don't know what follows ten ye've no business to ask him about it, he's not the schoolmaster," I said.

"One two three—" Christy began again.

"Hush up, fool," I said angrily.

Christy stopped talking.

"He can't help it he's a idiot," John said. "Born that way, wasn't ye?"

Christy said what he'd heared me say of him a hundred times. "I an't a idiot. I'm only simple."

John laughed like he'd never heared anything so funny, and Christy smiled again.

"Look at that smile, what a grinagog he is!" John said.

"An't a soul in the village wouldn't rather see Christy's smiling face than yers," I answered him, and he scowled.

Then the squire called John to bring him his horse, and I knowed it was time to do what I must.

3

"WHERE WE GOING, Kit?" Christy asked again when we was once more tramping down the road with our teeth achatter.

"Mr. Dean's," I said, grim as the gray sky.

He stopped dead in the road, and I saw the same obstinancy in his face I'd showed to Mam in my own. "I don't want to go, Kit."

I knowed I must be careful, for Christy could be stubborn. I did not want him to settle his arse upon a rock and refuse to stir.

"Why, ye needn't worry, Christy. I'll be with ye every minute. Anyways, he never killed a boy yet."

"But I don't remember my lesson."

I'd forgot Christy's lessons. Often when we saw Mr. Dean he tried to teach Christy something, and promised him a groat if he knowed it next time they met, but of course he never did know it. If we but had that coin now! It was worth the same as four pence.

"I can help ye to remember it, Christy," I said. "'Twas from the Bible, Book of Proverbs, don't ye recall? 'The fear of the

Lord is the beginning of knowledge: but fools despise wisdom and instruction.' "

I'd laughed out loud when Mr. Dean said it, and he smiled, too. It was like we was in league against Christy, and later I felt bad about it, but good, too.

"I don't want to go, Kit."

"Well, ye're going anyways, and ye're going to know yer lesson this time, and Mr. Dean'll give ye a groat, won't that be nice? We'll get a bit of firewood, and Mam'll be so glad and grateful."

"She'll be grateful to me?"

"Course she will. Now, say it after me. 'The fear of the Lord.' "

" 'The fear of the Lord.' "

" 'Is the beginning of knowledge.' "

" 'Is the knowledge.' "

" 'Is the *beginning of* knowledge.' "

" 'Is the *beginning of* knowledge.' "

That went on all the way to Mr. Dean's, which was a mile or more along the road to Chelmsford. Christy was a good walker, not swift but innocent and enduring, like cattle took to market. Twice he spoke the verse perfectly, but only right after I said it myself, and I couldn't do that in front of Mr. Dean. I wondered would Mr. Dean give him tuppence even if he got it a bit wrong.

"There it is," said Christy, for we was in view of Mr. Dean's farmhouse now, with its many gables and its raised design of scallops upon the whitewashed plaster. Only the squire's manor house of yellow brick was grander.

As we came near I saw Zeke Bailey carrying a bucket; it was

him who looked after Mr. Dean's livestock. He waved a hand at me and called out, "There's football Saturday afternoon. Can ye play?"

I shook my head and jerked a thumb at Christy, and he nodded and kept on to the barn.

Zeke and me was of a age. We used to play football together with the other boys of the village, whilst I kept one eye on Christy, who was likely to wander. The last time we played, the match growed so fierce I forgot to look toward my brother, and when the game was done we'd searched a hour before we found him sobbing and shivering by the creek. Since then I dared not play football anymore.

"Is Mr. Dean at home? Will it trouble him to see us at once?" I asked Betty, the scullery maid, when she opened the door.

"It would trouble *me*," she said. "We're baking this afternoon."

We followed her into the floury kitchen, where Susan, the cook, was patting the dough just so, making it all ready to bake. There was another loaf on the molding board, and more dough in the kneading trough. Betty went quick to work and raked the embers from the round brick oven near the hearth. The heat was lovely. I reckoned the wood they used was from the very hedges Mam spoke of; they say hawthorn is the sweetest wood for baking bread.

Christy sidled toward the warmth of the oven, and I pulled him back by his coat to keep him out of Betty's way.

" 'The fear of the Lord is the beginning of knowledge: but fools despise wisdom and instruction,' " I hissed at him, and I meant it.

"*Now* I'll ask if Mr. Dean can see ye," Betty said, once the bread was slid into the oven on the blade of the peel.

We was nearly thawed by the time she came back, and Mr. Dean after her. He was not dressed for the fields, but had his wig and waistcoat on, like he expected company. I wondered did I disturb him from important matters, and was uneasy at the grave look he turned to me.

"I hope you have not come to ask me for more money so soon as this," he said to me.

"No, sir, but Christy has worked hard remembering the Bible verse ye taught him, and would like to say it over and have his groat."

Mr. Dean looked at me so intent I wished we had not come. The thing had seemed full honest and honorable when first I thought of it, but I saw Mr. Dean was thinking differently. I knowed I ought to tell him how it was at the cottage, and why we needed more of his charity, but instead I found myself saying, "Never mind, sir, if ye think not."

"If your brother can recite the verse, of course I will give him the groat," Mr. Dean said. "Can you do it, Christy?"

Christy stared at his shoes, and I stared at them, too. The broke one had a piece of twine tied around it to hold it closed.

"I am waiting, Christy."

"The verse. Ye know it, Christy, ye've said it a dozen times today."

"The fear of the Lord?" Christy asked, making sure he understood what was wanted.

"That's the one!" I said to encourage him.

And he rattled off in a pure, confident way, "The fear of the

Lord is the beginning of fools, but they despise wisdom and in-struction."

"I'm afraid I cannot give you a groat for that, Christy," Mr. Dean said with a big smile.

"I'm sorry, sir. I thought he had it."

Mr. Dean put a hand on my shoulder and said, "You were right to try. Circumstances this winter are extreme."

My heart lifted, for it sounded like he was on his way to giv-ing us a little something. But just then Zeke came into the kitchen still wearing his hat, and before he saw his master there he said to Betty, "The heifer has died."

Then there was a moment of awful silence.

Mr. Dean was the one to break it. "Kit, I will speak with you another time. Betty, bring my stick."

"'Twasn't my fault, sir!" Zeke cried out as Betty hastened to the parlor without a glance at him.

I was sorry for Zeke, but more sorrier to see my chance of a little firewood take wing. There was nothing could be done about it, though. I made my bow, and nudged Christy so's he'd bow, too, but instead he blurted, "Circumstances this winter are ex-treme," like he was trying to memorize it.

Mr. Dean turned on him with a look that seemed to take back every good turn he'd ever done for my family.

"He can't help it he's a idiot, sir," I said. I grabbed Christy by the hand and pulled him after me, and then we was outside again, none the better for having walked all that ways.

We'd not been long in Mr. Dean's kitchen, but in those few minutes the sky had growed low and dark, and the air so cold it hurt to breathe. Then Zeke commenced howling, so we knowed

Betty had got to the kitchen with the stick. It was a piercing sound, and I'd have flinched to hear it, only I knowed he was making a show of it to persuade Mr. Dean he was in pain, that he might leave off the sooner. It was what I did myself in the days when I was beat.

"I an't a idiot. I'm only simple," Christy said.

"Ye're idiot enough to be the ruin of this family!" I said, and went on ahead without waiting to see if he followed. I walked fast as I could in the dark shade of the hedge, and the faster I walked, the angrier I growed. Maybe it was losing the chance of a groat, or maybe it was the way he kept me from playing football, or maybe it was because I'd checked my wrath so many times that day already I could not do it another time.

But I couldn't use the heat of my temper to warm the cottage. Mam was waiting on me, counting on me, to bring back something combustible. I looked up at the hedge, that great living fence that divided Mr. Dean's fields from Mr. Hayter's, thinking of how much wood it held. It was three or four feet thick and nearly twice my height.

Christy was coming along behind me, but more slower. "I'm sorry, Kit!" he called after me, for he knowed I was angry with him.

His voice was forlorn, which I could never abear. As I turned forgivingly toward him, my eye seized upon a piece of dim sky peeking through a hole in the hedge. A great, gaping hole. I stopped. We wasn't the only poor family in the village, and someone had come here before us—Robert Fryer, most likely, trying to keep his old father alive. They got nothing from the parish, for Robert was growed and could work if he would, but mostly he drank instead.

I stared at that circle of sky, trying to think. On the one hand, I knowed that if I did as Robert had I'd be throwing away my hope of someday being better off than I was now, for what man rises in life by stealing? 'Twas against the commandments, and against everything Mr. Dean had taught me, too. On the other hand, Mam was waiting for me. 'Twas my duty to care for the family, now that Dad was gone.

"What is it, Kit?" Christy asked me.

"Wait a minute, can't ye? I'm thinking."

We might not be catched. There was no one in view just now. But it was a ways to the cottage, and if we went on home with our arms piled high with wood we would most likely meet someone before we got there, and who was to say how forgiving that someone might be?

But it wasn't the thought of a whipping what kept me frowning at that bit of sky. It was Mr. Dean's kindness and encouragement. It was wanting to be the sort of boy he thought I was.

Only we had to live. Ye couldn't get past it, we had to live.

That's what was on my mind when the bird fell dead at my feet.

I bent and picked it up. The warmth hadn't faded yet from its feathery corpse, and I could feel it through the rags wrapped round my hands.

"What happened, Kit?"

"Froze to death, maybe." I was thinking how long it'd been since we'd ate meat.

Christy looked up into the sky like it was going to start raining dead birds. Then he looked at the pig trough in Mr. Hayter's field on the other side of the road and said, "We *never* burn pig troughs in the grate."

That was true enough, and anyways, it wasn't our trough, it was Mr. Hayter's. But there's other things not meant for burning what can be cast into the fire in extremity.

"Come, Christy," I said, and his face gladdened when he heared my cheery voice. For I knowed now how we was going to cook that bird.

4

WHEN MAM SAW what we brung and what we didn't, she
looked like she might cry.

"Don't worry yerself, Mam," I told her. "We'll burn the
trenchers. Or if they'll not make a lasting enough fire, then we'll
burn the trestles what hold up the tabletop."

"But, Kit, what'll we use to buy new ones when those have
gone?"

"We've enough trouble today without thinking about tomorrow," I said.

So Mam cleaned the bird of its feathers and cut it up and put
it into icy water along with some turnips and carrots and a little
crumble of dried herbs, whilst I set about splitting up the wooden
trenchers we had ate off of so many times. When that was done I
put the last of the kindling on the hearth and wondered what to
do for tinder. After thinking on it for a bit I went for our Bible,
which was maybe irreligious, but it was only half a Bible, having
been tore in two by someone long ago. We'd already tried to

pawn it but could not. We none of us could read it anyways, though I could sound out some of the words if they wasn't long.

Christy hung behind me, worrying, whilst I tore pages from the Bible. "What story ye burning, Kit?"

"God knows," I answered him.

"Ye won't burn the brothers story?"

He could have meant Cain and Abel, or the Prodigal, or Esau and Jacob. I used to think the Bible had more stories about brothers than any other subject. But I knowed it was Joseph and the coat of many colors he had on his mind.

"Doesn't matter, Christy. Even if the words was burned up, the story'd last after."

I leaned the sticks against each other so that they circled the kindling, took up my flint and steel, and let fall a prayer, for 'twas nearly dark now. I struck the one against the other, but did not get a spark. I failed a second time, and a third. The fourth time I missed the steel in the dark.

"It an't the brothers story, is it, Kit?"

"I told ye I don't know!" I said, striking again.

But he couldn't be easy about it, and kept asking till I finally told him we was burning the Ten Commandments. That satisfied him, and on the next try I got a spark, and it catched the dry paper and began to flame.

Christy stared at my sticks and said in a wondering voice, "We *never* burn trenchers in the grate."

"This is a winter of nevers," I answered him.

Pretty soon we had us a better fire than we'd had all winter, if truth be told, for we hadn't the means to buy seasoned firewood, and the green branches we usually burned spit and smoked in a terrible way. But the trenchers was old and made lovely flames. Mam hung the pot from the chimney bar, and we pressed near to the fire. We had to pull at Michael to bring him close, where he sat pale and limp as a wilted plant.

"Come, Brother, hold yer hands up." I took his hands in mine and held his little palms to the warmth, and he sighed with pleasure.

We had to burn all the trenchers we owned to get that bird cooked through, but it was eatable at last. Christy had broke our earthenware bowls long ago, so we ate from the ladle till we'd each had four turns. Then Michael and Mam had a fifth turn and there was just about a ladleful left.

"Ye can have it," I said to Christy. "I'm near to satisfied, any-how."

"Nay, Michael needs it more," Mam said.

"Why, Mam, he's had his fifth turn. I been counting."

"What's turns to do with it? He that needs it must have it."

Christy looked from one to the other of us with a anxious lit-tle smile, and then at the last morsel of stew with pure longing. As for Michael, he seemed hardly to care; he was leaning back against Mam with his eyes closed, like he was ready for a nap.

"It an't Michael's been out in the cold," I said, reasonable.

"Why, then, they can share it," Mam said at last, and gave a bit over half what was left to Michael, and then the final dribble to Christy.

We passed the chamber pot among us and settled down on our pallets to sleep, wanting to drop off while the room still had a bit of warmth. But it was one of Christy's restless nights; he kept turning over and the blanket would follow him, so's I had to jerk it back. I stood it as long as I could and then gave in. "What's fretting ye?" I hissed at him.

"Are ye sure we didn't burn the brothers story, Kit?"

I sighed. "If I tell it, will ye settle down?"

"If ye tell it, I'll settle down," he promised.

"All right, then. Once there was a man named Jacob—and sometimes he was called Israel, so he had two names. And he had two wives; they was sisters. The pretty one was named Rachel, and the plain one was named Leah. Leah had many sons—"

"Tell about Reuben."

"Leah's oldest son was Reuben, he had a kind heart. Rachel only had two sons, Joseph and Benjamin. Jacob loved Joseph best, and he gave him a coat of many colors."

"How many colors, Kit?"

"The Bible doesn't say that part. Only God knows."

"Did it have red?"

"Must have had red."

"Did it have blue?"

"Only God knows, Christy. But I'll guess if ye like."

He always wanted me to guess.

"I'm guessing it had red, and blue, and green, and yellow, and orange, and violet."

"Violet's my favorite color, Kit."

"I know it is."

"Wish I had a coat of many colors."

"Wish I did, too. We could use it tonight, couldn't we?"

"Tell more, Kit."

"Well, Joseph's brothers hated him because their dad liked him the best of all. 'They could not speak peaceably unto him.' "

I gave that line just how the preacher did, because I always liked it. There was plenty of folks couldn't speak peaceably unto Christy, and then there was some—like John Frith—I had trouble speaking peaceably unto myself.

"But Reuben didn't hate him," Christy said.

"Joseph had a good many dreams, and he knowed how to tell their meanings. He had a dream that he and his brothers was binding sheaves of wheat in a field, and his sheaf stood up straight, and all the other sheaves bowed down to his. And he had another dream that the sun and the moon and eleven stars bowed down to him. The sun and the moon was his father and mother, and the stars was his brothers. 'And his brothers hated him for his dreams, and for his words.'" That part was how the preacher said it, too. "One day Joseph went out to where his brothers was herding sheep, and they saw him coming from a long ways, because of that coat. And they decided to kill him and throw his body in a pit and say evil beasts killed him."

"What sort of evil beasts?"

"Any kind. The Bible doesn't say. But Reuben said, Let us not kill him, but put him in the pit where he may chance his luck, that way there'll be no blood on our hands. So that's what they agreed to do. And when Joseph came close, they took his coat and throwed him in a pit. But then some men came along on camels, they was going to Egypt, so the brothers resolved to sell Joseph to be a slave in Egypt. It was Judah's idea. They sold him for twenty pieces of silver."

"Why didn't Reuben stop them?"

"He wasn't there anymore."

"Where did he go?"

"The Bible doesn't say. But he wasn't there because later he came to the pit expecting to find Joseph in it; he meant to save him, but Joseph wasn't there. And Reuben was so upset he tore up his clothes."

"What about the coat, though?"

"The brothers killed a goat and put its blood on the coat of many colors, and took it home to their father and said they found it. And Jacob was so upset *he* tore up his clothes. All his sons and daughters tried to comfort him, but he said he was going to mourn till the day he went to his grave."

"And what happened to the *coat*, Kit? Was it tore up, too?"

"The Bible doesn't say. Maybe they burned it."

That wasn't the end of the story, but I never tried to tell it any further. Once that coat was done, Christy lost interest. That night he just settled down under the blanket, thinking it over, and finally he said, "*We're* brothers. I'm Joseph and ye're Reuben."

That tickled me. "What makes ye Joseph? Where's yer coat of many colors, then?" He'd nothing to say to that, and I kept on with my teasing. "If ye're Joseph, I'll be certain to tell ye my dream tomorrow morning, and ye can tell me its meaning."

"I'm Joseph and ye're Reuben," he said again, using his stubborn voice.

Then we went to sleep. Christy dropped off first; I guess it eased him to know ye can't lose one of God's stories just by burning it up. I lay there with my hands clapped between my thighs so's to keep them warm and listened to the breathing for a minute: Christy and Mam and Michael and me, filling the house up with our sighs. I thought about the brothers story, how rich that family must have been to go tearing their clothes up like that.

And I thought about the rest of the story, how in Egypt Joseph was a man of consequence, and told the meanings of dreams and knowed the future, and when his brothers showed up asking for help it was Joseph kept them from starving. In short, Joseph had nothing but bad luck whilst he was with his brothers, but as soon as he got away from them he prospered.

I'd have wagered a armload of firewood that the same thing would be true for me. I was a winning fellow, else why would my betters trouble with me? If there was no Christy to hang on me like a burr on a stocking, who knowed what Mr. Dean might do for me? It might be he'd find a master for me in Chelmsford or Braintree, a smith or a baker or a linendraper, perhaps, and pay the premium so's I could be prenticed. And when I'd learned the trade he'd set me up in a shop, maybe, like I was his own son, for he and Mrs. Dean hadn't any children. I pictured myself showing off baize and broadcloth, calico and crepe, to the fine folk who would come to buy of me. I'd buy worsted for Mam, so's she'd have a warm gown, and for Christy I'd buy a suit of black cloth. (I'd forgot there was no Christy.) And one day Kate Haddon would come in, and I'd show her a length of silk as blue as her eyes . . .

After that my thoughts strayed, and by and by I slid into what I call jumble-land, where real things turn into dream things whilst ye're just able to notice them doing it, and from there I went in and out of proper dreams all night long.

Toward morning I dreamed I was all alone in front of a blazing fire. I felt like I'd just stole a pig, as guilty and as glad. I could hear Christy calling to me from the other side of a barred door, only he was calling me Reuben: "Reuben! I'm cold, Reuben!" I let him go on hollering, for I didn't want to leave the warmth to let him in. Then I was breaking sticks off Mr. Dean's hedges, till suddenly Mr. Dean was there with me asking sternly what I meant to do with them. "They're for chastising Christy," I said, and he smiled and said I was a good brother to take so much trouble. Just then I felt a terrible pain in both feet and I knowed that evil beasts was chewing on them, one upon the left and one upon the right, and I looked down, very curious to see which kind of beast they was, but at that moment I woke, for there was a great and sudden noise—like the crack of a cannon, men said of it later, though I'd never heared a cannon myself.

"What can it be?" Mam whispered. "What has happened?"

There was another great crack, and after it another, and several more.

"What is it? What does it mean?" Mam cried out, more louder.

"I think my feet are froze," I answered her. They was stinging terrible inside their yarn stockings. Then I sat up and gasped at what I saw, for the frost had come within.

The dawn had broke and there was a pale light over all. It showed the hoarfrost that turned the blankets white, and lit the ice that glittered in the thatch. The piss had froze in the chamber pot and the ale in the bucket.

"Is it the end of the world?" asked Christy, sitting up beside me. His words turned to white before his mouth.

"It's winter, ye dolt," I told him, and then I made him take his stockings off so's I could see his toes wasn't froze, but they was pink enough, so he put them back on and his shoes, too.

"Michael has slept through everything, little dear," Mam

said, and touched his face to wake him, but he didn't stir. "Michael, Michael, wake up, child! Wake up!" Mam said, affrighted. She patted him on the cheek, none too gentle. "Wake up! I've got a tart for ye, Michael!"

Which was a lie, though I knowed she'd have done anything she must to make it true if only he'd roused. I would myself. My heart was like a woodpecker's hammering, and my guts was twisting. He didn't rouse, though, only lay limp and blue.

"Is it like the bird, Kit?" Christy asked.

Which was too much for Mam, and she turned on him. "It should be *you* lying here, ye great idiot! Ye're the one who took the food from his very mouth!" Then she gathered Michael's body into her arms and began to moan. "Why has God took my very hope, my whole, brave boy that was clever as a clerk, and left this clod of dirt to be my son? It's Christy ought to be dead, Christy, Christy, God forgive me but it's true." After that she broke down weeping.

Christy didn't try any of his smiles on, just pulled the blanket up a little as though he hoped her words was too large a size to get through the weave of it.

I knowed if I went to her it would be me she'd turn on, but I did it anyways, reckoning that sometimes it's a son's duty to let hisself be cursed. I pulled her away from my little brother's body and made her stand, and ducked back when she went to slap me so she only got my chin, and then I wrapped my arms around her whilst she sobbed against my shoulder. Every now and then she'd break off and tell me why it was my fault Michael died, and how I was a good-for-nothing sinner worthlesser than my twin, for at least he knowed no better. I didn't try to argufy, just let her rage. But her words came into me like bad meat and wormed their way through my gut, twisting and cramping, for I knowed they was true. I was of little use to her or to the world, if it came to that, and it was all on Christy's account.

At last she pushed me away and wrapped Michael in his blanket. I took up the axe and began to split a table trestle.

"Go on," Mam said. "Chop up the benches, too. What does it matter?"

I made no answer, but built up a good fire. After a little Mam told me to fetch Mrs. Hill, who lived nearest, and then to go on to the church, and tell the sexton we'd be needing a grave.

"Shall I leave Christy, so ye'll not be alone?" I asked her.

"Christy! What good to me is Christy!" she said. "What good is either of ye to me now?"

By then the house'd warmed and the piss was melted. I went outside to empty the pot and thought I would perish of the cold, cutting wind that was blowing and moaning. There was no snow, but the frost glittered on the ground, and a queer gloom lay over all. I stood there hunched against the wind, near doubled with suffering from Michael's death and from what Mam had said to me. Then it came to me that it wasn't Mam's words snaking through my entrails, but last night's stew, so I took the pot inside where I could squat without freezing my backside, and pictured Mam's bitterness leaving me in that same easy way. For surely, I said to myself, a mother will say things she doesn't mean when her grief is new.

But later I learnt that she did mean them.

Mrs. Hill knowed nothing of what made the great noises that

waked all the village. But before the church many men was gathered round the large oak what growed there, and me and Christy
pressed in amongst 'em.

By God, it was cold. No one in Essex had ever saw a winter
like that one what began in 1683 and lasted into the new year.
Soon folks was saying it was the coldest England had ever been,
and telling stories of rivers that froze and cattle that died and of
the preacher's ink that turned to ice so he could not pen his sermon though he sat at fireside. And it was the same everywhere,
they said, north to Cambridgeshire and south to Kent and in the
West Country. I know for a fact it was the same in London Town.
The same, but different, the way soup is different from a dream
of soup.

But all this knowledge was yet to come. That morning we
knowed only that the trunk of the oak tree was split, and had a
cleft that was not there yesterday.

"The oak outside the tavern is the same," Mr. Lowry said.
"And two of the walnut trees."

"And the oak by the smithy," the blacksmith said.

"And the one outside my place," said the cooper. "But 'twas a
branch what split, and has fell to the ground."

So I learned 'twas the splitting of the trees what caused the
great noises that waked me from my dream.

The sexton said the grave would take several days to dig, for the
frost was deep and he'd no one to help him break the frozen
earth. We kept Michael's body in the second chamber, what had

no fire, and stayed warm by burning the table board that had laid upon the trestles. "What will become of us?" Mam said when the axe split it in two, but after that she didn't speak again.

On Sunday morning we stood at the back of the church with the other humble folk. Most of the village had turned out, which showed the seriousness of our strange weather; we had all come to hear what it might mean. The squire and his wife was in their pew; John Frith stood at the back with us. Mr. and Mrs. Dean was there. He wore fringed leather gloves and carried a big fur muff, and she had a fur tippet wrapped round her neck.

Reverend Cook fixed us with a stern eye and said the weather was a judgment, and that we must consider what part we played in bringing God's warning upon us, and must mend our ways. It seemed everyone there had the fidgets; I supposed they was wishing they hadn't done all last week the things they meant to do over again next week. Leastways, that's how it was for me most every Sunday, for when Reverend Cook said what a sin it was to dwell on the pleasures of the flesh, I believed him in my heart and was so shamed I thought my prick would never rise again, but if I chanced to see a lady's tight-laced bodice whilst I was filing out of God's house, there it went poking up again, no matter how I hated myself for it. And then I growed angry, for I was doing my best, and it seemed to me it was the fault of the ladies who showed off their bosoms the way they did. Reverend Cook preached from time to time about women's lusts, and warned us menfolk not to let ourselves be catched by their nets and traps, which kept me cautious around females. They was like wild pigs, I reckoned, unpredictable, and always looking for a way to do some damage.

Of course, that Sunday I had something worser on my conscience than my unregulated prick, for I had starved my brother to death. The thought of it made my guts twist with grief. I wondered if it made a difference to God that I had starved him for Christy's sake, instead of my own. It seemed to me I ought to get some credit for that. Wasn't we always told to help the lame and the blind? And though Christy wasn't neither, he might as well be. Anyways, I was hoping that was God's view of things, but for caution's sake I aimed to be as pure as possible for a time, and I kept my eyes on the stones under my feet as I left the church that day.

Then Mam said she had people to see and sent us on home without her.

She was gone the best part of that day, which was rare in her. She didn't go much into the world except to church or when extra servants was wanted somewheres for a day or two. I kept a fire going all the while, first burning the hutch we used to store our ragged clothes, and then the chest what held our blankets when we was not using them. I wondered what would we do when all the furniture was gone. We'd not much left, only the benches.

Christy wanted to play Buying of Mustard to pass the time, but we could not, for it is played with a trencher and the trenchers was burnt. So we played Cropping of Oaks instead, sitting tailor-fashion opposite each other on the benches and striking at one another till one of us toppled. We played a goodly number of rounds, and then we was too sore to go on, so we was quiet awhile.

At last Christy said, "An't it sad Michael's gone?"

I said it was, and between us we remembered a few sweet

moments our brother had gave us, and I cried, though my twin did not.

"And is he with God now?" Christy asked me.

I said he was.

"What will he have for dinner there?"

But that was a question for a scholar, so I didn't answer him, but fixed us some porridge for our own dinner, and when his belly was full Christy lay down on our pallet and began to drowse. He was very fond of a nap. After a bit of waiting I got a unsettled feeling, and to calm myself I picked up what was left of the Bible and looked at some of the words that was more shorter: *man* and *that* and *fell*. I could read *"It came to pass"* but I never found out what it was that passed.

After a little Mam came in the door carrying a sack. She set it down and I heared the clunk of wood against the floor.

"Why, Mam, where did ye get it?" I asked.

"Mrs. Curtis gave it to us. I'm to go to her tomorrow."

I picked up the bag and began to feed the fire with sticks while I thought this over. "How many days?" I asked at last.

"Regular," Mam said. "To live."

I straightened up and stared at her.

"You an't breaking up the family?"

"It's broke up already, and not by me."

"Don't despair, Mam! We'll find a way. Once this cold is done I'll find steady work, and we can buy a table—"

"Ye've got steady work already. Ye'll go to Mr. Dean's. He's took a fancy to have a butler, or a footboy, or some such thing. And ye'll feed the livestock as well."

"But what of Zeke?"

"He went back to his mother. He will not work for Mr. Dean, he says he was beat too much."

I was to go to Mr. Dean's! A powerful wonder filled me at the thought of it. Regular warmth and regular meals, and Mr. Dean there all the while to show me how to better myself. I pictured us with our heads bent together over his account book, adding up my wages as I saved 'em—I'd not spend a farthing of it. Could I save enough to pay a premium, and become a prentice? I imagined Mr. Dean's encouraging hand upon my shoulder. No doubt he would be a stern master, and there would be some beatings as I learned new ways, but I knowed I would not be beat so much as Zeke Bailey, for he was a slow, blundering boy. Anyways, what did beatings matter? If they came I would take them without a protest, and show him that I could put his lessons to use.

Then I was struck by what it really meant—that Christy and me was to part. I wondered could Mam really take care of him the way I could. And what would I say to him? How was I to tell him the yoke between us what was made by God so many years ago, the double harness what kept him on the move at the same time that it slowed me down till I was near crazed from it—how was I to say that that yoke was broke forever? But even as I troubled over it, something singing and glad rose in me at the thought of being finally free.

"Christy'll miss me," I said, to hide my gladness.

"Nay, he's to go with ye, and help ye with yer duties."

"Why, he can't, Mam, he an't fit for it."

"His back's not broke, is it? He can do what he's told."

But that's just what Christy couldn't.

"Mr. Dean hasn't patience enough for Christy," I said.

"Patience! What has my patience taught him? Perhaps when he knows there's a stick waiting for him he'll learn more faster!"

"Ah, Mam," was all I said, but she thought I reproached her.

"I'm doing the best I can for the both of ye!" she burst out. "I always have done, and what's been my reward? I wish I'd never saw yer father, I wish I'd stayed in service in Chelmsford and was there now, making tarts in Mrs. Cobb's warm kitchen, instead of suffering in this frozen hell!"

Her loudness woke Christy, and he raised his head up like a sleepy hound, but we neither of us minded him.

"It's cold in Chelmsford, too," I said to Mam.

"It an't cold at the Curtis place, and it an't cold at the Deans," she answered me.

"What is it, Kit?" Christy asked.

Mam sat down upon a bench and covered her cheeks with her hands. I looked into the golden heart of the fire, like I could find there what I most needed.

"What is it, Kit?"

I spoke to Christy in my most cheerful voice. "Why, Mr. Dean's to give us a groat after all. And Mam is so glad and grateful."

5

Now, Christy," Mr. Dean said to my twin. "It is time for you to grow up. You are a little boy in a big boy's body, but it needn't stay that way. I'm going to teach you what you must know to be a help to others. Do you understand me?"

Christy kept his eyes fixed on his shoes, but mine was everywheres. We was standing near to a four-poster bed of mahogany with curtains of gold. On the other side of the room was a oaken table set with four silver candlesticks, every one of 'em with a beeswax candle in it and every candle lit, though 'twas early in the day. It was lovely not to have the greasy smell of tallow candles burning, and to see the dancing candle fire in a fine looking-glass that hung upon the wall. The hearth was large and grand, and within it the flames was so great ye'd think a body in that room could never shiver again. All the same, Mr. Dean wore his greatcoat, as if he had just come within. He kept his hands in his pocket slits as he studied my twin's hanging head, and after a bit he said, "You may look at me, Christy."

Christy looked at me instead.

"Mr. Dean is yer master now, ye must do everything he says," I told him.

So then he looked at Mr. Dean.

"Do you understand me, Christy?" Mr. Dean asked again.

"Yes, sir," Christy said, which meant nothing. He was always pretending to understand a thing.

"Then we have made a good beginning," Mr. Dean said in a satisfied way. "Kit is right, you must do everything I tell you, and everything Mrs. Dean tells you, and everything Betty tells you. We will take special care to explain your duties well. But, Christy, if you fail to do what we ask, you will get the stick. Do you understand?"

"Yes, sir."

It seemed to me the best moment to venture a word. "If ye please, sir. Perhaps for the first day or two I might help explain things to Christy. I've a good bit of practice putting things so's he can understand them."

"Nay, that is just what we must bring to a halt. You have been your brother's worst enemy by standing between him and the world, Kit. Christy must learn to understand others without your assistance."

I gaped at him before a glimpse of myself in the mirror made me shut my mouth quick, for Mam herself would not have knowed me from Christy with my jaw hanging open that way.

"I'm sure you have done your best, Kit," Mr. Dean said kindly.

My poor best, my futile best, is what he meant to say. His words was like a blow, nay, like the mirror that hung on the wall, showing me my poverty and vanity together. All those years of towing my brother behind me in all weathers, and training him to take his cap off when I did or to keep his eyes on the ground when a pretty maid was by—all my helping only hurting, that was what Mr. Dean meant.

I was sunk in the shame of it, yet I could not keep from saying, "I fear there's things he just an't able to learn, sir."

"We shall find out. Perhaps if we are consistent and persevere he may surprise us."

"Yes, sir," I said, and hoped it was true. After all, Mr. Dean had been at university. I told myself it was natural he would know things I didn't, even about my own brother. Maybe he knowed a way to make things stay in Christy's head instead of falling back out through his ears as they always seemed to do.

Mr. Dean's house was like a paradise—if heaven is on the icy side. We was gave linens what was to be washed for us every week—not new, but sound—together with coats and breeches that hadn't a tear in 'em, though they was much patched. They was scratchy, being made of linsey-woolsey, but they was still lighter and cleaner than the ancient rags we took off. Christy had whole shoes, and both of us had gloves. For outdoor work I was gave a heavy coat and leather breeches and stout boots. The boots was too big for my feet, but Betty gave me rags to stuff into the spaces, which did two duties, for they helped keep out the cold, as well. We was never dressed so fine in all our lives, and the clothes was ours to keep.

We had more to eat in the first day than we'd had in the three days before, and tastier, too: beef and veal what was roasted upon the spit, and apples from the cellar, and as much bread as we liked. The rooms was full of candlelight, and the pallet in the kitchen where we slept was ironed with a warming pan before we lay down on it.

The bed curtains in the Deans' chamber was golden silk, and the hall was hung with scarlet Turkey carpets. There was a painted picture there, too, all brown and green. I could not keep my eyes from it, and at last I made out that it was a view of men hunting. I laughed out loud, for I felt I'd been took to another place without stirring a step. I liked the portraits of Mr. and Mrs. Dean what hung in the parlor even better, though I'd saw such things before. Imagine that a man may die, and his likeness live after him! Such paintings was like a velvet coat or fingers heavy with rings; they let folks know where a body stood in the world.

In the portraits, Mr. Dean looked stern, and his wife sad, and looking at them I thought again about the children she did not bear him. John Frith laughed at Mr. Dean when our betters was not near, and said 'twas clear he did not give his wife her pleasure when they coupled. "If ye cannot warm the cellar, the seed will not sprout," he said. Of course, I knowed that a woman's seed must join a man's before she can breed. But I took Mr. Dean's part, not aloud, but in my thoughts, for it seemed to me that women in their lust put great demands upon men, and to meet them might not be easy.

Not that Mrs. Dean seemed lustful in any way. She was a odd match for her more grander husband: a small, hurrying, worrying woman whose apron was always soiled. Our first day there she came into the kitchen and looked from Christy's face to mine as though she sought a difference between us.

"Oh, dear. Can ye not make him close his mouth?" she asked me.

"Yes, mistress, but I cannot make him keep it closed," I answered her.

"Don't mind, then, never mind." She flapped a hand at me and looked again from me to my brother. Christy was staring at the scarf she wore round her neck, what had took his fancy. It was the softest, warmest wool I'd ever saw, the same blue as the evening sky in summer, and in the next days I learned she wore it everywhere she went, even churning butter or climbing the ladder to the cheese loft, for the warmth of it, I reckon.

"Do ye like it? Ye may touch it," she said kindly to my twin, and held out the hanging end of it so's he could pet it with his fingers. "Ye're to have livery, ye know. Green and black."

Livery! Like John Frith! I felt like a rooster when its breast feathers puff up.

But Mrs. Dean sighed. "The master thinks 'twill cause a stir, to have ye and yer brother identical."

"How can it make a stir? Everyone in the village has saw us both a thousand times and knows we are twins, however we are clad."

I spoke before I thought, and then looked at her all in dismay, for I ought not to have said such a thing about Mr. Dean's idea.

But she agreed with me. "Just so," she said with a quick nod. "Mr. Dean likes his experiments, however, and nothing can be done about it. Ye never bottled wine, did ye, Kit?"

And then we left Christy with Betty, and Mrs. Dean told me what a butler must do. There was many casks of wine in Mr. Dean's cellar, some from France, and some from places in the world I had not heared of: the Rhinelands, the Canaries. They could not be kept long in bottles without turning, so I was to fill only one or two bottles at a time, and only when they was wanted.

"Ye're to lay the table as well," she said. "And in time ye'll have the care of the silver plate, if ye earn Mr. Dean's trust."

John Frith was just a footman. I was to be a butler!

"It an't yer true work, mind," Mrs. Dean said. "That's caring for the livestock. The livery's only for guests, and this butler nonsense, well, 'tis a fancy of Mr. Dean's."

So then my breast feathers settled a little. But I'd still have thought myself in paradise, except for Christy. For he did not take to paradise so well as I.

All my life, even when my dad yet lived, 'twas my duty to take care of Christy to keep him from harm. I'd groaned and carped about the trouble he made for me, but I did my duty anyways, and took a kind of pride in it in the end. But now I could not do my duty anymore.

On our second day he was sent alone to fetch the household's ale, which he was to put upon account. But he came home without it, for when the alewife asked how much he needed he could not remember. He was not beat much that time, only a few swats with Betty's broom. He was sent back for it with the number of gallons written on a paper, and did not lose it, praise God. But as he trudged along the road toward the farm with two buckets hanging from the yoke over his shoulders, he met Robert Fryer, who asked if it was Mr. Dean's ale. When Christy said yes, Robert told my poor simple twin that Mr. Dean had sent him for it. So Robert went off with the ale and Christy came back without it a second time, and that time he was beat severe. He cried out for mercy, but it did not stop the beating, and finally he just sobbed like his heart was as tore up as his skin. It made me sick to hear him, for he was not like Zeke, who knowed enough to pretend a pain he did not feel. In the end Robert Fryer was had up on charges, but I was long away by then.

After that beating Christy was too frightened to be of much use. No matter what instruction he was gave, he stood as though rooted, for fear of doing something wrong. Susan and Betty took pity on him, and kept him in the kitchen with them as best they could, but even there he came to grief. Once he dropped a whole pie into the fire, where it spilled and burnt. When Susan told Mrs. Dean of it, our mistress fretted and worried, but at last said, "Say nothing to Mr. Dean; it shall be our secret." And she patted Christy's shoulder before she left the kitchen.

After that no one tried to make Christy useful, but only pretended he had turned the spit or scoured the pots, whilst really he had sat on a bench near the fire and remarked upon the marvelous heat of it, or told over and over again how we had burnt our trenchers on the night Michael died.

Michael was buried on Thursday. The parish paid for it all, from the tolling of the death knell to the beer and bread what was shared after. He was brung to the grave site in the parish coffin, but being so little he slid about in it and knocked against the side. When we reached the churchyard he was took out and put into the grave wrapped in his tiny winding-sheet. The service was read quick as can be on account of the cold, and then we was eating and drinking and being fussed over by Mam. She had new clothes, too, and was cleaned up, and ye could tell she was eating regular from the plump of her cheeks. All the same, she looked sad, and tired enough to drop. She asked us was our bellies full, and Christy began saying all the good things we'd had to eat at the Deans', and she looked so satisfied with herself I couldn't abear it.

"He's been beat twice," I said.

"It an't on his mind, though," Mam said.

Then she went home with her mistress and we home with our master.

Friday was a fearsome cold day. The trees was silvered with ice and the sky was low. The sheep kept close together in their pens, and the goats burrowed into the loose straw in theirs. In the stable the long winter coats of the horses made them look as furry as bears. Ice glittered in their whiskers, and the frozen balls of dung was like stones neath my boots. The cows was huddled together for warmth. I mucked their manure into piles, that it might help warm the barn, and set buckets of water before them I had carried from the well; thank God the deep well water had not froze. Even so I had to break the ice on top that had growed in the time I went from well to barn, and when I carried the milk back with me it likewise formed a crust of ice upon it.

When I was through I went into the kitchen to warm myself. Everyone was buzzing and bustling, getting ready for company. I was holding my hands to the fire when I heared Mrs. Dean's voice coming from beyond the kitchen door. Ye could tell from

the sound of it she was distressed. Susan and Betty and Christy
had fell silent to listen, and I listened, too.

"Let Kit take care of the wine; Christy can take the coats
from the guests when they come in," Mrs. Dean said. "'Tis
enough for him, poor boy."

"No man will take his coat off in weather like this," Mr. Dean
answered. "Anyways, Christy is my project, you know. I made a
wager with Mr. Hayter that I could train him to be useful in a
week, and I don't intend to be the loser."

"But not the glassware, husband! 'Tis Venetian, so fragile!"

"Then he must be careful with it, mustn't he?"

And he walked into the kitchen whilst we was all looking at
each other in dismay.

He had brung us our livery, which was most handsome; even
Christy looked well when he had dressed in it. I reckon a bit of
black braid upon the shoulder makes any man more comelier.
Betty took Christy into the parlor so's he could see hisself in the
looking glass, and after that he could not keep a grin from his
face. As for me, I sneaked into the hall and took a long, admiring
look at myself in the great mirror what hung upon the wall there,
and wished Kate Haddon might see me thus. 'Tis true what they
say, that clothes are the making of a man.

"Now, Christy," Mr. Dean said gravely. "This is a special day
for you. I am going to trust you with an important task. Are you
ready?"

"Yes, sir," he said.

"You are to carry the wine goblets. Can you do that?"

"Yes, sir."

"Not full glasses," Mr. Dean said, as though that made all the difference. "You need not trouble about spilling. Only the empty vessels."

"Yes, sir," Christy said.

But I knowed he heeded nothing that was said to him, for he was grinning through it all.

By dinnertime my brother had been told ten times to handle those goblets careful. Mr. Dean told him friendly-like, and Susan told him stern, and Betty nearly begged him. I told him myself, and said if there was no breakage I would take him to see the animals at midnight come Christmas Eve, for some say that they speak in that first moment of Christmas, and praise the Lord. Christy was excited to go, and promised over and over to be careful, till I felt bad to have said what I did, for if he failed 'twould only deepen his desolation.

At first things was fine. The guests laughed to see me and Christy dressed up, just as they was meant to do, and everyone said how clever it was. I stabled the horses, and Christy carried in wood for the fire. There was a great dinner, with a boiled leg of pork and venison pie and biscuit cakes and a trifle and cheese. And wine, of course. Sack and claret in bottles, but that was drunk at table from pewter mugs, and did not worry me.

'Twas during the caroling that things got difficult. There was the guests, red-faced from wine and from singing whilst Noah Perkins fiddled, even Mrs. Dean had growed warm, and her scarf had fell from her neck to the floor neath her chair. And there we was, dressed just alike in our green jackets with their black braid. Mrs. Dean gave me the signal when the wine was ready—a claret mulled with sugar and spices, and served in a great bowl. I was to ladle it most careful, that I might not splash the hot stuff upon our guests, but before that I must carry it in and circle the room with it whilst Noah Perkins played a kind of heralding music that made everyone look up. I held it high like I was bade to do, yet my eyes was half the time upon Christy, who was across the room, as though my looking at him could keep us from calamity. That's how I came to be watching him when it happened. He was not bade to circle, as I, but only to go straight to the table I would come to at last. He walked so slow and careful, and hanged on to the tray so tight, that I thought he would do it, but then Mr. Pearson called to him—called to me, really. But he'd mixed us, and thought I was my brother. "Christy! Here!" he called out. Christy swung round quite heedless. A goblet fell and he tried to snatch at it and so doing dropped the tray. There was six goblets upon it to start, and every one broke.

I nearly dropped the bowl I carried, not from surprise but from despair. I was sick with shame at having such a brother, and with anger at Mr. Dean for making him do what he could not, and with fear of what would happen to us both. The caroling had stopped and everyone gave little cries of pity or blame.

"Dear me!" said Mrs. Dean, and clapped her hands to her red cheeks.

"Now, there is a useful fellow," Mr. Hayter said with a broad smile.

I set the bowl upon the table and went to Christy, thinking to help pick up the sharp pieces, but Mr. Dean stopped me with his hand. His grip was fierce, and I knowed he was angry to have lost his wager.

"Remember what I have told you, Kit," he said. He let go my

arm, but his voice had just as much a hold on me. "Christy remembers, don't you, Christy?"

Christy smiled a foolish, guilty smile.

"Answer me, boy."

"Yes, sir," Christy said.

"Then you know what you must do."

The truth was he hadn't the least notion, but Mr. Dean had turned back to his guests, so I inched myself close enough to whisper, "Clean it up, ye dolt."

Then the singing commenced again, whilst Christy picked up the pieces as best he could. His hands was covered with blood by the time he finished, and he was sent to Betty in the kitchen to have them wrapped in rags. I went for pewter mugs and ladled the wine into them, and served and bowed and carried. "I'm so sorry, for Christy's sake," Mrs. Dean whispered to me when I brung her a mug of punch.

Soon the snow began, and the guests growed anxious and made to leave, though 'twas early yet and they was meant to stay to supper. I brung their horses from the stables, and Mr. Dean went into the yard to help fix the lanterns to the coaches. As I led out Mr. Hayter's horse I heared Mr. Dean say to him, "You will see. I will make a servant of him yet."

His words was unwelcome to me, for I'd hoped he might learn from tonight that there was no use trying with Christy—hadn't I tried all my life?

And there was still his beating to be got through.

"Bring my stick to the kitchen," Mr. Dean told me the moment we was within.

"Must ye beat him, sir? It an't his fault, sir, ye know it an't. God made him that way."

He looked at me amazed, like I was one of the oaks what had burst. "Do you teach me the ways of God, Kit? I did not think you had such effrontery."

What answer could I make to that?

"I beg yer pardon, sir," I said with downcast eyes. "I was wrong to ask. He is my brother, though."

I brung the stick, and was bade to stand by whilst Christy took off his livery and had his beating, which I did do, and Betty and Susan also, though Betty stopped her ears that she might not hear Christy's screams so clear. I wished I might as well, for he screamed my name more than once, and each time he said it Mr. Dean hit harder, like it was my name he wanted most to beat out of my twin. But that he could never do, for I was King to Christy.

I stood with my eyes closed but my ears open, clasping my hands tight together and wondering how long it would take Mr. Dean to learn what everyone else could tell in a glance: that my brother was not made to take care of others, but to be took care of. And Christy screamed, and fell upon the rush matting on the kitchen floor, and curled his tenderest parts together, but Mr. Dean leaned over him and beat him still, till at last he was satisfied.

He straightened hisself and handed me his stick. "Christy has learnt something tonight," he said. "And he will remember it, unless you make him forget his lesson by giving him too much sympathy. You will not do that, will you, Kit?"

"No, sir."

"Very well, then. Here is a shilling; you must share it with Christy, though. Do not spend it now, save it for your Christmas revels."

I promised him that I would, and he went to console his wife for the loss of the glassware.

Christy lay turned from me on his pallet, sobbing, whilst Betty dabbed a rag against the wounds on his bleeding back. She is good to him, I thought, as I took off my livery and put on the clothes I'd been gave the day I came. It vexed me that she could do more for him than I could myself, and I made a noise with my tongue, but Christy heared it and stilled his sobs.

"Kit, is it you?"

"It's me, Christy."

"I broke the glasses, Kit. Now I cannot hear the animals speak." And he burst out sobbing again.

Betty took her cloth and moved away. "Poor soul. What a cursed day 'twas that he came here."

Susan grunted. "They was freezing and starving," she said. "An't ye glad to be in front of a warm fire, boy?" she asked me.

I told her I was, and told it to myself, too. How could I say different? I'd a full belly, and clothes where once I wore rags, and a fire to hold my hands to. I'd a whole shilling to squander how I liked, and my world was filled with bright colors and dancing lights. 'Twas not so bad a life, seeing where I'd come from. Not so bad for me, I mean to say. Worser for Christy.

I sat down on a bench by the fire and tried to think of the good things the future might bring, the way I used to do. But instead I growed every moment more angrier with Mam, who had broke apart our family, and with Mr. Dean, who knowed more about the New World than he did about a boy like Christy. But I was angry at Christy, too, for being the sort of creature he was. What a fool I'd been to think I could make my way with him tied to me like a bell to a harness. There was no more hope for me here at Mr. Dean's than I'd had back home at the cottage.

Was it right that all my hope must be sacrificed for my brother, when I could do nothing for him but stand by whilst he was beat?

I felt a great *nay* growing in me, for what angered me most of all was seeing my fate before me like a long road with no paths branching from it what might lead to better. I told myself that our fates an't ours to make, but even as I said so I dreamed of walking right out into the falling snow, walking all night till I got to a better place: a inn what smelled of roasting chestnuts, maybe, and beyond it, a great city filled with hurry and bustle. London Town. That was where hope lay, for such as me. I could never rise in the same village I'd growed up in, amongst people who could not look at me without seeing Christy.

But to run away to London Town in this weather, with nothing but the clothes on my back and a shilling in my shoe—'twas impossible. Yet how far had doing possible things got me? I could not abear the possible anymore. If I could not make my way to London, I would sit in the snow till I froze, and come that way to heaven itself, God willing, and there I would never again have to hear my brother cry whilst I did nothing.

Before long Betty and Susan went to bed. I kept my seat by the fireside, and listened to the sounds of the house dying away as people tucked themselves under their rugs and blankets. Of a sudden I got a picture in my mind—put there by the Devil, I reckon—of Mrs. Dean's blue scarf, lying under the chair where she had sat in the parlor. A scarf like that might help a boy through the cold miles to London, and might be sold for a goodly sum once there. The idea of it shocked me. Even supposing I was willing to throw away piety and obedience and the chance of rising lawfully in life, how could I take from the woman who'd showed us such kindness the very thing she seemed to like the best? She would not mind me having it, I thought, but I knowed it was the Devil speaking.

So I sat there, knowing right from wrong, and then I chose the wrong, willfully, with naught to excuse me but despair, which is a sin, they say. I lit a candle from the fire and crept through the soundless house to the parlor, where folks had sang and drank a few hours since.

The scarf was still there. I picked it up and let it lie for a moment in my hand, just being a servant who picks up after his mistress. Then I hid it quickly neath my clothing, and was a thief.

In the kitchen I lay down on the pallet with Christy, and petted his yellow hair what was as matted as my own.

"Don't cry," I said to him. "And I'll tell ye a story from the Bible."

"Will ye tell me the brothers story?" he asked.

But I did not like to tell him that one, for I was not Reuben, who was so kind. I was not Reuben, and I would not try to protect my brother anymore.

"I'll tell ye the story of the animals on Noah's ark."

"But they did not speak," Christy said sadly.

"Perhaps they did, when no one was by. Perhaps they spoke among themselves, and wondered how long the fearsome weather would last, and said to each other that they couldn't abear it anymore."

"When the frost breaks, will we go back home, Kit?"

"I don't know," I said, which was a lie.

But he settled, and listened as I told him the story of Noah, till by and by he seemed near to sleep. I tucked the blanket round him and said, "Are ye warm enough?"

"It hurts," he said.

"'Twas meant to," I answered him.

"Betty says she has a ointment what'll help, tomorrow."

"She's kind, an't she?"

"Is it Sunday tomorrow?"

"No, the day after."

"Must I walk to church, then?"

"If ye're able."

"I don't think I'll be able, Kit."

"But ye'll see Mam at church."

That thought made him happy, and he finally let hisself doze.

I waited till 'twas nearly dawn, though I hardly slept, only lay there thinking of my resolve. I did not think of the moment Christy would wake and find me gone. Instead I told myself that he'd not be wanted at the Deans' once I was away, that he'd be turned back to Mam, or boarded with another family of the parish what would be kinder to him.

When it was time, I rose and dressed. I put on every stitch

that I'd been gave, saving the livery; one layer upon the next, so's to stay as warm as I could, and over them I put my coat and boots and gloves, and I clapped my sugarloaf hat upon my head.

"Be well, Brother," I whispered as I stood above our pallet, but it woke him.

"Where do ye go, Kit?" he whispered.

"Why, to feed the cows, same as every morning," I said.

"Come back and tell me what they say, will ye?"

"Christmas an't come yet, Christy. They'll say naught but 'moo.' "

And those was the last words I spoke before I left him.

6

MY HEART MISGAVE me the moment I stepped outside the kitchen, for the cold was so bitter it seemed like a weapon in the hand of God. The first breath I took tingled in my chest; the next one gave me pain. I covered my mouth and nose with my gloved hand, and waded through the drifted snow to the barn; it clung to my breeches in a armor of white. In the barn I did my duties, not for any good-hearted reason, but so that the lowing of the cattle might not betray my absence to Mr. Dean. I held my palm to the muzzle of a cow, willing that the ice there might melt quickly, for I was in great haste to be upon the road before I was discovered. Only a few days before I'd scorned to take sticks from the Deans' hedge, even to save my life, and now I had took something so costly I would surely hang for it if I was catched. And I was twice a thief, for I had also stole from the kitchen a venison pie, a whole one, still in its dish; it was neath my coat, against my belly. I got it out now, broke the crust, and brung a handful of meat to my mouth. The rest of the pie I scooped into a piece of rag and tied it to a stick. I left the dish in the barn, and the milk. It had a crust of ice on it before I stepped outside.

Though it had snowed considerable 'twas not enough to alter the countryside, praise God. I could see the bell tower of the church, and using it to guide me, I made my way out of town as quick as I could. As soon as I passed the cottage what marked the end of our village, I took Mrs. Dean's scarf and wound it round my face so it covered my mouth and nose, which brung me great relief.

I'd walked that road many a time, bound for market, first with my dad, and when he was gone, with Christy at my elbow. Dad and me made good time, reaching Chelmsford in two hours despite of our jaws clacking all the way. He was a talkative man, was Dad. With my twin 'twas harder—everything was harder with Christy. But now all that was past.

I'd never walked the road alone, nor on such a day as this was. But then, there never was such days as this before.

I knowed not what terrible thing might overtake me that morning and keep me from ever coming to London, or even to Chelmsford. Perhaps I'd sleep that night in prison. Or it might be the weather that catched me, a icy blizzard what first blinded and stung me, and then made me sleep still and quiet till I was waked by the horns of Judgment Day. But come what might, I vowed I would make my way toward London while I'd the strength to do it.

When I began there was no light in the sky, but only a promise of light what made the snowdrifts shine blue. 'Twas like some story world, all ice and doom. Many of the trees I passed gaped where they'd burst, and the fields was littered with fallen branches. Now and then I saw the dim shapes of birds what had fell dead from the sky. Once I saw a bright spot and wondered at it till I drawed near enough to see it was a fox, froze stiff. I thought of other times I'd passed this way, how the hawthorn hedges bloomed white and the birds sang whilst the brook made its own music. Now there was a stillness such as I'd never knowed, no sound, no motion, no stir of wind, only my own harsh, aching breath, as if I was the only one yet alive.

Praise God my feet stayed dry, on account of the boots Mr. Dean had gave me. But my legs was quickly wet from wading through snow, and I ached from the labor of my slow steps, what sank sometimes up to my knees in the drifts. At first it was nearly a satisfaction to me to be suffering again, as the poor are born to do. There was a kind of triumph in it, like I was the one punishing, and not the one punished; and it was a counterweight to thoughts of Christy, which did torment me when the snow was not so deep. But it an't in my nature to endure suffering long, and soon I was cursing the snow and the ice and everyone but He who sent it. Yet I knowed I *must* endure it. I imagined I was Dick Osborne, the peddler, and that the snow that clung to me was the same as a pack upon my back. But Dick did never carry his burdens through such terrible cold. Each breath I took sucked the scarf to my lips, and when I breathed out it went back. The water from my breath froze to ice upon the wool, and the tips of my nose and ears stung most painful, whilst the insides of my nose burned with cold. I looked often behind me, to see if any man or horse broke the stillness, but there was none.

The longer I walked, the colder I growed, and before I'd

went a mile my toes began to numb. Where the snow was not drifted I runned, stamping each foot upon the road as hard as my strength did allow, but my throat was scorched with cold and I could not keep going. I stopped, panting, and dropped my stick that I might open my clenched fingers inside their gloves. They was slow to obey my command, but at last did open, and close, and open again. I looked down the road and saw a curl of pale smoke before me, which gave me hope; I took up my stick and hastened toward it.

When I found the cottage the smoke came from, I went up and stood against the timbers that built it, to warm myself. I wondered what the hour was, and that made me wonder what Christy did. Then I wrenched my thoughts from him, for a man cannot walk forward always looking behind, or he will trip and come to ruin. I ate a few bites of venison. It was froze through, and all the savor had went from it. I finished it even so for the good it might do me, and set out again.

So it went as the time crept by. I was sure of my way, but the landmarks passed so slow I feared I would freeze before I came to Chelmsford. If a fox in her bright fur could freeze, why not a boy? I ached from toe to crown, except my feet and fingers, which was numb. I could not even feel my hand upon my walking stick, but I kept a grip on it even so.

Once I stopped to sit upon a fallen log, and after a moment lay down on it and there fell asleep for a few chill minutes; I know not how long. When I woke I could not open my eyes, which I did not understand at first, but then I came to know that my eyelashes had froze together. I took off my glove and blowed upon my hand, then cupped it over my eyes, and all the while kept trying to open them, till at last they did open. I put my glove back on and let myself think of Christy. Did Mr. Dean's anger turn upon him, when it was found I'd gone, was he beat bad when he had not yet healed, did he scream my name? The thoughts themselves was like beatings. My remorse was so great I groaned with it, then hanged my head in despair. I'd not the heart to put myself again upon my feet. I raised my head and looked about, wondering if I looked upon the place I would die.

"Our Father, which art in heaven," I began, and said it through, and after it I began my Creed, that I might prepare myself to meet God. But then it came to me that the future was not yet writ, after all, and as for the past, it might not be as I imagined it.

I did not wish to die alone in that frozen place. If I could have undone it all, and gone back to Mr. Dean's warm house and tucked the scarf back under the chair, I reckon that's what I would have chose. But 'twas too late for that, and I could give nothing to Christy by turning round except the sight of myself being hanged, which would be more harder for him to bear than beatings. And so I took to my feet, stamping them, and clapping my gloved hands till they hurt, and vowed not to think of my brother again.

I never met a soul upon the road, coming or going, though I was so watchful for pursuit. My way passed through two villages before it came to Chelmsford, and when I reached the second of them I paused, and stood against a warm wall. I wondered did I ought to knock and be let in, and save myself from freezing. I had not far to go, and believed I could make it to Chelmsford if I so wished, but what would become of me after that? I knowed I could not walk all the way to London in this weather and arrive a living boy.

But I did go on, and hoped every bend in the road would bring me a glimpse of the bell tower of the church, and at last, thank God, it so happened. When I had saw it I stopped behind a tree and told my frozen fingers to take Mrs. Dean's scarf from my neck. At first they would not do it, but I kept trying and after a little they did obey me. I hid the scarf neath my coat, sorry not to have it covering my face, but knowing a boy like me and a scarf like that did not belong together. Once I was to a privy I would hide it neath my shirt, where no one was likely to see it.

I had never before been to the Golden Lion, which was the coaching inn. It was a grand building, with a forest of chimneys and a sign what arched over the roadway. I'd heared there was beds enough for fifty to sleep there all in a night. It did not cater to such as me, but I knowed they would not turn me from the kitchen when the cook heared how far I'd walked through the cold world.

And so it was. She exclaimed over me, and bade me sit a distance from the fire that I might not grow sick from the sudden heat. Some pies had just been took from the oven and the savor of them was all through the kitchen; one sniff made my hunger spring up.

"What's in 'em?" I asked.

"It an't for beggars," she said. "But I've some soup ye may have."

"I an't begging," I said.

But the cook brung the soup anyways. I took off my gloves and opened and closed my fingers a few times, then commenced to eat without saying a word about the cost. The first mouthful was lovely hot, but it cooled too quick.

"How came ye to walk such a ways?" the cook asked, very curious.

"I am London bound," I replied. "Can ye tell me the fare?"

"London bound!" The cook laughed. "Why, the fare is seven shillings, nothing to a lad such as yerself, I suppose."

Seven shillings, and I had but one!

"Have ye any work for me?" I asked without much hope as I finished my soup and wiped my mouth upon my sleeve.

"That's for the innkeeper, Mr. Slingsby, to say," the cook replied, and pointed me through the door.

I told my toes to move within my boots, and rejoiced that they obeyed me, though they stung most bitter. They had swelled, and pressed against the rags, and I longed to take my boots off and take the rags away, but could not do it now.

I took my hat in my hands and made my way into the inn proper with careful steps. Things was very gay there: there was holly and laurels hung about, and a great many men was talking and laughing before the fire, and drinking healths to one another in wine.

"I'm looking for Mr. Slingsby," I said to the boy behind the bar.

"Him in the black wig," the boy said, pointing.

Three men was argufying near the hearth.

"It cannot be safely done, sir," said Mr. Slingsby. He was fat as a pig and red as a rose, with eyes as tiny as peas. "'Twould be daft to try."

"He calls you daft, Joshua," the tallest man said with a sour smile. Both hands was clutching the knob of his walking stick, what he held before him.

"There is no such thing as safety, Mr. Slingsby!" the man called Joshua said.

He was a fair man, plump in a handsome way, and he was dressed as fine as any man I ever saw. He wore a wig of flaxen curls, and his coat fit him like a gown does a maid, though his shoulders was hunched over. It had pocket slits so low they was nearly to his knee. A bright green handkerchief hung from one slit, and his cravat was green, too, and so was his stockings. I knowed at once he was from London Town.

"Are not all fates in God's hands?" Joshua went on as I stared. "We might cower three weeks in this inn and die of a pestilence or burn to death in our beds before we set out for London."

"I said nothing of weeks, Mr. Fowler, sir," Mr. Slingsby said. "The weather must break in a few days."

"I cannot wait a few days; I must be home for Christmas. I remind you that our places in the coach have been long reserved. You have had my money all that time, was it for nothing? Come, man, your driver knows every step of the way."

"The snow is bound to be drifted in places. If you should overturn—"

"We will not be the only ones upon the road," Joshua said. "If the coach upsets, and we cannot right it ourselves, someone will be by in a short enough while to help us do so."

"There's no knowing, sir," said Mr. Slingsby, sounding stubborn. "'Twould be different if you had another pair of shoulders with you to clear the drifts. But with only yourselves and the women I cannot see my way."

"Do you hear, Nathaniel?" Joshua said to the tall man. "If you had not dismissed Sam before we came, we would not be in this pickle."

"The boy was a thief. Or so my landlady told me."

"If you would take more care when hiring, you would not need to discharge one boy after another in this way."

"I own I did not need much persuading," Nathaniel said, as though the other man had not spoke. "He was always groveling and whining. I cannot bear to be fawned over in that way."

"Think of what you are saying, Brother. Obedience is the most essential virtue in a servant, nay, in all of us, for 'tis God's command—"

"If you are going to sermonize I will withdraw."

I'd been waiting for a chance to speak, but I saw I had to make my own chance, so I spoke out strong and clear. "I've a strong shoulder, sir."

"And what of it?" Mr. Slingsby growled at me. "Speak when you're spoke to, boy."

But Joshua looked me over with a keen eye. "And are you bound for London, lad?"

"Yes, Mr. Fowler, sir, but I haven't the fare."

"Who are you and why do you go? Don't lie to me, now."

"I am the widow Mary Chidley's son Kit, sir. My brother Michael died of the frost and my mam has gone into service and there is no hope for me here. I want to go to London and there better myself."

"And your clothes? Do they belong to you, or are they the property of your last master?"

"To me, sir."

"And every word you speak is true?"

"Every word, sir." Which was no lie, for I was so used to honesty I had been fool enough to give my true name.

"Well, Nate. Do you like to hire him?" Joshua asked.

Nathaniel had been watching me the while, not with the earnest gaze of his brother but with lazy, sideways-looking eyes. Now he looked at Joshua amazed.

"*I* hire him? For what reason?"

"Why, to replace Sam."

"I am in no hurry to do that. I have resolved, on good advice, to be more careful in hiring my servants."

Joshua's face turned red and vexed. "You are the most contumacious man I have ever known! You make trouble for the very sake of it!"

"Why do you rant?" Nathaniel asked. "Hire him yourself, if you care to."

Joshua looked troubled. "My household does not need another servant. I like not to bring him to London and set him adrift there. He may fall into evil ways."

"No, sir, never, sir!" I said eagerly. "If ye but take me to London I'll find someone who is needful of my help, God willing."

Joshua stood thinking it over. At last he shook his head. "I cannot cross my conscience," he said.

"I think it is your purse you will not cross," Nate said.

"Think so, if you must." He sighed a sigh as heavy as he was hisself, and turned back to Mr. Slingsby. "When can we go, think you?"

But I did not hear his answer, for Nate came near me, and stood so that he blocked my view of Joshua and the innkeeper, and theirs of me. I'd have drawed back if I dared, for his teeth was black and stood out against the pallor of his long face. He wore no wig, and though his own hair was tied from his face, many hairs had come free and wafted where they liked. Nothing about him was fine, save his walking stick. But I did not dare to give offense, so I stood where I was.

"You admire my brother's piety, do you not?" he asked.

"Not so much, sir, for it keeps me from London Town."

He smiled at that. "If you came with me, I doubt you would remain long in my service. My future plans are uncertain."

Hope came rising up so strong it made me giddy, like I'd drunk too much ale. I spoke very careful, being sure to say each word clear, as though I feared that giddiness, like ale, might thicken the tongue. "I care not, sir. Once I am in town I can make my own way."

"Are you sure of that, lad? You will have no settlement there, and no right to assistance from the overseers till you have worked in the same parish for forty days. I cannot promise that you will stay so long in my service, and this is no weather for sleeping on the street."

"I will take my chance, Mr. Fowler, if ye let me."

He nodded in a satisfied way and turned to his brother. "I will hire him after all, Joshua, since you think him fit for it. On your head be it if he proves a rascal."

"He is not a rascal—are you, lad?" his brother said with a earnest look.

I said I was not, which was the first lie I told him, for an't thieves rascals and rascals thieves?

"He is impertinent, and should not interfere with his betters," Mr. Slingsby said, but no one paid him any heed.

"I believe you, boy," Joshua said to me, and to his brother, "I will dine with Gertrude in our room. You had better make sure the boy has something to eat before you join us."

"I am not in the habit of starving my servants," Nate said.

And then Joshua clumped heavily up the stairs.

I stared after him till Nate said, "What do you look at? Have you never seen a fat man climb stairs before?"

"He is the finest-dressed man I ever saw," I told him.

"It is how he gets new business. He is a tailor. But mind, lad, he is not the one who hired you, and the minute you answer to him and not to me I will throw you from the coach into the snow and leave you there to freeze. Do you understand me?"

"Yes, sir."

He crossed to the bar then, and as I followed him I saw for the first time that he was lame, and used his fine stick to walk. I followed after him, and tried not to let him see I was lame as well from my painful toes.

Nate paid for a hearty dinner for me, and sat by, working his way through a jug of wine, whilst I swallowed one warm mouthful of pigeon pie after another.

"Tell me your name again," he said as I ate. And when I did he said, "Did you ever see a painted picture, Kit?"

"Why, there is one there, sir," I said, pointing, for above the bar hung a portrait of a handsome man in a dark wig and a lace collar.

"Yes, of course," he said, staring at it as though it was a traitor's head upon a pike. "Horrid thing, isn't it?"

"No, sir, why should ye think so?" I asked with surprise.

"It is a portrait of Benjamin Slingsby." He nodded toward the innkeeper, who was yet standing before the fire.

I own I was surprised, but all I said was, "Flattery an't the same as horridity."

He laughed, and said I was a honest man but had not got taste. "I am sick to death of all this face painting," he added. "'Tis an easy, lazy way to get a living, feeding the vanity of the rich. God gave more beauty to this English countryside than to all the men and women in England together."

I thought that over, but could not agree. I reckoned some bits of land was pleasing to the eye and others was not, the same as with people. The difference lay in this: looking at a waterfall or a green hill filled a body up, but gazing at a beautiful maid made that same body hungry all through. I did not say so, however, for that an't the sort of thought to be shared with a master.

Instead I told him, "I have saw a picture what was not face painting."

"What, at another inn? What is your village, boy?"

But that I dared not say. "Hunters and a deer, it had. Mostly green, but some of the green darker and some so light 'twas near to yellow."

That made him peer at me, and I wondered was the wine

dimming his sight. "You are a boy that can use his eyes," he said after a good look. And then, "This will surprise you. I am a picture-drawer myself."

"Are ye, sir?" I said with courtesy, for 'twas clear he was vain of it, though I knowed not why. His brother, the tailor, was surely a more prosperous man.

"I am," he said with satisfaction.

After that he showed me his room upstairs and told me I would sleep on the truckle bed there, what was kept under the big one. I stared, for I had never slept in a bed before. My head was awash with wonder at the sudden turn in my fortunes. Death had not took me, though I made myself ready for it; instead I had a full belly and was to sleep in a bed close to a warm fireside; I had employment and a way to London and the hope of rising in life—who but God could say how far?

But before I took myself to bed I used the privy, and there I saw the scarf I had near forgot. Then all that I had left behind came rushing into my head: my brother, whose fortunes had got worse as mine got better, and Mr. Dean, who knowed by now what sort of boy I was. But that was past, and I must think of the future. I tied the scarf round my middle, neath my shirt linen, and reminded myself that though I slept in a bed, the innkeeper knowed my name.

7

I SUPPOSED I would ride with the coachman, for I had often saw John Frith on the outside of the squire's coach. But Nate said 'twas too cold for that. So it was that the next morning I followed Joshua's wife, Gertrude, and her maid, Priscilla, out to the coach with two great boxes, one upon each of my shoulders. I was to put them within after the ladies had settled, and then go back for more, but Mrs. Fowler was slow to arrange herself, and the minutes I stood there waiting in that bitter cold stretched till I thought time itself would snap. She sighed, and fussed with her skirts, and looked all about at the places the boxes might be put.

Then it seemed she had forgot me, for she seized Priscilla's arm and said, "I was never so glad to leave a place behind. That innkeeper was as great a swag-belly as ever I laid eyes upon. And those tiny peepers in that great noddle of his, did you ever see the like? He is ugly as a carp, no matter how much he may tiffle up to have his portrait painted."

I did not know I gaped till Priscilla spoke to me through the open coach door. "What a hobbledehoy you are. Did you never hear a Londoner speak before?"

"Leave him be," Gertrude said. "He is only a country cokes, bless the poor fellow. Here, you may put the boxes down just there, boy, and fetch the rest."

I did not know what a cokes was, but guessed it could be no good thing. Still, I did not mind her saying it half so much as I minded what her servant said. I wished there was no masters present, so I could have gave back what I got, and as I carried out the rest of the luggage I picked what words I would have said if I'd had the freedom.

At last we was ready to go and the horses walked forward. I had never rode in a coach before. It was like a little room upon wheels, with a door and glass windows what kept the weather from getting at us. It ought to have fitted eight, but every inch of space was crammed with the boxes what held the belongings of the Fowler family, and more boxes was strapped behind. Nate and Joshua and I sat upon one seat, and Gertrude and Priscilla sat opposite to us. Mrs. Fowler was pink-cheeked and bright-eyed, but ye could not call her pretty, for her nose was so tilted ye could see straight into her nose holes. As for Priscilla, she was a small, dark girl.

Mrs. Fowler looked out the window. "I do think we could get to heaven itself faster than to London."

"I can arrange it if you like, madame," Nate said. "At the first sign of a ditch I will throw my weight toward it, and we will perish in a trice. You know I am ever at your disposal."

"That's enough bounce from you, saucebox," she replied.

"Death and resurrection are not subjects for foolery," Joshua said. "Are you quite comfortable, chicken?"

"I am as comfortable a chicken as ever roosted, my duck," she answered.

And then we was all silent a ways whilst the coach rocked and jostled along. I gazed out the windows at the countryside we passed and moved my aching toes about in my boots. I had took the rags out. My feet would not have fitted if I did not.

After a time Gertrude said, "As sure as day I will die of boredom if we do nothing to pass the time. What shall we do, Mr. Fowler?"

There was two Mr. Fowlers present, but 'twas not her husband she looked at.

"We might say gliffs," my master answered her.

"Oh, I know one," she said. "Dick drunk drink in a dish. Where's the dish Dick drunk in? Now you shall say it, Priscilla."

That gave me a chance to look at the girl who had spoke so rude to me, though not a long one, for she said the gliff easily. I had only time to see that her eyebrows was like the wings of some great dark bird crossing the breadth of her forehead, and that her hair was of the same black. I could see it where it pulled away from her face, before it disappeared under her white hood. Though she was such a little thing I guessed she was a year or two more older than me.

Nate also said the gliff very quick. Joshua said it right but more slower than the others.

Then Nate said, "'Tis your turn, boy. Just say it once, very fast, without taking a breath. Dick drunk drink in a dish. Where's the dish Dick drunk in? Like that."

I took a deep breath and said, "Dick drunk dish in a dink. Where's the dish Drick drunk in?"

Everyone laughed, and when the laughter was done Mrs. Fowler said, "If not for you we could not have made a game of it. Not without opening the wine, you know, for the rest of us have heard it before."

"Then 'tis only fair that I have more chances," I said. "Two more." I spoke more bolder than any servant should, but I wanted to show that serving maid that I was not a dullard. Before they could argufy I said carefully, "Dick drunk drink in a dish. Where's the dish Dick drunk in?"

"You did not need both your chances," my master said. He looked pleased, like it was him who learnt the gliff so quick.

"In good sooth, I do believe there were enough fleas in my bed last night to turn a white dog black," Mrs. Fowler said, and yawned. "I slept very ill, didn't you, Priscilla?"

"Very ill, madame."

"I could sleep all the rest of the journey, I am so tired."

And then she leaned against a cushion and fell asleep, just as she said she would. I was amazed, for the coach rocked and swayed enough to make a boy lose his breakfast. I dared not close my own eyes. Instead I looked out the window till my neck ached. Also I sneaked many glances at Priscilla, thinking how she made sport of me and studying on her eyebrows, till one time I catched her sneaking a glance at me. Then we both did color and look into our laps.

We rode in silence for a time, and I fell to thinking of Mr. Slingsby. How long before Mrs. Dean found that her scarf had gone with me to Chelmsford? How long before the innkeeper was asked had he saw any runaway boys? And he not only knowed I had went to London, but in whose company I traveled. 'Twas plain I must leave my new master as soon as we came to our journey's end—he had near told me he would not keep me on, anyways. I'd been so eager to go with him I never asked what he would pay me—it might be he would leave me without a farthing at the gates of the city. The shilling Mr. Dean had gave me was yet in my boot, but likely it wouldn't last long when I was on my own in London Town. I wondered how to find the place for clothes sold secondhand; I would need to rid myself quickly of Mrs. Dean's scarf, not only for the money it would bring, but so that it might not be found on me if I was seized.

For a hour or more the coach rode easy, but for a little slipping and sliding now and again. I was just thinking to myself that Mr. Slingsby's worrying had been all for naught when the coachman yelled at the team to halt, and we found that a great drift of snow blocked the road.

"If only Daniel were here," Mrs. Fowler said. "There is a strong lad."

"Kit is taller and more broad in the shoulders," Nate said.

I knowed not who Daniel might be, but I resented him anyways, and vowed to prove that if I was a hobbledehoy, at least I was a useful one.

That was the first of many drifts, but between us we was able to clear them all. Mostly I shoveled, but twice I helped to uncouple the horses and lead them around to the back of the coach, where they was harnessed up again and pulled the coach back from a ditch. They was only little ditches, thanks be to God, and the coach never did overturn. It was painful cold, but we warmed ourselves eating and drinking, for the Fowlers had brung dinner enough for three days, together with much wine for the masters, and ale for the servants. And though my toes ached when I walked, I walked but little.

We was only halfways to London when night fell, and we surely would have perished if we had tried to travel in the dark, or if we had stayed the night in the coach. But the coachman knowed just where there was a town with a inn. We was none of us sorry to be keeping close to the fireside that evening. There was a great argument at supper, between those who believed the frost would break next day and those who believed it would not. Joshua Fowler did not take a side, but said gravely that we must all pray that the sun would not shine warm enough to melt the snow, for if it froze again after, the roads would be paved with ice.

Maybe God heared our prayers, or it might be our will fell with His. Anyways it did not warm, and our second day of traveling was mostly like the first. There was halts and delays, but also times when we rode without a stop for a hour or more, and I had more chances than I liked to listen to those brothers argufy. Christy and me did never quarrel.

Once Joshua suggested we sing to pass the time. I heared him eagerly, for I am a little prideful of my voice.

"What a pity Daniel is not here," Gertrude said again. "He and I do harmonize well together."

"I will begin," my master said. "My song is 'The Difference Between Widows and Maids,' and it is sung to the tune of 'The Wanton Wife of Westminster.' "

"We shall sing one of the psalms," Joshua said.

But Nate began: "'For maidens are wanton, and oftentimes coy; / But widows are willful and never say nay!'"

"For shame, Brother, you have forgot yourself! My wife is present, and her maidservant as well."

Nate looked at Gertrude and said, "I have drunk too much wine." Then he lifted his bottle and drank from it again.

"This is a paraphrase on the sixth psalm," Joshua said. "And can serve as a prayer to God to ease this severe winter. I believe most of us may know it."

Then he sang out, and as I knowed both the words and the tune, I joined in. All eyes swung toward me, but they looked away again when I did not stop.

"'O heal! my bones with anguish ache,'" I sang, though I was more troubled by anguished toes than anguished bones.

When the psalm was done, Joshua said, "Well done, boy. I have seldom heard finer."

"Shall I sing the harmony, sir? I believe I can."

"My throat aches," Gertrude said. "I had better not sing anymore."

So we traveled awhile in silence, and after a little Mrs. Fowler nodded off, and then her maid, and finally my master. I was not next to him, for when last I shoveled, Joshua had climbed back in before me. When Joshua saw that his brother slept, he turned to me and spoke in a low voice.

"I know my brother too well to suppose he has given you any counsel about the dangers of London," he began.

"He did give me some warnings, sir," I said, thinking of what Nate had said about my settlement.

"And left many more unspoken, I vow. Did he tell you of the

dissenters that crowd the city? Presbyterians, Conventiclers, Baptists, Quakers—there is no end to it. Boys that have come from pious homes sometimes find themselves curious, and think there is no danger in listening to a sermon cast at a different foundry—but there *is* danger, boy! Many, many lads have been led to damnation that way. You must go to church every Sunday— a proper church, mind—whether or not your master does so. My brother is not so careful of his soul as we all wish he was. But your duty to your master is not so important as your duty to God, you understand that, don't you, boy?"

I told him I did.

"And to please God we must regulate our passions. 'Tis dangerous to feel too much—too much anger, too much pride, too much ambition, too much love." He dropped his voice more lower at the last word, and I could not help looking across at his wife and her maid. But both seemed yet to sleep.

"Because I know my brother will not do it, I will speak to you of women," Joshua said gravely. "You can have no idea of the number of lewd women that throng the streets of London. Some lads go to Cheapside or Moorfields thinking to jeer at these nightwalkers, but they are not prepared for what they see. The strumpets paint and powder themselves into a false beauty, and display flesh that should always be modestly covered, and the lads who thought they would laugh instead burn with lust, till they come home having spent their last farthing on these degraded creatures. How sorrowful the boys are, when they come to their senses! I have seen it too often."

He paused a moment to ponder it, and I could see he felt it

deeply, and feared for me. I was grateful for his feeling, and vowed I would keep a great distance between myself and all women. But before I could say so, he spoke again.

"What is worse is that it does not end there. For the unluckiest, it does not end there." He shook his head. "Though he may despise the whore he has coupled with, and despise himself for yielding to her enticements, yet a youth will often go again and again to such women. He cannot help himself, once he has begun to walk this road. There have been good lads, apprentices with their futures before them, who have ended on Tyburn Tree—on the gallows, I tell you, Kit—because only robbery could produce the great sums needed to keep a mistress in the City. Remember that, I beg you."

"I'll remember every word, sir. Thank ye for your kindness."

"You're most welcome, boy. And remember this, too: there is nothing so valuable as a modest maid. A maid who guards her eyes and her tongue will also guard her virtue. This is the only sort of maid I allow to be a part of my household; all my serving maids are modest girls—they have been told that at the first sign of immodesty they will be cast out, and that I will do my best to be certain they are never employed again. Among such modest women you will always be safe. There, I have done at last. Good luck to you, boy."

I thanked him again, and fell to thinking over his words. 'Twas not my first warning against women, I'd heared many such from the preacher. Anyways, everyone knowed how lustful women was, and especially the widows, like Nate sang about in his song. John Frith told me once that he had had his fingers in

Widow Scott's coney. When he said so, I did wish that I could say as much, and now I thought that as I was London bound, perhaps if I should see him again, I might have come to manhood in between, and be the one with most to tell. Then I blushed that God had saw me thinking such a thing, and vowed I would have nothing to do with lustful women. I was a thief, perhaps, but I would not be a fornicator.

Yet I could not keep from wondering what it would be like to touch a woman there. What glorious pleasure it must bring, that youths did do it again and again, though they lost their lives by it, and damned their souls.

I sneaked a glimpse of Priscilla, wondering if she truly slept or if she heared it all. Was she as modest as Joshua said? Was it modest to call a lad a hobbledehoy, and to sneak a glance at him whilst her mistress slept? Or did she guard herself when the master was near, and play when he was not?

By and by we came to another drift, and the men climbed out of the coach to answer nature's call before raising a shovel, whilst the women answered nature's call within, and handed out the pot. We settled into digging. It was labor what made me ache all through, but most in the back. However, there was this to be said for it: it warmed my blood.

The drift was quickly lessened, and the brothers went back into the coach, leaving the last of the snow for the coachman and me to level. I straightened for a moment and put a hand behind me to rub a place what was hot with pain. As I did I found myself looking at a piece of distant sky where a brown gloom hovered over the land. It was not like any storm I had ever saw brewing, and I was fearful that it was some doom come upon us from the next world. I stared and stared, till the coachman said, "Work, boy, ye was not brung along to look at the countryside."

"Yes, sir. But what is it, sir?" And I pointed.

"Why, that's London Town. That's the smoke from the coal folks are burning to keep themselves from freezing. I can't abear it myself, but they say ye get used to it in time."

And I was struck with wonder, and almost with fear, about the place I'd been dreaming after so long.

As we drawed nearer to London the air growed sharp with a cindery taste, and I began to cough, though the others did not.

"You become accustomed to it," my master said to me.

I stared through the coach window into the distance and made out a great, curved shape that rose into the hazy sky: taller than treetops, taller than church spires. "Why, what is it, sir?" I asked.

My master did not even look where I pointed. "'Tis St. Paul's Cathedral, Kit," he said. "And every visitor to London marks the wonder of it."

We jostled our way along the road, now passing many houses. There was dirty mounds and hillocks at the side of the road, and after a bit I saw that they was of snow, and that the road had none. We began to meet with other coaches, and people shouted from one coach to another.

"Happy Christmas!"

"Happy Christmas! Have you ever seen the like of this weather?"

"The Thames is frozen! It will be worse than '77!"

"I hope Agnes has begun the pies," Gertrude said to Priscilla. "For once they are prepared they must be sent to the cookhouse to be baked."

"I wonder how Daniel has done with the suit for Mr. Vaughan?" Joshua said.

"I hope we need not wait long in Gracechurch Street for a hackney coach," his wife said.

"No, my chicken, for any coachman will be happy to take us to Middle Temple Lane, when he can so easily find another fare at Temple Bar."

"And what of me?" Nate asked. "Covent Garden is yet some way from there."

"You can hire another hackney at Temple Bar."

"Then we are here?" I asked, looking through the glass, for we had entered a lane, more broader than any I had ever traversed, and the coach shook so over the stones of the street that our very words trembled as we uttered them.

"Yes, Kit," Nate said. "You are in London Town."

8

I HAD SAW London many times in my daydreams, and it was like and yet unlike the town I came to at last. I'd saw fine houses, and there was fine houses, but I did not see in my mind the smoke what spewed from their chimneys and turned the very air to brown. I pictured hurry and bustle, and there was hurry and bustle, but I didn't think of the thunderous din that bustle would make. There I was, my legs still rocking from the motion of the coach, my throat tickled and my breath rattled with coughing as I thrust my head forward to hear what my master shouted at me through the open door of the coach. But instead I heared the angry barking of many dogs, the ring of a hammer upon metal, the crying of babies, church bells tolling, and men and women bawling words I understood not. I wanted to drop to the stones and cover my head, for it seemed like Judgment Day had come upon us. But no one else was a bit troubled; they only climbed out of the coach and shook themselves like animals what leave the water.

It was a moment to get faint-hearted, if I'd been the faint-hearted sort. But folk from all of England had found themselves able to breathe, and to hear, and even to prosper in this great city. What they could do, surely I could do as well.

"I am more glad to arrive in London than a libertine at a bawdy house," Nate said.

"Brother!" Joshua said very sharp. Then he spoke more sweeter, saying to his wife, "You had best go within, my chicken. Send Francis out to help Priscilla and Kit with the boxes."

So Mrs. Fowler went into the fine brick house that rose behind a fence of blackened snow, and Priscilla hauled up a box and went after her mistress.

I looked at the luggage piled around me and wondered which was whose.

"I see no reason Kit should help you with your boxes," my master said. "He is my servant, not yours."

"I will give him sixpence if he does, which should be reason enough for him. Isn't it, Kit?"

Sixpence! I looked at Nate.

"If it will not exhaust you," he said to me. "You will have to carry my box a long way upon your shoulder."

"Surely you will hire a hackney in this weather!" Joshua said.

"I have hired a servant; that is extravagance enough."

Joshua made a noise with his tongue and turned away. "How came I to have such a brother?"

"The very question I ask myself."

I'd have interrupted even if I'd naught to say. "I can do it, sir." I spoke as if to both, so that neither should know to which my "sir" belonged. "Shall I follow where Mrs. Fowler went?"

But I was not answered, for the door had opened again, and there was Priscilla, and with her a prentice such as I never saw before. He was comely and clean, and dressed as fine as most masters did in the village I left behind. He even wore a wig of black curls what bobbed as he walked.

"Happy Christmas, sir."

"And to you, Daniel."

"We feared you would not come in time for it, with the weather so severe."

"I was resolved to celebrate at my own fireside," answered his master. "What of the business?" His rounded shoulders made him seem to lean forward toward Daniel as he spoke, and added to his eager look.

"I measured Mr. Brown, but have not cut the cloth yet. Mr. Vaughan's suit is near to done. I hired an extra man for two days, sir, that we might not fall behind on the liveries for Mr. Fitch."

"Could not Francis . . . ?"

"He has not yet quite enough speed with his needle."

The door opened as he spoke, and a boy my own age came out, more taller than Daniel and very handsome in figure, but not well dressed. He wore no wig, but had many fair, tangled curls upon his head.

"Francis, this is Kit. He will help you with the boxes," Joshua said.

Then the brothers and Daniel went within, and Priscilla after them, bearing on her arm the basket what held the leavings of our dinner.

"You are to be Mr. Nathaniel Fowler's new boy?" Francis asked me.

"For a little."

"He cannot keep a boy for more than a little," Francis said. "He is as hard to please as a breeding woman. Here, I will take this box, you can carry that one." He talked on as we worked. "Mr. Joshua Fowler is different altogether; he is a sober, shrewd businessman and a very fashionable tailor. He has made clothes for Judge Jeffreys and for the Lord Mayor. He keeps four apprentices, I am the newest; I have served only a year of my term, so I am mostly sent on errands and to do servant's work. I black the shoes, and am even put to making beds with Priss. And since the frost has come I bring the water from the pump, for it does not flow through the pipes. But Daniel finishes his apprenticeship in a few weeks, then he will be a journeyman. He is going to give a banquet for all his friends. I suppose that my master will take a new apprentice then, and I will spend more time sewing seams. It is not hard work, you know, only it hurts the neck. These go into the workshop; Mr. Fowler brings worsted home whenever he visits his father in Norfolk; it is sold cheaper there."

I saw my chance of a word, and seized it.

"For baize he must come to Essex, it is wove in some of our villages, ye know."

He looked at me in some surprise. "You are from Essex, then? And newly come to London, that I can tell. If there are things you do not understand about our ways here you've only to ask me, I was born in Watling Street and have never been farther than Richmond in all my seventeen years. I can tell you where to have your pocket picked and where to see a pickpocket hanged, where to go coney-hunting and where to see the whores flogged.

To the right, and through that great door—yes, here we are."

We was in a big room with a good many windows, but of course the sun did not shine. To give more light there was lanterns with candles in 'em set all around, and on the floor two boys in aprons sat cross-legged with their shoulders hunched whilst they wove their needles through the bright lengths of cloth that lay upon their laps.

"Ralph works on Mr. Vaughan's suit; there are only the buttonholes and such to be done, and Humphrey on livery for Mr. Fitch's servants," Francis said. "Blue, of course, not red. Red is only for the servants of the nobility."

"Where is Daniel?" I wondered.

"Oh, at fireside with our masters, most likely," Francis said.

"There is not light enough in this room for a man to find an elephant he has misplaced," Humphrey said. "And it is Christmas Eve."

"We must wait for Daniel's word before we stop," Ralph answered him.

"Daniel does all the work of a foreman," Francis said as we left the workshop. "But he has not the pay. I think he would be glad to stay on here after his term is served if Mr. Fowler would pay him a foreman's wages, but of course he will not."

"And what of Daniel's suit?" I asked him as we walked. "Did he make it hisself? 'Tis very fine."

"Yes, that was lucky," he said. "We had a remnant of broadcloth from a commission for Judge Jeffreys." He looked over the garments what Mr. Dean had gave me and shook his head. "What a pity your clothes have so much wear left in them. You'll get nothing new of Nate Fowler till you are in rags. He cares naught for fashion or bettering himself. He prefers to spend his time drinking ninny-broth and studying the difference between upside-down and topsy-turvy."

I knowed not what his last words might mean, but what he said about my clothes I understood well. I thought to myself that when I sold Mrs. Dean's scarf I would dress myself more finer, and then I was sure to find a more fashionable master and a greater chance at betterment.

Next we took boxes into the house proper, which was more smaller than Mr. Dean's, and somewhat sooty, though 'twas very fine. We made three trips to the upstairs chambers, and Francis talked all the while of how clever and prosperous the one brother was, and how foolish and odd the other, till I wished with all my heart it was Joshua who hired me. Being as Francis had bade me ask him questions, I did, and learned that *ninny-broth* was coffee and that someone who *tiffled up* dressed hisself very fine and that a *noddle* was a head.

"And what is a cokes?" I asked him.

"Why, that is the same as a ninnyhammer. A fool. A simpleton, you know. I think we have but one trip left to make."

He led the way and I was glad, for it meant he could not see the angry blood in my face. Mrs. Fowler thought me a simpleton—like Christy. Did her husband think so, too? Did Priscilla?

"Have you finished with the boxes?" my master said, coming up behind me. "We must go soon."

"Nearly, sir."

"I will take leave of my brother, then."

He went, and Francis led me once again out the front door to the place where the driver had stopped. The coach was long away by now, and night had fell. But to my surprise the blackness was not complete; Priscilla stood on her tiptoes as she placed a lantern in a niche of the outside wall. The lantern was tin but two sides was of horn, and through them ye could see the candle glowing, casting round it a circle of light with Priscilla at the center of it. For a moment I could not take my eyes from the strange, sweet sight of her.

"'Tis the law here in London," Francis said. "Householders who live in principal streets must set out a light from dusk till nine of the clock, unless the moon is full. It is an aid to the watch." He lifted a box to his shoulder. "This is the last for our household," he said. "The other is your master's. Will he dine with us tomorrow, think you?"

"I know not," I said, wondering would I still have a master by then.

"Then happy Christmas," he said, and went within.

Priscilla did not go with him, however. Instead she came near and smiled at me.

"You are a hardworking fellow," she said.

"That is what hobbledehoys are good for," I answered her.

"Aren't you a saucebox! You have not been long in service, I reckon."

"Long enough to know my duty."

"But not long enough to know your advantage. You are still angry because I called you a hobbledehoy, but you ought to thank me. If I had not scolded you, my mistress would have done so, and then she would have held it against your character for as long as she knew you, but instead she was able to pity you and to speak in your defense. Now every time she thinks of you she will remember her kindness, and 'twill bring a smile to her face. At the same time, she will think me a valuable servant, for I made certain she was treated with respect."

This was a new way of looking at things for me, but I saw the sense of it, and felt foolish that I had not saw it before.

"Are you angry with me still?" she asked.

I looked at her very steady. "Nay. I am not angry now."

But maybe she was a modest girl after all, for she looked quickly away from my eyes. "I am glad of it," she said, and went into the house.

Before the door could close after her, I heared the voices of the two brothers saying their farewells to one another, and then Nathaniel came out of the house, and I was alone with my master.

We took a hackney coach to Covent Garden after all. "I may as well pay for a coach as for a linkboy to carry a torch," my master said as he limped toward Temple Bar, but I guessed his leg pained him and he could not abear to walk.

Temple Bar was a great arch the coach passed under when it brung us, and the place where the hackney coaches waited. To the left and right of it there was small arches what allowed foot traffic to pass without slowing the coaches as they thundered through, and many people had writ letters or doodles upon the wall there with mud or charcoal. I stopped a moment, as if to rest myself, though I did not put down the box. Partly 'twas for my master's sake, to spare his leg, but also I was curious to see if I could recognize any words by the flickering lantern light.

Nate saw what I did. "Can you read, Kit?" he asked in surprise.

"No, sir. Only a few words. 'Man,' " I said, sounding it out. And then, " 'No.' What is the rest of it, if ye please?"

"Oh, you wish to be educated, do you? Temple Bar is the place to do it, to be sure, as it is so near to the Inns of Court, where the lawyers practice." He pointed to each word as he said it. " 'The lawyer Richard Hardcastle is no honest man.' Someone was not happy with the fee he was asked to pay, just as I will not be happy with the fare the hackney driver asks. Yes, there is a very high class of buffoonery before us. Here someone has written in Latin, that is to say, in dog Latin—Latin that has been played with and corrupted. 'O mirum Fartum / Perigrinum Gooseberrytartum.' Shall I translate that for you, Kit? It might come in useful someday."

"It might. Ye never can know, sir," I said with a grin.

He laughed aloud at that, and I could see he began to like me.

When we reached the hackney, it was as my master foretold. He spoke sharp with the coachman, who wanted him to pay more than the law allowed because it was Christmas Eve (said Nate), but at last they agreed on the fare and soon we was flying through the night—toward Death, it seemed to me. For the driver could hardly have saw his way by the light of the lantern what swung so wild, and he lashed his horse and cursed and took the turns so sharp 'twas a miracle of God that we was not upset on those wintry streets.

Nate Fowler lodged on the second floor of a building that fronted the street. The landlady, a widow called Mrs. Larkham, lived on the floor neath him with her grown son and his wife and baby. Mrs. Larkham was a great pillow of a woman; she did not like the look of me, and said so. I could feel the hopeless guilt upon my face as her great fleshy eyes searched it, and was ready to confess all and be took off to the gallows. But my master told her he had knowed my family for long years and that my honesty was proved. I barely kept myself from looking at him in wonder as he belied hisself, and it crossed my mind that between the two of us, I might be the honester man.

When we had climbed the stairs I followed my master's leading candle through two rooms into the sleeping chamber, where I slid his box from my shoulder. By and by a large, awkward girl came with coal, and a fire was lit. She was called Sophy, and her face was more pitted from smallpox than any I had ever saw; Nate said (after she left) it was like a turd full of cherry-stones. Later I learned to pity her, for he could not abide her, and hastened her from the room when she wished to linger. I knowed not if it was her ugliness or her innocence he could not abear, for she had no opinions of her own, but agreed with whatever was said to her.

After a little the room growed so warm that I took my coat and gloves off, and my master did the same. Then I unpacked his box, and we shared some biscuits he had took away from his brother's house.

"And now, Kit, I have kept my promise, and brought you to London," he said.

"Yes, sir," I said, took aback. "Must I leave tonight, sir?"

He smiled, and then growed serious. "The truth is I do not need a servant, except when I am working, and I have had few commissions of late." He pondered that a moment. At last he said, "You may stay with me till Twelfth Day—the feast of the Epiphany—and if I have no work by then I will give you a crown and my blessing. But if someone commissions a painting from me, and you and I suit each other, then I shall give you three crowns come Lady Day and on every quarter day afterward that you remain with me."

"Thank ye, sir," I said as I made my bow.

Three crowns every quarter day! How I wished I might stay with him. Four quarter days in a year and four crowns to a pound—that made three pounds in a year, over twice what Mr. Dean meant to give me, and my keep besides. The only thing better was to be a prentice, and for that I must have a premium. I wondered what I would gain when I sold Mrs. Dean's scarf, and wished I'd asked Francis what sort of premium his father had paid Joshua Fowler when he began to learn the art of tailoring, though I knowed almost for certain 'twas not within my reach. But I might find a place with a master of a humbler trade who asked for a lower premium. However, that needed more than money; I must also find someone to recommend me, as I could not ask friends or relations to do it. If only I could stay where I had landed! If I could prove my character to Joshua Fowler, he might recommend me to another master. Or perhaps I could make a friend of Daniel, who would soon be finished with his term, and he might write a letter for me. Even my present master might help me—if he knowed anyone useful. But it wasn't likely

I'd find someone to give me a character whilst wandering friendless through London Town.

Yet how could I stay, with Mr. Slingsby knowing my name and my master's as well?

"I fear the chance of my finding a commission is not large," Nate said to me. "You had best keep your eyes open for other employment, Kit."

Then he said he was tired.

"I will have a truckle bed brought tomorrow," he said. "But tonight you must share my bed."

"That's kind of ye, sir."

I blowed out the candles before I undressed, lest the dark of the scarf wrapped round me show through the white of my shirt linen.

My dream that night was of two coaches, one chasing the other through the streets. At first I was in the one chasing, desperate to catch up, for the other had in it fine clothes what would well become me. And they was meant for me, the clothes; they was mine by right. I couldn't abear the unfairness of that coach running away with them.

Then, as is the way with dreams, it seemed I was in the first coach, the one chased, and now I was desperate to get ahead of the one behind me. *Who chases us?* asked Nate, who was with me. *Is it Mr. Dean?* But I answered him, *No, 'tis Christy.* And then I was all in horror, for I'd not meant for him to know about my simple brother. When I woke I felt the relief of it all through me, that I had not told anyone about him after all. Then I felt shame, and then wondered how my brother did, and then chased all these thoughts away and brought my mind back to those two coaches.

I remembered how Joseph in the Bible could say the meaning of dreams, and wondered could I do the same. If dreams be messages from God, it seemed God was telling me that Mr. Dean did not pursue me after all, and that it was safe to stay with Nate Fowler, or anyways to travel with him awhile. God had picked out a fine fate for me in London in spite of my wrongdoing, and fine clothes to go with it. Was it so?

All that day I gazed at men in their Christmas finery like I was looking to find the clothes that was in that coach. We worshipped at St. Paul's Church in Covent Garden, where my master's plain coat with its buttons of horn looked almost Quaker-like amongst the ones in the pews there; many of those had buttons made of brass and was trimmed with fur and tassels.

It was well I had clothes to occupy my mind, for though the sermon was long, one person or another hacked and coughed during every sentence the preacher uttered, causing me to miss the sense of it. I was glad when we was through and bound for Middle Temple Lane. I was eager to see Joshua Fowler again, and most especially his prentice Daniel, that I might begin to make a friend of him, but I ought to have knowed better. Joshua and his wife and brother and Daniel and Francis and every one of the prentices and even Priscilla was all at table together, laughing and drinking healths and eating Christmas pie, whilst I sat in the kitchen eating my portion with the cookmaid and scullery girl. My disappointment was so bitter it spoiled what pleasure I might have took in the feast.

"An't there manservants here?" I asked Agnes, the cookmaid.

"What good is a manservant, unless you've a private coach?" she answered me.

"Mr. Nathaniel Fowler keeps a manservant."

"On account of no prentice will sign with him."

Which I did not like to hear.

'Twas a long afternoon for me, for after dinner there was games, and I heared the laughter and fun of them but could not join in. Dorothy, the scullery maid, tried to get me talking of Essex whilst I waited for my master, but I knowed such talk to be dangerous, and gave short answers. Soon she stopped her trying, and I had no one to speak with, and when we left that evening I'd had not so much as a greeting from Daniel, or from Priscilla either.

9

BEING MR. FOWLER'S servant was a thousand times more easier than being Mr. Dean's. There was no cows to milk nor hens to feed, and 'twas Sophy who carried the coal and emptied the pots and collected the soiled linens. I brought my master his things when he called for them, or carried them for him that he might have a hand upon his walking stick. But my greatest duty was to wait upon his will and whim whilst he prattled in the coffeehouses and taverns, or played at Christmas gambols late into the night with his friends. I stayed up with him, of course, and got the benefit of it, for folks was generous with tips during Christmastide. I kept the coins I was gave in a knotted rag what had been within my boot, and soon it made a mighty jingle when shook.

My master's favorite tavern was the Bear in Drury Lane, near to our lodgings. He often found other picture-drawers there. They all had the same white faces and black teeth from working with the minerals their paints was made from. It began to seem normal to me for a man to look that way. George Pearse was one such man; he worked at the Royal Theatre in Drury Lane, making pictures of orchards or oceans that the audience might imagine they was where they was not. Nate's other great friend was Petrus de Lange, who was Dutch. My master was always praising the Dutch for their paintings, which surprised me, for back home people jeered at that nation.

Together the three men would speak of Godfrey Kneller, who was the court painter for King Charles; or they would laugh at men who had caught the venereal disease, which they called Covent Garden gout; or they would tell the tales they had heared about the fearsome weather we all suffered from, or exclaim over what things cost on account of it. Now and then my master took a sudden whim for something, tobacco, maybe, or new drawing pencils, and I was sent off to find the thing he lacked in the welter of streets around us. Those streets! There was thousands of them, or anyways hundreds, crossing and curling and leading one to the other like they was determined to make a body lose his way. But I learned them soon enough—some few of them, I mean to say. I reckon there was not a soul in that great city who knowed them all.

It was so cold I did not think it could grow more colder, but it did. Innocents' Day was so bitter we shivered even at the fireside of the Bear, and at last made our way homeward through the icy streets as quickly as we dared.

As we came near to the door of our lodgings we saw a beggar waiting there in the gloom. His linen was filthy and torn, and one hand was wrapped in rags. The other he kept hidden neath the tatters of a woman's shawl. I supposed my master would give him a groat and shoo him away, but instead Nate embraced the man with glad cries.

"Tom!" he said. "Why do you not wait within, away from this devilish cold?"

"The girl would not let me," said the other.

"Come," Nate said. "Let us sit by the fire and talk."

"Nay, that visit can end in just one way. Only give me a shilling, that I can buy something to warm my insides."

"You are speaking nonsense. I am not going to let you go away in this weather without knowing where you lay your head at night. You may freeze to death."

"Aye, if fate is kind."

But my master hushed him and we all went up to Nate's sleeping chamber, where I added coal to the fire.

"Here, I am going to wrap myself in my blanket; you had better wrap yourself in one, too," Nate said.

"At least I will not leave it lousy. The lice have died of the frost."

Nate handed him a blanket—my blanket—and Tom wrapped it around hisself with his left hand. His right was gone, and part of the right arm as well.

"Where do you sleep, Tom?" my master asked.

It went on that way, whilst I grumbled within, for I was not so sure Tom's lice was gone, and I guessed that I would soon be sent to a cookshop for his supper, for which trouble I would get no tip. And so it fell out.

But it did not end there. As Tom finished his veal pie—a

whole one, mind, which he ate by hisself—my master said to him, "You must stay with me till this weather breaks. I will not have you freeze."

"Don't, Nate," the man said, beginning to cry. "Do you not remember how it was last time? 'Twill be so again, you know it will. Only give me some wine, before I go."

"I remember," Nate said. "But 'twill be different this time."

Then he poured wine for both of them, whilst I sat shivering near the fire, and wondering if Tom was to sleep with me, as Christy used to do.

He stayed four nights, and he slept with me. I did not grow more itchier than I was before, so maybe the cold did kill his lice. But that was not enough to make him welcome in my bed, what had seemed so strange to me when first I lay in it, but which I was now so accustomed to that I was jealous of every soft corner. And I was resentful, too, that while Tom was with us my master stayed much to our lodgings, and I was kept busy running for food and wine. I had no time to hunt for brokers of secondhand clothes, nor for proper masters, nor had Nate Fowler time to seek a commission. The days till Epiphany was growing more fewer.

Except that first night I did not see Tom sober. Once he touched the wine he could not keep from it, and Nate did not gainsay him, but spent his own shillings on one bottle after another. I was the one sent for it, and I brung it back with ill grace, and sometimes took a swig of my own upon the stairs, less because I wanted it than because I wanted him not to have it.

Once when he had not yet drunk enough wine to send him into a stupor he went into the room that was Nate's workshop. I was accustomed to it now, but the first time I was there I thought that I had never before saw a room so strange. Against one wall was a table filled with pans and pipkins and crucibles and basins and glass bottles what had stoppers in them, and from the ceiling six or seven bladders was hung, like they was being sold at a fair; my master used them to hold his colors when they was wet. There was also a press with shelves that was piled with canvas cloth and a great many sticks, and another cupboard with a blue checked curtain before it, what held my master's finished paintings, which I had not yet saw. On top of that cupboard was a great slab of stone, some foot and a half square, that was black and gray and white and green all mixed together. My master said it was his grinding stone, made of marble, and that I must not touch it on any account.

Tom went straight to the cupboard with the blue checked curtain before it, and I wondered would he touch the grinding stone, and what my master would say if he did. But instead he pulled aside the curtain and began to look at Nate's paintings. My master did not say nay, to him or to me, so I stood by and looked in my turn.

"Your color is muddy here. You did not grind the verdigris fine enough."

"Perhaps."

"And this—a farmhouse, is it meant to be? Or a water mill? It might be either."

"That is why it remains unsold, no doubt."

"And this—oh, Nate, Nate." He gave a drunken laugh. "I think you must hate women, you paint them so ill."

I saw his meaning, for the woman painted was brown and freckled.

"I used yellow ocher with the vermilion to color her flesh, the way I do when I paint peasants or seamen," Nate said. "But 'tis very like!" Then he began to laugh, and his friend laughed with him.

"You have no gift for portraiture, Nate."

"I do not deny it."

"I would have done wonderful portraits. I would have put every pretty feature that woman had upon the cloth, and smoothed out every bad one." And he began to cry.

"I know, Tom," my master said, as tender as a woman might.

On the first day of 1684 we woke to find Tom gone, and the green marble grinding stone was gone as well.

"A pox!" Nate cried. "Why must he take the grinding stone? He knew how I prized it!"

I flinched at his words, like they was aimed at me, for I knowed how Mrs. Dean loved her blue scarf, and wondered did she rail at me this way when I'd took it from her.

"After all the wine I poured down his greedy gullet! He might have taken anything, my books, my lute, the silver candlesticks from the parlor—I would not have begrudged him my very coat and gloves, to keep him from freezing," my master said. "Oh, Tom, Tom!"

He sat down suddenly upon a stool and put a hand upon his forehead.

"Shall I call a constable, sir?" 'Twas the last thing I wanted, yet I thought I must ask, or he would wonder why.

"A constable! Nay, certainly not."

I was relieved, but curious. "Surely 'tis a costly thing, sir."

"He has a claim on me," Nate said. He stood again and shook his head like he could that way throw off his painful thoughts. "When next I am given a commission I will buy another from the place that makes tombstones. Thank God he did not know where I keep my amber, that is the costliest color I use. Do not mention this to Mrs. Larkham, Kit; she is always certain that I am harboring thieves in her house."

And so you are, I thought, not in a clever, satisfied way, but with a great sigh in my heart.

And so we came to the eleventh day of Christmas, and Nate had no commission. As we was walking to the Bear that day the streets seemed more icy and clamorous than ever, and more thronged with paupers, many of 'em missing a leg or worser. "Kind Christian gentleman, won't you relieve my suffering?" one said to my master, tugging on his sleeve, and Nate stopped to give him a groat, and bade him get within doors. I wondered would I end the same way, and it troubled me, for I knowed not if I had the pluck and hardihood to beg of strangers. I wished I knowed where to rid myself of Mrs. Dean's scarf. My master had showed me the places he might one day send me, such as the ironmonger he went to when he needed a new crucible, and the stationer he liked to buy pencils from, and the apothecary where he got turpentine. But I had not saw a pawnshop. Ought I to ask my master where a clothes-broker was to be found, or would that rouse his suspicion?

We came to the Bear, but as we went in Petrus and George was coming out. "Have you heard?" George asked. "There has been a wager; someone will drive a coach across the ice of the Thames."

"You do not mean to go down there?" said Nate, and I knowed he thought of his leg.

In truth he did not go as quick as others did, but Petrus and George walked more slower that he might join them. By the time we reached the river a merry crowd was gathered there, and the coach, drawn by six horses, was halfways across the span of the Thames.

All those around us was betting, and a boy in blue livery wanted to make a servant-sized wager with me, but I would not. My future was so perilous I dared not lose any of the little I had, but more than that, I could not judge of my own desires: if the ice held, there was a chance of a frost fair, like nothing I had ever saw or would ever see again. But if the coach broke through, it would be a great spectacle and drama and a satisfying lesson for us all.

"It is sound—they will reach Lambeth safely!" someone cried.

"Hold, they are slowing!"

"No, they reach—they are there!"

And they was. The crowd broke, and people rushed upon the

ice, many sliding and falling. Among them was a girl in a blue cloak, and suddenly I saw it was Priscilla. I began to raise my arm, meaning to wave it and perhaps catch her notice, but my master looked at me as if to say nay, and I stopped myself. Just then she fell, and a lad near her helped her gain her feet, which made me cross with my master. Who was he to give me orders with his eyes, when today was my last day in his employ? If not for that look it would have been me that was near to her by the time she had fell.

"Do you remember Abraham Hondius's painting of the frozen Thames in '77?" George Pearse said. "That was a fine landskip. Do you suppose he will paint it again?"

"I would like to paint it myself," Nate said.

But I hardly heeded them, for I'd saw who it was that helped Priss to right herself, and knowed that all the waving in the world would not have served me; for it was Daniel.

That afternoon I was gave a few hours' holiday, for my master said he would not need me till nightfall. The moment I was free of him I began almost to snatch at those who walked by me, demanding to know where I might find a clothes-broker. Angel Alley, said one man; Bear and Ragged Staff Yard, said another; and a woman said Rosemary Lane. I knowed where none of those places was, but then someone said there was a shop near to St. Paul's Cathedral. St. Paul's! That great dome what rose high above the scampering life of the street! No landmark in London was easier to find, and I hastened toward it, glad to have a chance to see the whole of it.

Then for a little I forgot my errand, only craned my neck and stared, agape, and prayed a little in thanksgiving that I'd been brung far enough in life to see it, even should I die tomorrow. Some things are like that, I reckon, grand enough in themselves to satisfy a soul entirely, at least for a little while.

I was not alone there, for the place was thronged with criers and beggars and all manner of folk. One lad tried to make a wager with me on a game he played with three balls and a cup, but though Nate had not warned me against women or dissenters, he had warned me against such play as this. I reckoned the boy knowed by my clothes I was a country cokes, and began to think of what I would wear when I had sold my scarf. I saw a boy in livery near to me—saw him and opened my mouth to call to him, for he had not saw me, and I meant to ask him if he knowed where the clothes-broker kept his shop. But then beyond him I saw his master, a stout man in a fair wig what reminded me of the squire back home. And the boy's livery was gold and black, like the squire's.

I runned. A fool thing to do, or maybe not, but anyways I did it. And suddenly the courtyard of St. Paul's was alive with shouting and pointing. They was chasing me, I would be catched, the scarf would be discovered, I would be hanged, I would never again see Christy, and he would wonder all his days what became of me. Those was the thoughts I had as I took my first running step, and my second was the leap of one who has the Devil at his heels. I runned by a man who heared the clamor and throwed hisself at me, but he slipped on the ice and missed. I slipped, too, making great, wild steps upon the icy street, but did not lose my feet. I runned into a alley so filled with pigs I could not go through it, but must turn and run out again. There I stopped, panting, much took aback, for the people who was chasing me had now crowded round another figure.

"Pickpocket," said a serving maid. "Caught pinching a purse." She carried a pail half filled with something what was froze solid. "What was *you* running for?" she asked.

I made no answer. The pain in my chest and throat was terrible, each breath seemed to tear at my flesh.

"Be off, then, or I'll call the constable," she said, and took her pail away.

I could not see the stout man, nor the gold-and-black livery, but my terror did not leave me. Now I went as slow as before I went fast, like my creeping movements might escape all eyes. I trembled with fear, and my eyes growed wet, though praise God the tears did not spill over and freeze upon my cheeks. I inched my way through many streets before I saw the foolishness of it, and began to walk again with dignity.

That night after the candles was pinched I lay thinking of my fate, and wondering if the boy in livery was John Frith, and if it was, where in London I might best hide from him. I knowed not if the boy or his master had saw my face before I runned. There might be constables looking for me, or there might not. I might meet John Frith anywhere I went, or I might not. What should my first step be when I left Covent Garden tomorrow?

I spoke into the darkness. "Will I leave in the morning, sir, or stay till dinner is past, maybe?"

He said naught for a long moment, and I wondered did he sleep.

Then he said, "There will surely be a frost fair."

That turned my thoughts. "With jugglers, sir?"

"Oh, much more than jugglers. 'Twill be like nothing you've ever seen—and a great subject for a landskip. Abraham Hondius will certainly paint it. Others will, too."

"And yerself, sir?" I asked as I began to understand him.

"The scene fills my mind, though I have not yet laid eyes on it. I can think of nothing else. I have been to an innkeeper who has given me a commission. Now you will learn something about painting!"

"Then ye'll be keeping me on, sir?"

"Of course," he said. "I'll be needing you."

I was filled with relief, knowing I did not have to take that first step alone next day. All the same, I could not keep from thinking if there was one place in London John Frith was bound to go, 'twas the Frost Fair.

10

THE FROST FAIR was put up so quick it seemed a fairy thing. The Thames was wondrous to gaze upon of itself: a shining white plain of ice. But now it looked to have a little village built upon it. There was many booths planted in a line, each made of frieze blankets hung from the oars that the watermen could not use till the river was itself again. One booth sold gingerbread and another spiced ale, and there was hot pudding pies and brandy-balls and tobacco. Beyond there was boats pulled by horses what had their hoofs wrapped in linen that they might not slide upon the ice. There was boys playing football, and jugglers, and some people throwed snowballs. Then there was men who had a sledge tied with a rope to a stake put through the ice, who towed it round in circles so that it spun merrily, whilst the people sitting within laughed and screamed.

And on the south bank, near to the Old Barge House, there was my master and me and all the things I'd carried for him: a clever wooden stand he called a easel, what had his canvas cloth stretched tight over its frame of sticks, drawing pencils, a stick of charcoal, and some fine white breadcrumbs for rubbing out his mistakes. We'd brung a charcoal brazier, too; I kept a fire in it and heated stones within, as my master bade me.

When all was arranged, my master drawed off his gloves.

"Ye'd best keep them on, sir," I said to him with dismay. "Else yer fingers will freeze."

"Did you give advice so freely to your last master? No wonder that you were desperate to get out of Essex."

"Beg pardon, sir." But the truth was that he liked me to talk, and encouraged me. I reckoned that he was lonely, not for the company of equals, for he had that in plenty, but for someone he could teach, like a prentice.

"No one would buy a painting made by a gloved man. Drawing requires fine control. I will warm my hands with the stones when I need to, or put my gloves on and wrap myself in our blanket awhile. Or you can bring me a dish of chocolate or coffee from one of the stalls from time to time. Indeed, why not now?" Already he opened and closed his fist, like his fingers was stiffened.

"The watermen are charging tuppence to use the stairs, sir," I reminded him, for the coachman had said so. Also, I did not wish to go upon the ice, for though I could not see the garments of every figure that crowded the fair, I was near to certain that some of them was livery.

"What matter, so long as I am the one who pays? When I send you upon the ice I'll give you tuppence, and if you yourself choose to go it shall be your tuppence. Here, go, and while you are about it look closely at those men on skates, and when you return tell me what you have observed."

"Ye'd do better not to trust my eyes, sir. Can't ye do it yerself?"

"I trust your eyes more than my leg," he said, swatting his lame one to show me what he meant. "Come, you needn't be afraid of falling, a strong young lad like yourself." And he handed me a coin for the stairs and one for the coffee.

So I walked out onto the ice, telling myself no one would notice one more boy at the fair. At once I slid, but did not fall; then I slid and did, but I hardly cared, for I was looking through the crowds for stout men or liveried boys. I had not saw any, though, by the time I came near to the Dutchmen—and then I forgot for a moment about John Frith. There was six or seven on skates that day, including Petrus, who winked at me. They was beautiful to watch; they glided by like they was birds in the sky, or boats upon a river, whilst the blades of their skates drawed shapes upon the ice, as a diamond writing ring leaves letters when it cuts window glass.

But when I had brung coffee back to my master, and tried to tell him about the men on skates, he shouted, "Do not tell me that they are birds or boats! Look at the thing itself!" And he gave me another tuppence for the stairs and sent me off again.

So I went back to look at the thing itself: the arm, the leg, the skate, the flying ice. Then he was more satisfied, though I could not see that what I told him changed his drawing.

After that I went when I was bid, whether to look at the things he painted or to fetch him chocolate, and I never saw John, till at last I reckoned he was back in Essex where he belonged, and 'twas my own fancy that put him at St. Paul's. Of course, his master was bound to come to London in the spring, but I need not trouble over that now. If a boy is to live he cannot always be looking behind him, at brothers and scarves and squires.

My master's picture growed quickly all that first day, and the next day we brung colors: white lead and blue bice, each in its own bladder, and folded papers filled with fine-ground powders he called umber and ocher and other strange names. Also linseed oil, and oil of turpentine, and a wooden board he called a palette, and many brushes. I watched with interest as I tended the brazier to see what he would do with these things, but my interest made him cross, and he bade me go upon the ice and amuse myself. However, he did not like to give me a tuppence for the stairs, and I liked not to spend my own—till I spied a blue cloak, what changed my mind.

I hastened as quick as I could down the stairs and across the frozen Thames toward the fair, always keeping that blue in sight, till I catched her up, and indeed, 'twas Priscilla.

"I did not think to see you here," she said with surprise. "Have you been dismissed?"

"Nay, Mr. Fowler paints a picture of the Frost Fair—he is there, upon the bank." I pointed across the river. "He has nothing for me to do at this moment, that is all. And yerself, what do ye here?"

"I am on an errand for my mistress," she said.

"What do ye buy for her?"

"Vinegar," she said, and we laughed, for there was none at the fair.

"Need ye hasten back?"

"Nay, half my duty is to bring my mistress news. Have you any?"

"Well—my master has got a commission from Mr. Webb, who keeps a tavern in the Strand."

"Yes, she will like to know that. What more?"

I thought of Tom and the theft of the marble grinding stone, but reckoned my master would not want that told, and a servant must always keep his master's secrets.

"I haven't heared much, but now I know ye're wanting news I'll listen more keener. Why don't we walk a little, and see the sights of the fair?" And I offered her my arm.

But she cast down her eyes and shook her head, and said she must be going, though she'd said so lately that she needn't.

"What of *yer* news? What of Daniel's banquet?" I called after her, but she heared me not, or so pretended. I wondered did she leave me because I was a country cokes, or for some other reason.

By the end of that second day my master's canvas was done: buildings and the shadows of buildings, sky and ice, the blanket booths and the coaches going by, and dozens of tiny figures amusing themselves, while in the very middle of it all was three men on skates. I was surprised how quick it had all come into being, and for the first time thought my master a clever and artful man.

The next day Nate had a fire built in the workshop grate and set his canvas near to it to dry. Then he left me there to tend it whilst he went to the tavern. Tending a coal fire an't so easy as tending a wood fire. The thing must be always poked and stirred to let the air in, and when first I came to London I near despaired of learning to do it, but by now I was comfortable at it, and not afeared it would die.

When my master left I was glad of the peace, but before a hour passed I own I never was so bored. I was troubled, too, that Nate had so quickly done his work. I could not but wonder what help I could be to him when the thing was finished.

I went into the parlor and stood at the window, watching folks trotting past, thinking on what sort of a painting they might make: here a parson, there a milkmaid; here a laughing lord, perhaps; there a miss. At least, I reckoned from her fine clothes she was a miss, I mean to say a young woman whose keep is paid for by a man who visits her when he feels lusty. Nate said there was many such living in Covent Garden; there was bawdy houses, too, nearby in Long Acre. One such miss appeared three times in the street, and looked anxiously up and down it, before she was catched up by the youth she waited for, who was dressed as fine as she was herself. I was thinking over what Joshua Fowler had said to me in the coach, about prentices who ruined themselves keeping whorish girls in London, when another youth turned into the lane, and I saw that it was Daniel. Without a thought I snatched my coat from its peg and runned down the stairs.

"Daniel, it's Kit, Mr. Nathaniel Fowler's boy," I called out when I was near to him.

He heared me not, and followed the lane where it curved into another. But I was resolved, and hastened after him.

"Daniel! Daniel, it's Kit!"

At last he heared me, and looked round with a frown.

"Who are you, boy, and what do you need of me?"

"I'm Kit, Mr. Nathaniel Fowler's boy," I said again.

He frowned at me a moment more, then said, most impatient, "Yes, Priss said she had seen you about. What is it you would know?"

Priscilla had spoke of me! The interest of that stopped my tongue for a moment, but I found it again quick enough.

"I thought perhaps ye looked for my master. I can tell ye where he is, if that's aught of good to ye."

"My master does not send me with messages for his brother. I am come to measure a merchant for a suit. Is there something more?"

I could not say: *How might I turn from me to you?* which, in truth, was what I wished to know. I said instead, "I am wondering if ye might give me counsel, sir, on how I may better myself."

"I cannot help you with that. Give good service, I suppose, and hope to move on to a better place."

"I wish I might be a prentice, instead of a servant."

"That is not so easy. Can you cast accounts?"

"I can do sums, sir."

"And can you read and write?"

"I can read a few words."

"Well, find someone that can teach you to read more. Reading opens many doors. That's my advice."

A ragged-dressed woman came abreast of us just then; her hands was purple and white from the cold, and her eyes was bold but they was desperate, too.

"Warm me up with a pint, countryman, and I'll see to it you're warm as well," she said, in the same kind of voice a beggar uses.

He smiled back, and took the glove from his right hand.

Then he did put the back of his hand against her cheek. I watched amazed and shamed as my prick rose, and thought of what Joshua had said about his pious household.

"Why, how will you warm me, love, when you're so cold?" Daniel said. "Tell me how?"

Then she told him. I had never heared such words from a woman before, and the shock of them did add to my lust as I waited to see what answer Daniel would make.

With a look of triumph he threw his head back and spat upon her face; the spittle froze on her cheek. She screamed at him, and he called her a strumpet, and wished pox upon her privities, till she hastened away, crying foul words at us as she went.

Daniel smiled again, much satisfied. "And do not waste your earnings going coney-hunting," he said. "That, too, is my counsel."

Then he strode away, and I did not try to hold him.

A whore was the last thing I meant to spend money on, the thought of it did not even cross my mind till Daniel lifted his hand to that woman's face. But now I did stop to imagine the touch of a woman's coney. I wondered why it was called after a rabbit, and would it be so soft as one, and what it must feel like to put my thing altogether in hers. Perhaps after I sold my scarf— but no, that money was for my premium, that I might someday be impatient with servants in the street, as Daniel was with me. I filled with shame to have catched myself thinking such sinful thoughts, and hastened upstairs, wondering did the fire still burn. It did, and I burned as well.

∾

My master and me was both in a ill-humor that afternoon. We was like flies what have been trapped by a window, buzzing and bumping vainly at the glass. My own humor was on account of my meeting with Daniel, but I knowed not what accounted for his.

At last he picked up the drying canvas and took it near the window, where a little gray light did yet enter.

"The men on skates look like wasps."

"They are more taller than wasps," I said.

"What a comfort you are," he said, and I could tell he meant the opposite. "Bring me a candle."

I brung one near to him and held it so's he could more better study his painting.

"What do ye look for, sir?"

"Today I saw the picture Abraham Hondius is working on. It is a thousand times better than mine."

"It matters not, sir, so long as Mr. Webb cannot pay for his picture."

He gave me a look such as I used sometimes to get from Christy: hurt and surprise mixed somehow with cunning.

"Bring my knife, please, Kit."

'Twas on the table, where he opened the oysters we ate for dinner. I brung it to him, thinking he might mean to scrape a bit at a single spot of paint upon the cloth. But instead he plunged the knife straight through the picture and drawed it down with great strength and fury, and then did the same again, and yet again till the whole of it was destroyed, whilst I stood watching him, as a servant must.

"That is how much it matters!" he said, like he had won a wrestling contest.

It seemed like it was my hope of betterment that was so rent, and my feelings burst from me.

"Sir, sir! Is it a madman I serve? Is that why I carry yer things for ye, that ye might tear up what ye've done? Where are ye taking me, sir, tell me, please! For I cannot live without hope, no one can."

"*You* to live without hope! Why, you selfish, ignorant creature, you know nothing of despair except how to inflict it upon another! What sort of fool will taunt a man with his insufficiency, and then regret the cost?"

I stood trembling before him and the truth of the matter began to fall upon me like snow. I saw that the words I'd meant as a comfort was instead a torment to him, and they was the reason for his mad act what had ruined his chances and mine, too. It was strange to me that a man could be so prideful as to care more for his skillfulness than for his bread. No wonder that his brother could not abide him; he was not fit for company. I was as sure of my rightness in this as I was of the Creed, but all the same a cold grief numbed me clean through, for I had failed in my service, failed because my master was beyond my understanding. And now what would become of me?

"I am owed a crown, anyways," I said, most sullen. "A crown and a bit more, if ye're an honest man, but I'll take the crown at least."

"That is the sort of boy you are, then, the kind who walks away just when needed most. I might have known it. I wish that I had left you begging your bread in Chelmsford, 'tis all you're fit for."

"An't ye sending me away, sir?"

"Why would I send you away when I have great need of you? For I must begin anew tomorrow and do all my drawing over again."

His anger had left him, and he sat down sudden upon a stool near the fire. I could see from the way he moved it that his leg ached.

He was silent for a little, then said, "'Tis easy to see why God made great artists, but why did He also make worthless painters of no talent such as myself?"

I thought for a moment and said cautiously, "*Did* God make ye a painter, then?"

"He did."

"And did He make me a servant?"

"As good a servant as I am a painter," Nate said, and then gave a bark of laughter, which startled me.

We was abed early that night, yet lay long awake, each listening to the other squirm and toss.

"Is it yer leg hurting ye, sir?" I asked my master at last.

"Nay, not that. Or yes, perhaps a bit." He kept silent a little, then said, "I wish you could read to me! It eases me to hear a few sonnets in the evening."

"I know a fair bit of Scripture, sir, if ye'd like me to recite a psalm, perhaps."

"Nay, nothing in that Book will solve my problem."

I was glad he refused me, but wondered what problem he meant: the problem of his painting or the problem of his aching leg or the problem of his brother—or yet some other problem.

"I only wish I *could* read, sir. I would rather learn that than anything."

"Ah, yes, your education. Why are you so keen to learn reading, Kit? Are you thirsting for works of philosophy?"

"I mean to rise in life, sir."

"To rise in life! I advise against it. That is my brother's aim, you know, and he spends all his time telling pretty lies to his betters, or listening to gossip about men he never meets, and spewing out gratitude. Is that any kind of life?"

"'Tis the life of a servant, sir, only more comfortable-like," I told him.

He laughed. "I think you are too honest to rise in life, Kit. But if you are determined, I will help you learn to read. Remind me of it when we've time."

Which cheered me a little, and soon I slept.

11

I THOUGHT WE would begin his painting again next morning, but Nate said he would take a day's holiday first, and that turned into two, and then three. I reckoned he was afraid to start again, like a boy who falls from a horse. I was troubled, for if the thaw should come he would lose his commission. But 'twas not all bad, as he interested himself in teaching me to read, though in a way I believe no other man ever did.

We was in a privy, I upon my hole and he upon his, and he asked me to pass him some bum-fodder what had been left there for the wiping of one's arse—printed pages torn from books no longer wanted. I gave him some, and kept some to study, thinking to pick out the simpler words as I struggled to get rid of the pork pasty I'd ate at dinner yesterday. That reminded him of his promise, and he began to help me with the pages I held. But some was printed in what he called Roman type, and some in a manner he called black letter, which gave me much confusion. At last he

told me we would come to that later, and settled meanwhile for
more coarser lessons.

"Look here. What can you read, Kit?" he asked, pointing at
the wall.

It was covered with words, but I knowed only a few of them.

"Listen, then," Nate said when I only grunted. "For 'tis
much to the point. 'No Hero looks so fierce in Fight / as does the
Man who strains to shite.'" Then he laughed and raised his
breeches, for he had not had such a hard time of it as I.

He waited for me in the street, and when I was through making fierce faces I raised my breeches as well, and studied the
words he had pointed at, till I was sure I would know every one
of them again.

So it went all through London. In one boghouse we read:

Because they cannot eat, some Authors write
And some, it seems, because they cannot shite.

And in another:

Damn their Doublets, and confound their Breeches,
There's none beshit the Wall but Sons of Bitches.
May the French Pox and the Devil take 'em all,
That beshit their Fingers, and wipe them on the Wall.

Though, of course, whoever wrote it had done the same hisself.

But privies was not my only primers. We used windows, too,
where folks had writ with diamond rings upon the glass. Those
was more genteel, and I learned to read:

That which frets a Woman most,
Is when her Expectation's crossed.

Once whilst we sat in a tavern Nate said, "Ah, this inscription is well done. I have seen the same engraved on a summerhouse window. You can read it by yourself, can you not?"

"Why, there's nothing but letters, sir."

"Try reading it, and we shall see."

So I read aloud: "'I, C, U, B, Y, Y, for me.'" By the time I was done I saw the idea of it, but could not make out the Y's for a moment. Then it came to me, and I read again: "I see you be too wise for me."

"Excellent! I thought you could do it."

Which made me feel as proud as if I'd read the Gospels right out loud.

The tavern we was at that day was not the Bear; Nate had not went there once since he tore his painting. I knowed he did not wish to speak with other artists, or with anyone who might tell him his place was not at fireside but on the south bank of the Thames. So we ranged far from Covent Garden, and went to chocolate houses and taverns I had not saw before.

One of these was the Harp and Ball, near Charing Cross. It had many rooms, and fires in all of 'em, and was crowded with men who liked to wager on the throw of the dice. Nate had brung a book, for he meant to teach me about printed words. But I hardly heared him, because of the great din, and instead of teaching me he soon growed interested in what was there writ. I was not sorry

when he shooed me from him, but went to watch the gamesters,
for there was great excitement there, and loud cries from all each
time the dice clattered on the table. A red-faced man with a griz-
zled beard won again and again, but never smiled; a man with a
long head and a dark wig had lost much, he never smiled either.

Someone brushed near me and I stepped aside that he might
pass, but to my surprise 'twas a she, a woman in a ragged cloak
held tight about her. She'd come from the room beyond, and I
knowed what she must have done there. I looked to see who she
had done it with; but no one appeared, and my eyes went back to
the dice.

A few minutes later, I was again brushed, for I stood near the
door to that inner room, and must step aside for anyone who
came out of it. I looked to see what sort of man he was, knowing
he'd just been with a low woman. He was dressed like a gentleman, with a fur muff and a beaver hat, and he had on his face the
great smile that the gamesters lacked. He did not leave the tavern,
though, as the ragged woman had. Instead he pushed ahead of
me, so I must fall back, and took my place watching the throw of
the dice, and after a while said he would bet.

But when he felt for his purse, he had it not.

"Thief!" he cried, and turned on me. "This boy brushed
against me and stole my purse!"

He seized me by the shoulder in a painful grip; I struggled
against it.

"I have not took yer purse, sir!" I cried out. "On my oath, I
have not got it!"

"Certainly you have it! Search the lad!"

All the gaming had stopped, and people crowded round. The vintner came from behind the bar and scowled at me.

"Who are you, boy, and why do you idle around in taverns instead of doing honest work?"

"Mr. Fowler, sir, help! Help!" I cried.

And only then did Nate look up from his book, and, seeing I was in distress, hastened to me.

"What goes on here?" he said, sounding greatly vexed. "This lad is in my employ, he is not troubling anyone."

"He has took a gentleman's purse," the vintner said.

"I have not, sir! I have not took it!"

"Well, that can be easily proved," Nate said. "He is willing to be searched, aren't you, Kit?"

Then he looked at the terror on my face and saw that I was not. The shock in his eyes filled me with shame, and I could not speak, but hung my head.

They began to search me. The vintner was the one undid the buttons of my coat, and the coat was then passed round among the men, all patting and poking it, to be sure 'twas innocent. They found the knotted rag what held my own small treasure, and jeered at it, and cast it aside, where Nate quickly picked it up. Then my doublet was took off, and the same done unto it, and my shirt linen was pulled free of my breeches. The vintner stepped back, then, and everyone waited for the purse to fall to the floor, but it did not.

"Why, where is it, then?" the vintner asked, and patted my breeches all round, including my most private places, but found naught but what was put there by God.

I waited for him to put his hands neath my shirt, and find the scarf wrapped round my middle, but he did not.

Nate spoke; his face was clear and easy now. "'Twas not so small a purse that we need look for it in his arse hole, I suppose," he said, and there was great laughter.

"He has passed it to an accomplice," the gentleman said, very angry.

"It is likely to be in the hands of that hag with the ragged cloak who left here a little while since," my master said. "You were with her in a back room, were you not, sir?"

Now there was yet greater laughter, and jeers, and the men returned to the table, and the game began again.

My master turned without speaking, and left the tavern, and I followed after, only stopping to pick up his book, what he had left upon the table.

"This is yours, I think," he said, and held out to me my knotted rag. I took it from him, and he did not speak again of what had happened at the Harp and Ball.

After that I knowed I must get rid of that scarf. So long as I had it with me I was in danger. Once I had sold it the danger would not go entirely, but it would be less, and I could walk with a lighter step, and need not blanch with terror before my master.

Since he had quit painting Nate had began lying long abed each day, in part because he drank so much of a evening, but also because he knowed not what to do with hisself once he rose. On one such morning I built up the fire for him, and then went to the privy, where I unwound the scarf and tucked it in the place between my shirt and coat, so's I could put a hand to it without trouble. Then I hastened down the stairs and out into the street. I knowed now how to get to St. Paul's the most quickest way: Drury Lane to Fleet Street and up Ludgate Hill. At the head of Fleet Street of course I passed Middle Temple Lane, and looked that way toward Joshua Fowler's house, thinking of Priscilla, but catched no sight of her, which was as well. But it might be that I would see her on my way back to Covent Garden, when my errand was done.

Once I reached St. Paul's I asked the first man I saw for the clothes-broker's shop, and though he knowed it not, the second man did. 'Twas not so close to St. Paul's after all, but one street over, in a quiet, narrow lane so shadowed by the cathedral that I reckoned it never saw the sun, even when there was one to see. I stood for a moment outside the shop, calming myself, and then went in.

The woman inside was writing something in a book what lay open on a counter; she looked up quick when she heared my step.

"Good morning, madame," I said as I bowed.

"I wouldn't sell that coat, boy, you'll freeze if you do," she said, fixing her eyes on it.

"It an't my coat I'm selling," I said. I reached into it and brung out the scarf.

I hadn't seen it but in the dark for many weeks, and had forgot the night-blue beauty of it. The woman had it quickly in her hands. She tugged at it to test the weave, and touched it to her cheek, and then she smelt it, which made me drop my eyes, for I knowed it smelt of my sweat.

"How came you by this piece of cloth?" she asked me.

"'Twas a gift from my last mistress," I said.

"Here in London?"

"Nay, in Essex."

She rubbed the cloth between her thumb and finger, and scowled at me.

"I am a pawnbroker. Do you know what that is?"

"Yes, madame."

"It is a kind of moneylender," she said, as though I had not spoke. Her words was very sharp and angry. "I loan you a little bit of money, and you give me this scarf as security, and I give you a ticket for it. When you are ready to repay the loan—and a little over it, mind, for my trouble—you come to me with the ticket, and I return the scarf to you."

I reckoned that was the way it was supposed to work, but in my experience it never did. Pawned things was as good as sold for one such as me.

"You understand, then, what a pawnbroker is?"

"Yes, madame," I said again, thinking it must be my country ways that made her explain things so slow and simple.

But she drawed herself up straight and shouted at me, *"I am a pawnbroker! I am not a fence! Frank!"*

I was bewildered and affrighted. I knowed not what a fence was, but I could see she meant harm to me, and I heared heavy, running steps from the back.

"I'll go then, if you please," I said, bowing again, and pulled at the scarf. But she would not loose her hold.

"What is it, Mother?" a man said as he burst into the shop from behind.

"He is no honest boy!" she said to her son.

"It is mine! Mrs. Dean willed me to have it!" I cried, and yanked the scarf as hard as I dared. But perhaps I did not dare enough, anyways I could not get it from her.

"Mrs. Dean," she said. "I will remember that name when I give evidence. Frank, call the constable."

So once again I runned, though only far enough to reach the crowds outside St. Paul's. There I slipped myself into the midst of them and tried to look at my ease; however, I never was so angry in all my life. I could not be more angrier if the scarf had indeed been a gift to me from Mrs. Dean; I think I had forgot for a moment that it was not.

'Twas a contest between my master and me that day as to whose spirits was the lowest. I had the more right to 'em, I thought, for I was a thief but had not got the good of being one, though the bad of it might yet lie before me. I had no prospects now beyond my service to Mr. Fowler, and where was that likely to get me, with him so odd and changeable?

But next day we was evened up, for as we was going out that morning Mrs. Larkham was coming in, with her market basket hung over her arm. "The frost has begun to give, God be praised!" she said in a high voice what quavered from excitement.

"It cannot be true. 'Twas cold as Muscovy last night," my master said.

"'Tis true enough. Eliza!" she called to her daughter-in-law. "The frost begins to give!"

"Then I am finished," Nate said.

The moment we walked outside we knowed from the softness in the air that Mrs. Larkham was right. We rushed down Bow Street and past Somerset House to the bank of the Thames and looked east toward the Temple Stairs. All was in disorder: many of the booths was gone, and others was being took down as we watched, whilst the boats and such was being towed toward shore. The ice was yet hard, and the Dutchmen on skates did not mind the scene around them, but continued to swoop and glide while they might.

"I am ruined. I am finished," Nate said.

"It may freeze again tonight."

"Nay. It is done. I am done. Let us go to the Bear."

He drank too much that day, and into the evening, till he was not fit to walk. I hired a sedan chair that he might be carried to our lodgings, and splashed alongside through the melting snow. One of the men helped me with him on the stairs. I tipped him for it, and we wished each other good fortune.

Nate puked much when first we came into our rooms, but after that he rested peacefully a good part of the night, and I did the same. About a hour before daybreak he opened his eyes and called to me to feed the fire.

"It an't day yet," I said, struggling up from sleep.

"'Tis near enough. I will sleep no more, at least. I have been awake this past hour."

He sat upon his bed and pulled his blanket about his shoulders, then gazed into the fire. "I dreamed a man with a chestnut wig gave me a great deal of money, many pounds, I do not know how much. 'What is it for?' I asked him, and he told me I was to paint all the good dishes of a feast for him, but he warned me to taste them not. I told him I could not paint, for all my colors had frozen, but he said, 'Ah, that is how I like them.' What do you make of it, Kit?"

"It is a foreseeing dream," I said confidently. "Mr. Webb is the man in the chestnut wig, and he will give ye much money when ye have finished yer painting of the Frost Fair."

"That is over with," Nate said.

"Nay, 'twill freeze again, and your colors, too, see?"

"And what of the good dishes I may not taste?"

"Why, that means the delights of the Frost Fair, for ye draw them but ye do not go upon the ice to enjoy the merriment, and ye must not, or some ill may come to ye."

He put his hands up to the sides of his head. "Ill has already come to me," he said. "What a headache I have got! Is there any ale?"

"I'll go for some as soon as the day breaks, sir."

I was so pleased he asked me about his dream I forgot my misery for a moment. I could not but think of Joseph in Egypt, and how he interpreted the dreams of those around him. But when Joseph came into my mind he brung his many-colored coat with him, and then I was pierced by the memory of Christy, and all my sorrows came back to me.

12

THE WARMER WEATHER lasted but two days. On Sunday morning when we left our lodgings a bitter wind drove through the lanes, and our way was slippery with frost, though the snow had gone.

"Ye dreamed it, didn't I say?" I said to my master.

"We will not reckon our chickens before they are hatched," he answered me, but he looked more cheerfuller.

And the next day those chickens did hatch, for all the booths was put up again, and there was taverns and coffeehouses with blankets for walls, where men sat at charcoal fires drinking and talking, just as if they was in Fleet Street. Every kind of ware was sold, earthen and copper and tin; ribbons and gloves; snuffboxes and toys. There was more kinds of diversions than I had ever saw: ropedancers and puppet plays and a man who walked on great stilts. A place was set up to bowl at ninepins, and another to play at pigeon-in-the-hole. The whirling sledge returned, and a boat on wheels was towed by some men whilst a man stood in the front of it beating on a drum, to warn people from its path. Some sat in chairs upon the ice and was pushed from behind by men on skates, that they might slide.

And in the midst of the revelry the Thames kept up its ordinary business, only instead of barges of coal going to Southwark it was sledges of 'em, and instead of taking a wherry from Westminster Market on the north shore to Lambeth on the south, men went by coach across the ice.

My master was happier than I had yet saw him. Maybe it was the joy of having his commission back, for there an't nothing so cherished as what was thought lost that is then found again. His drawing was not so quick as before, but 'twas very like, and what's more, it pleased him.

"I *see* it now," he said to me when he had put his pencil down to warm his hands. "Before, I did not see it. Look, look at the sky, and tell me what you see."

I looked. "'Tis a dark, scowling sky, sir."

"Do not be fanciful, look at the thing itself. What colors shall I use to paint it, think you?"

I looked more harder, turning my head from one side to the other to see the whole of it. "Why, ye'll need black and white and gray and blue and brown, sir," I answered him at last.

"Yes, now you use your eyes, now you see. I will mix white lead and burnt hartshorn—I cannot afford black ivory, that is made from the burnt teeth of walruses—and a bit of indigo; that will be my gray. I will use a little blue bice; it is very pale."

He rubbed his hands together. "That sky will have many colors in it, before I am done. And I will brighten things a bit, for this landskip has many sad colors in it. Red lake for this coat, and

massicot for the blaze—it darkens with age, but that will not matter so much in fire. For the yellow sail of the drum boat I will use
a bit of orpiment. It is a mineral; yellow arsenic is another name
for it. It does well for drapery, though 'tis tricky to use, for no
other color will overlie it well. I believe I have some still—I used
some to do the monstrous ugly gown that Mrs. Neil wore when I
painted her. Yes, I ground a great quantity of it in water, and
mixed but a little of the dried powder with oil."

"A painter is half apothecary, it seems to me."

"At least half! Though many have assistants who do that
work. Perhaps you will learn to mix colors for me one day, Kit."

I made no answer, and kept myself from looking his way, that
he might not know I thought of his black teeth.

"Oh, 'twill be pleasing indeed to paint again," he said, almost
like he spoke to hisself. "That is the part I love so well, to color
God's creation near to how He colored it Himself. You have
never seen the Malvern Hills, of course, that some call the English Alps. There is a spot so high that you can see the countryside for forty miles round: Worcester and Oxford on one side and
on the other, all the fruit orchards of Herefordshire, like a garden! 'Tis one of the most beautiful spots in England. We will go
there in the spring, when the apple trees blossom, and next year
perhaps to Sussex where the white cliffs rise from the sea."

He went on talking that way; it made me think of Dick
Osborne, who traveled round England with his ware. I found
myself wishing for spring, and for new places, and most of all to
be far from dark and dirty London, where no good had come
to me.

But just as I thought so I looked up from the brazier I tended and saw Priscilla coming toward us across the ice. I rose and went to meet her with a tumult in my belly.

"Your arm will not be much use to me," she said when I offered it to her, for I had fell twice in my hurry to reach her.

But she took it anyways, and something in her grasp sent my blood to blushing, and made me want to go slower toward the spot where my master worked, so's to keep that hand upon me.

When we reached him Priscilla curtsied and said, "If you please, sir, I've brought a message from your brother. He wishes you to dine with him in Middle Temple Lane."

"I cannot, I must use the light while it lasts."

"'Twill be roast goose, sir."

"He will have his fill of it, as I will not be there," my master said. He gave her tuppence for her trouble, and she curtsied and went upon the ice again.

I was vexed that my master did not accept his brother's invitation, for the spot on my arm where Priscilla's hand had squeezed me was all afire. But it was no use having such wishes, for things having to do with brothers was sore points with Nate, as they was with me.

"That sigh is from your heart," Nate said.

"Did I sigh, sir?"

"You need not be so eager to run after her. You will come to ruin if you listen to the siren songs of the female sex."

I was abashed that he read me so close, and hid it by sounding wronged. "I am only hungry, sir."

He turned his head to look at me. "Yes, all men become hungry, sooner or later, that is our curse. Go then, if you must. You can probably catch her up."

I was not so sure, myself, for the time since Priscilla left us seemed long to me, and I thought she might have got already to the Temple Stairs, which was at the foot of the lane she lived in. But I found her at the booth of a coppersmith, where she had stopped to look at a engraving there.

"Has your master changed his mind?" she asked as I went breathless up to her.

"Nay, I am bound for the cookshop in Fleet Street, and thought I would walk with ye a little."

I offered her my arm, and she took it again, which stirred me. But she would not look at me, which left me cast down.

"Mr. Fowler will be disappointed," she said. "Reverend North preached on Matthew 5:24 on Sunday. 'Leave there thy gift before the altar, and go thy way . . .' "

" 'First be reconciled to thy brother, and then come and offer thy gift,' " I finished, for I knowed that text well, though I did not like to think of it. Christy and me was not quarreling, perhaps, but neither was we reconciled. "Your master is a pious man," I said to Priscilla.

"He strives to be guided by Scripture."

"My master is cross at all that has to do with his brother, do ye know the reason?"

"He wooed my mistress before his brother did, but she would not have him."

I was took aback to hear such a thing, and did not answer for a moment. Finally I asked, "Because he is not comely?"

"Perhaps in part. Yet tailors have rounded shoulders from bending over their needles for so long, and porters have misshapen backs from their heavy burdens. All men bear the marks of their trade. The truth is my mistress could never be happy with so odd a man as your master is."

I pondered that a little. "Women always do love the man who dresses more finer, just as a hen loves the cock with the brightest crest." The moment the words was out I wished I did not say them, for I was certain she would see that Daniel was the cock I meant, and herself the hen.

But her mind was fixed on gossip. "She told him she would have him if he would paint more portraits, and those of fashionable people. But he said she must take him as he is, and she would not. He cannot have loved her much, if he would not change such a little thing."

"Is it a little thing?"

"If *I* loved someone I would do anything he asked!"

"But *do* ye love someone?" I asked before I could stop myself.

"Of course I do not." But she colored and looked down.

Then we was awkward for a moment. I thought to myself that I knowed who it was she loved, and could not stop myself speaking of him.

"How does Daniel? Does the end of his prenticeship draw near?"

"Oh, Daniel! He is like a boy before his breeching, that takes off skirts and puts on a man's clothes for the first time. No one in the household speaks of anything else."

It was not Daniel who made her blush! Was it me she thought of?

Just then I saw that we had came near to the whirling sledge, and a idea came into my head of a sudden. "Will ye ride with me on that thing?" I asked, nodding toward it. But in case she might not like to sit so near me, I added, "Or do ye fear to puke?"

"I am less like to puke than you!" she answered me.

So we sat together in the sledge and six brawny boys in a line took hold of the rope. The fair began to whirl around us, bits of color flying past, and as we swung round I fell against Priscilla, who laughed and pushed at me.

"I cannot help it," I said with what little breath I had, and I tried to sit more upright.

Then the sledge slowed, and I sat up. But the ride was not over, for now they began to pull the opposite way, and this time Priscilla fell against me, which I liked better, for now I was not honor-bound to sit straighter if I could.

"I suppose ye cannot help yerself," I said, looking down at her bird's-wing brows.

She cast her eyes down with a modest and miserable look, but she did not try to right herself. Her cheeks was bright and her body was soft against mine, and I wished the ride might last forever. It did not, however, and the moment it was over she curtsied without looking at me and went away as fast as the ice would let her.

I went back to the south bank of the Thames, but I could not leave off thinking of Priscilla's body near to mine, or perhaps I would not. I attended little to my master, and he spoke sharp to me. I could hardly wait for the day to be done and my master asleep that I might lie in the dark remembering the touch of her. And when at last that moment came I did not think only of what had passed, but of what never would: I pictured my hand upon her bosoms, and I wondered about her thing. My prick growed full and without meaning to I brung my hand to my mouth and blowed upon my fingers so as to warm them, like my body knowed before my mind what I would soon be touching. Then I was upon that road what is like a path deep in the woods, dark and fearsome and exciting, and so brambled on either side there is no getting off it till it leads where it leads. My breath and my hand was both quick as I gave myself ease, and afterward my muscles was slack with pleasure and my skin was warmed, and though I knowed I would burn with shame on the morrow 'twas not the morrow yet, and I did not even pass through dreamy jumble-land on my way to sound sleep.

Next morning I woke cheerful, and wondered how that could be. Hadn't I lost Mrs. Dean's scarf, and all my chance of betterment? Yet I imagined a future that seemed not so ill: seeing the English countryside with my master, or when we was in town, walking with Priscilla through whatever flowering places we could find—for even London must have something of greenery to it.

That is the human spirit, I reckon, to make new dreams as soon as the old ones is took away. But these ones did not last long, for but a few hours later I saw the squire on the ice, and John Frith with him, and this time I was not mistook.

I had been sent for chocolate, that my master might warm his hands, and had not yet got it when I passed by the printing press. It was a great attraction, for the printer was making cards with a person's name and the date upon it, and the fact that it was printed upon the frozen Thames, to keep as a remembrance of the

Frost Fair. Such cards was much the fashion, and I wondered did Priscilla want one. They was dear, but with all my tips and what I was owed for my service I might have enough, and what was I to save it for now?

From the other side of the press a stout man drawed near, and his boy in livery behind him, and I saw it was they.

Before I had runned, but a boy cannot well run on ice, and if he tries, 'twill only draw all eyes to him. Instead I turned round, very careful, slipped into the booth next door and then out the back side of it. From there I found a gap between the blankets and looked through.

John Frith was speaking with great excitement to the squire, and pointing the way I had went. For a instant I was as froze as the ice. Then I saw a barge was passing by, drawed by a horse; 'twas carrying many passengers under a great hoop of canvas. I grabbed on and swung myself up into the tail of the thing, and stepped forward that I might be hid by the canvas.

"Tuppence," the waterman said, then looked at my face and said, "if ye've got it. Had a fright, did ye?"

He'd have took a good story as his fare, I reckon, and knowed I had one from the white of my face or the sweat on my brow. But I gave him his tuppence instead.

The barge took me farther upriver than I wanted, so I had to walk back to Old Barge House to reach our spot on the south bank. I felt weak as a mewling baby when I stepped off that barge; the humors that had flooded my body in the fright of seeing folks from home had washed back out like a tide, and every step was a great labor. So it was that instead of thinking what I ought to do I only put one foot before the other and followed the

Thames, and sooner than I meant to be I was standing before my master, and had not got the chocolate, either.

He looked at me amazed. "Kit, what has befallen you?"

"I beg yer pardon, sir. I took a ride on a barge, and then could not get off again. I never got yer chocolate, sir, I beg yer pardon."

He looked at me long, and I knowed he wanted to ask me more, but instead he sighed, and said the light failed, and we would go now to his lodgings.

We took a hackney cab to Covent Garden. I was used to feel I was in peril every moment I rode in one, but tonight I felt safe anywhere that I was hid, and most especially at Mrs. Larkham's, after the outer door was barred behind us. But I did not see how I could ever go on foot into the streets again.

As we was climbing the steps to our lodgings laden with the tools of my master's art, Mrs. Larkham called out to him that a letter had been left for him that day.

"From my brother, I suppose," he said, and went on to our room, while I waited for Mrs. Larkham to fetch it.

"Mind you give it to him straightaway," she said, holding it out of my reach like I was a dog what might jump for it. "And don't go trying to read it on the stairs, boy, 'tis none of your concern, that's certain."

But at last she gave it to me and I took it upstairs to my master.

"We will let you practice your reading upon it," he said when I offered it to him.

He lay on the bed, and I drawed a stool close to the fire, wondering could I calm myself enough to do it. But we can do most anything if we must, I reckon, and after a moment I was catched up in the labor of it, and studied the writing with great doubt.

When I did not speak he did, thinking to help me. "'Dear Brother.' Does it not begin that way?"

"No, sir," I said. I knowed not what word I studied, but it could not be *brother*. I spoke slow, making the sound of each letter. "'Dear ff—ri—end.'"

"It is not from my brother?" He sat up in great haste. "Then give it here, at once!"

I did as he said and he read it quickly. A curse burst from him, and then, "Oh, Tom, heedless Tom! Bring me some ale, Kit."

He drank some, and I as well, and when he'd wiped his mouth upon the sleeve of his shirt he said, "Can you guess where Tom is, Kit?"

"In prison, sir?"

"Exactly! He is to be tried tomorrow at the Old Bailey, and wishes me to witness to his good character. But the offense! He does not name his offense. Please God it is simple theft."

"Why should it matter, sir?" I asked, wondering why theft was better than other crimes.

"Why, then he can receive benefit of clergy, and will not be hanged."

He saw that I did not understand.

"A man's first offense may be forgiven, if the crime be not too grave. Housebreaking or robbery they will not forgive, but theft they may, and only brand the thief in the thumb with an

F for *Felon*, that he might not be forgiven a second offense. It is called benefit of clergy, because hundreds of years ago it was a privilege of the clergy only. Now it can be pleaded by any man who can prove he knows his letters by reading a verse from the Bible, or for that matter, by any man who has memorized the first verse of the fifty-first psalm. It has saved so many men from hanging that it is called 'the neck verse.' "

A sudden hope clutched me. "Is it this one, sir? 'Have mercy upon me, O God, according to thy lovingkindness: according unto the multitude of thy tender mercies blot out my transgressions.' "

"Yes, that is the one. Now you, too, may receive benefit of clergy."

Which words lifted my spirits greatly. Yet with such a mark on my thumb could I ever again gain a master's trust? Was there any sort of honest work I could do once branded as a felon?

"A mark like that must count against a man all his life," I said to my master. "You, sir, would ye ever have a man with a brand in yer service?"

"Oh, Tom would not wish to work for me, he is too proud," Nate said, which was not what I meant to ask. Then he said, "I'll go early, for there is no knowing in what part of the day he may be tried."

"Why, ye won't witness to his good character, when he has took yer favorite thing from ye?" I was surprised and ill pleased, for I had no wish to go near to all those sheriffs and judges.

"He has a claim on me, Kit. We were apprentices together, once, and I know not which of us was the better painter." He stopped a moment, like something pained him. Then he went on:

"We argued, one day, about what pigment would best show the color of the sea, we spoke of ultramarine and Haarlem ash and blue bice . . . and to settle our argument we climbed upon a thatched roof and gazed out to sea. And then—this moment comes back to me often, yet I can never say just how it happened. I pointed at a patch of darker sea, and spoke of indigo, and my foot slid on the thatch, and there was a great scrabbling, and we fell. We fell."

Then it seemed he would speak no more, so at last I asked, "Is it how ye was lamed, sir?"

"Yes. My leg broke, and was mended by a surgeon, and in time my bones knit and my bruises healed. I never finished my apprenticeship. I never studied in Italy or in Amsterdam, as I meant to do. But I am yet a painter, as you see. For Tom it was different. He fell against a hoe that lay upon the ground, and suffered a great gash in his arm—his right arm, mind—and the wound grew blacker until the arm had to be severed by the surgeon."

He gave a great sigh. "We both argued, we both climbed, we both stood upon the slippery thatch, we both fell. But I am a painter, and he is not. Did you ever hear of John Bradford, the great Protestant martyr?"

"No, sir."

"No matter. When he was in the Tower of London, he saw a thief led off to his execution, and said: 'There but for the grace of God go I.' That is why he has a claim on me, Kit. Because it might have been me, but it was not."

That night I dreamed I was on trial at the Old Bailey. They said I had stole my master's coverlet, to keep myself warm. I did not deny it, but was let off anyways. "The circumstances this winter are extreme," the magistrate said. I rejoiced to be set free, and runned through the streets and lanes of London. Then I reached the Thames, and saw that all the ice had melted, and the river coursed free. I was afraid, for I thought I would be tried again, now that the severe weather had ended. And then I *was* on trial again, not at the Old Bailey but at some other place, and Mr. Dean was the magistrate. "Have mercy on me, according to your steadfast love," I said to him. But he said I had stole Christy's wits, and was to be hanged for it. "But I can keep the clothes?" I asked. "The clothes are mine to keep?"

I woke much troubled, and that morning whilst my master belied hisself within the Old Bailey and I waited for him in Newgate Street, I pondered what such a dream might mean. It did not seem so easy to understand as Joseph's dream of sheaves bowing down. But at last I made out that I would not be brung to trial so long as the frost lasted, or if I was I would be let off. I vowed that I would trust in God and fear not to go upon the ice or anywhere crowds gathered. All the same, I did not go to the Frost Fair unless commanded, and then my eyes was always open for servants in livery.

Tom was convicted of having took a silver tankard worth more than ten pounds, but without violence. He was gave benefit of clergy, as Nate hoped, and was sentenced to be burnt in the hand. Then my master and me went back to the Thames, where all was revelry and sport.

13

AND STILL THE frost held. The village upon the ice had become a city, with streets laid out on many parts of the Thames, though the main thoroughfare was yet the one that curved from the Temple Stairs toward the place we stood upon the south bank. Some people called it Temple Street, and others Frieze Street, on account of the blankets. Now meat was roasted in many booths of the Frost Fair; it was thought nothing to build a fire over that thick ice. Coaches did go regular upon the Thames, as many as fifty in a day, 'twas said.

One morning my master woke muttering of his dreams, and I begged him to share them, that I might once more display my powers of dream divination.

"I need no seer, for God was not the sender of this vision. 'Twas but a carnal dream."

I blushed and wished I had not, for it made me seem but a boy, and not a man who had his own dreams of that kind.

"They say hawkweed with succory is good for that," I said, hoping he had not saw my blush.

"'Tis a part of our nature, Kit, and has been since we left Eden. Some fight it, some glory in it, and some tread a middle path, though seldom without a misstep."

I had heared lewd speech in the streets, and fearsome warnings from the pulpit, but I had never heared carnal matters spoke of the way my master did.

He was untroubled those few days, by carnality or by any other thing, for his work went well, which made all things right in his world. He painted slowly but with great love, darkening the sky and lightening the ice, as though he knowed the frost would last as long as was needful.

Then one night when we undressed for bed he broke out in such cursing as I had never heared from him, and when I looked his way I was dizzied with fear.

A pink-and-red blotch spread across his belly.

"Is it the smallpox?" I asked.

"No, fool, 'tis the great one." And when I said nothing he spoke angrily, saying, "The French pox, the foul disease, the *lues venerea*. The venereal disease. Do you understand me now?"

"Yes, sir."

He sat upon his bed and put his head into his hands. "Oh, God. Oh, God. Perhaps I am wrong. I had a sore upon my prick a few months since, but it is long healed, and I have not been near a whore in that time. How can I have another case of pox? It cannot be. I worry for nothing. It cannot be."

When he did not speak again I asked, "An't there medicine for it, sir?"

"Medicine, yes. Guaiac, I suppose, or chinaroot, or sarsaparilla. My friend Andrew took such medicine till his purse was empty and his face began to ooze. He ended up taking a salivation in the foul wards at St. Bart's, where there are no fees. I saw him there once. His breath stank and he was so tired he could hardly stand, for if he but lay down the noxious mercury he had swallowed sickened him and made him rise to vomit. His teeth were gone, and he told me that he spit and puked all the day long, and that the surgeons measured it all. They say only mercury can cure the pox."

"And did it cure your friend?"

"It seemed to do so. But then he fell ill again, and died; I am not sure of the cause. I would rather die myself than go to the foul wards. I will use more discreet medicine so long as I can afford it."

"Yer brother will help ye if yer means an't great enough."

"No!" I'd never saw him look so fierce before. "Say nothing of this to my brother, nor to his servants, nor to anyone, not to anyone you meet, do you hear me? If you break confidence you shall never again find service in London. I will blacken your name throughout the town till you will be lucky to escape the gallows! Say that you understand me!"

"I understand ye, sir."

"I could not face him if he knew. Nor Petrus, nor George. How they would laugh at me when I was not by to hear it, and speak of my Covent Garden gout!"

I could not comfort him, though I did for him what I might. I called Sophy to iron his bed with a warming pan and helped him from his day things and into his nightclothes, and settled him for sleep. But he did not sleep, only lay with troubled breathing. Sometimes he made a great gasp and then was quiet again. Finally he did not try to restrain hisself but sobbed full out. I had not heared such sobbing since Christy was beat by Mr. Dean, and my heart was nearly as tore up for my master as it had been for my brother.

At last he calmed hisself, and said, "I am foolish. Most likely 'twill be gone by morning."

Then he slept, thank God. I lay thinking of what had befell him. My heart was sore with pity, but I own I was anxious, too, for a servant's fate is bound with his master's, and looking into the future, I could not see any good thing waiting there for me.

When he woke late next morning and lifted his linen nightshirt that he might use the chamber pot, those spots was still there. Nate cursed again, then shut his lips up tight like he meant no more curses to come through them ever.

"I shall not paint today," he said. "This must be taken care of at once."

We did not breakfast, but when dressed found a wall covered with bills, what my master looked over most careful. My reading was coming on, and I made out many lines of type. MOUSE-COLORED GREYHOUND LOST, one page read. Another said: RUN-AWAY SERVANT—and of a sudden my heart froze. ABOUT 18, it went on, BUT HE HATH THE LOOK OF ONE MUCH YOUNGER. GRAY-EYED, WEARS A PERIWIG—at last I breathed again. But there was many such bills upon the wall. My eye leaped from one to another: RUNAWAY APPRENTICE, TRUNK LOST OFF BACK OF COACH, WHITE GREYHOUND BITCH WITH BLUE HEAD LOST.

My master looked at a different bill, and at last my eyes came to that one.

AT THE SECOND HOUSE ON THE LEFT HAND IN PETERBOROUGH COURT IN FLEET STREET YOU MAY HAVE A PRIVATE, CHEAP, AND SPEEDY CURE FOR THE VENEREAL POX.

He turned and limped away whilst I followed.

"Find a chair for me, Kit."

"To what quarter, sir?"

"The Globe, in Fleet Street. That is near to Peterborough Court."

We spent the best part of the morning laying hold of that medicine, for my master was resolved that no one he knowed should see him go within the surgeon's house, nor come out of it. Before we was done I had went as a spy into every shop in Fleet Street, and even into a boghouse; I had learnt the use of secret knocks, and lent my coat to my master for a disguise, though I had his, what was warmer, whilst he had mine. At last Nate laid hands on the parcel he so wanted, and we changed our coats and walked along as master and man.

"Secrecy makes a man hungry," my master said.

"There's a cookshop in a little way, sir."

"I am sick of eating from cookshops, and taverns, and of things bought from criers."

"Then dine with yer brother. Ye know he's been wishing it."

"Yes. Yes, I shall dine with my brother," he said to my great surprise.

He did not call a chair, as we wasn't far from Middle Temple Lane. Instead he took my arm, as he sometimes did, and hanged on to it as if he was a old man. We walked a bit in silence, and then I dared to ask him what the doctor said.

"Oh, he is confident of my cure, of course. How else could he induce me to spend so much on the medicine he sells me?"

"May God grant it, sir."

We walked the rest of the way in silence. The door opened just as we reached Joshua's house, and Priscilla came out, all dressed in her warm things. I saw by her basket that she was bound on a errand for her mistress, and was aggrieved, like she did it deliberate that I might not idle with her whilst Nate was here.

"Is your mistress within?" Nate asked her as she made her curtsy.

"Yes, sir, she's in the parlor. Shall I take you to her?"

"Nay, I'll find my way. Kit, I'll not need you for some time; go with Priscilla, and see if you can be of use."

He looked at me with lifted brows, and I bobbed my head in thanks, but he did not yet free the arm he had held so tight. Instead he brung his head close to mine and whispered, "Take care! Though they are sweet to touch, they carry fire in their coneys!" Then he let go my arm at last, and I opened the door for him.

His ill-chose words warmed my face in spite of the cold as Priscilla and I set forth. They was maybe true of bawds and nightwalkers, but I was sure they could not be true of her. She was quiet at my side, and those bird's-wing brows was pulled together, which made me wonder if she heared him.

"Where are we bound?" I asked her.

"To the stationer's in Chancery Lane," she answered me. "For sealing wax."

"That is ill luck," I said.

"How so?"

"'Tis too near—we have only to cross Fleet Street and we'll be there."

"You are mad to wish to be longer upon these frozen streets," she said. "But take heart, the stationer's shop is at the far end of Chancery Lane, almost to Holborn."

I was between being disheartened and being vexed that she would not understand my meaning, and wondered how I might change the way she thought of me. Then came a great chance, for just across Fleet Street was a tavern, and as we passed it I saw scratches in the window, and stayed to see if I could read what was there writ.

"Why, you cannot read, can you, Kit?" Priscilla asked.

"My master teaches me," I said, and the wish to show her my powers swelled in me. I studied the words a little and at last I read them out:

Here I did lay my Celia down;
I got the Pox, and she got half a Crown.

I was so pleased to have read it well that at first I did not take in the meaning. Then I did, and at the same time I heared the name Priscilla in my head where the name Celia belonged, almost as though I had read it aloud. My face growed warm again as I remembered my master's words, and from her silence I reckoned she did remember them, too.

I spoke to lay a false scent. "I pity the men whose reason is overmastered by such poxy whores."

She did not answer me, but began to walk again.

When I could not abear more silence I said, "How is Daniel?"

"Every woman who gives the pox *to* a man has first been given pox *by* a man," she said.

I was took aback, and knowed not how to answer her. I supposed that it was true, but what was also plain was that no maid ought to be doing anything what might give her the pox.

Before I could choose my words she spoke, turning the subject. "How is your master? Does his work progress?"

"The buildings have been painted, and London Bridge, and all the booths of Temple Street. Now he must color the people, and the entertainments. The whirling sledge, he an't painted that yet."

As I named the sledge I put my hand under her elbow, like to steady her, but really to remind her of when we was throwed against each other. But we'd got to the stationer's.

"As you are so ready to be out in the freeze, I will go in alone," she said, and left me there.

The ice was within me now, as well as without. She was vexed, or she was modest, or she did not fancy me—what did it matter which was true? I crossed my arms and stuck my gloved hands into the pits of my arms and stamped upon the icy pavement till she came out, and then we walked together back to Middle Temple Lane without a word between us.

Next day Nate and me was back at our spot near the Old Barge House, but he was much changed. His zeal for his art had left him; he was distracted, or, when not distracted, irresolute. Once when he had put his brush down to warm his hands a little, he gazed upon the scene he painted and said, "Look at how they do, Kit, is it not strange? Not one can keep his feet with ease, they slide and slip and fall and clamber up again. Some are covered with bruises, some break bones, and a few have drowned. Yet still they crowd the ice. Why do men do what is so likely to bring them harm? Is it not mysterious?"

"Why, all folks must have sport," I said. "Bodies want exercise, and minds want novelty. 'Tis natural in us."

"To our sorrow," he said, and gave a great sigh.

Then I saw that he did not speak of what passed upon the ice, but of his own lust and what followed from it.

My master was not the only one changed. Where he was grieved, I was angry. I did never like the whores of London Town, not the fine-clad misses, nor the bawds who lived in the brothels of Long Acre, nor the nightwalkers who drifted through the lanes when darkness had fell. Truth to tell, I feared them not a little, like they was witches what could curse my limbs till they withered. Or maybe 'twas my own weakness that I feared, for my pintle often growed stiff as I passed 'em. But where before I feared, now I hated; they seemed vile to me, and I resolved that I would spit when I saw one, as I'd saw Daniel do.

January twenty-third was the start of Hilary term, and lawyers wearing caps and dark robes flocked from the Inns of Court down the Temple Stairs to the ice. There they hailed coaches, and rode in them to Westminster Stairs, that they might stand before the court at the King's Bench, or do other business at Whitehall Palace.

On the same day they baited a bull upon the ice. They did not wrap its hooves, and the maddened thing slipped and slid, but at last got a dog upon his horns and tossed it wrathfully.

I felt as wrathful as that bull, and wished I had a dog to toss upon my horns as well.

14

I CANNOT FINISH."

At first I did not heed my master's words. They came only faintly to me, for I squatted by the brazier, and my hat was pulled well down to cover my ears. It seemed more colder to me than the day before, and when we stepped outside that morning I wondered would the world end in ice, after all. The coal smoke was so thick in the air a body could not see across the street, especially where the lanes was narrow and the houses high. Here by the Thames 'twas not so foul; I could see clear to the Temple Stairs. Indeed, just then I saw a blue cloak at the top of them and wondered was it Priscilla. But I could not stay staring when my master spoke, so I broke my gaze and rose from my haunches.

"I cannot finish," he said again. "The thaw comes."

"Why, what put that in yer noddle, sir? Have ye been to a astrologer?"

"It warms me." His brush was dropped to the ground, and he began to unwrap his muffler. "They had best get the booths down before the ice melts. All my work in vain. Help me with my coat, Kit." He fumbled at his buttons.

"Ye're ill, sir!" I said, much alarmed. "Sit upon the bank whilst I fetch a chair."

He looked puzzled, but sat upon the folded blanket as I bade him, and I runned to hail a sedan chair that might carry him back to our lodgings.

I got him to our chamber and into his nightshirt, and tucked the coverlet about him so that his arms lay within its warmth. But he brung his hand out again and clapped it to his ear. His pallor had got worser, and his face looked near to bloodless now.

"Does yer ear pain ye, sir?"

"Yes, my ear, and my throat as well."

"I will go for a apothecary, and then to fetch yer brother."

"No apothecary," he said. "No brother."

His eyes was closed, and there was sweat upon his forehead.

"Ye must have a apothecary, sir."

"No apothecary." He moved his hand from his ear and laid it upon his belly, where the ugly blotch flowered neath his nightshirt. "No brother."

Then he slept.

I tucked his hand back neath the blankets, then poked the fire, so that it would not go out while I was gone. I knowed not where a servant's duty lay in such a case, and could only do what my heart bade me.

Mr. Wills was a apothecary in Drury Lane. He was pallid like my master, with many teeth gone and the rest dark; he was of short stature, with a head more wider than it was high. But he was a seasoned man, with a serious air and a quick step, and by the time we was up the stairs of our lodgings I had told him of the fever and the ears and the throat, and he was nodding and whispering things to hisself.

My master opened his eyes when we came into his chamber.

"No apothecary," he said in a angry way, and his voice had more strength in it than I expected, which heartened me.

"My master is afraid ye will lift the covers from him, and that he'll die of the chill in this pinching weather," I said.

"Well, well." He had took his gloves off and now rubbed his hands together to warm them. "A full examination is in most instances best. Still—fever, ears, throat—and the weather *is* a hazard. There is no indication of smallpox? No pink or red spots upon the skin?"

"None, sir. I'd have noticed."

"He can use his eyes, can Kit," my master whispered with a small smile.

Mr. Wills bent over the bed and brung his strange, earnest face close to my master's. He touched the spots before the ears, and my master cried out. Then he pressed some spots upon the throat.

"I am so warm," Nate said.

"You must have more blankets, that you may sweat profusely, and help to restore the balance of your humors," Mr. Wills said. "I think you had better be bled, as well. I will send the surgeon. And I will make up some drops recommended by Nicholas Culpeper, millipedes boiled in oil. Very efficacious for pain in the ear. Also a gargle for his throat, made with ale-hoof, burnt alum, and honey. Well, well. We shall see."

He said he would send his prentice with the remedies, and left us.

My master pushed his covers away, and I pulled them back, much alarmed.

"I think I am better," he said.

"Ye must do as ye're bid, sir."

I tucked the blankets round him again, and as I did he put his hand upon mine. His was dry and rough, and hotter than anything I'd touched since the frost came.

"Who is the servant and who the master?" he asked in his hoarse whisper. But before I could answer he added, "Thank you, Kit."

And I knowed what it was he thanked me for.

Mrs. Larkham's cook made a venison custard for him, what soothed his throat, and after he ate of it he was better for a time, and could speak without whispering. He asked me to bring his painting, which I did do, though I vowed I would not bring his knife if he bade me.

But that he did not ask for. "I wonder how many paintings I have done in my life. And not one of them worth preserving, unless the one I work on now." The painting fell to his chest, and I took it carefully from him. "Though there is one portrait . . . of my brother's wife, did you never see it in their home? She was not his wife then, of course, only her father's daughter. He made a present of it to Joshua when they married. My whole heart is in that picture."

The remedies came, and I put one drop in each ear, as the apothecary had bade, which made my master cry out. The gargle soothed him a little, however. Then the surgeon arrived, and Nate's bright blood was let into a bowl and took away, which did exhaust his little strength, and he slept. I sat at his side and prayed that he might live.

But while he slept his fever rose again, rose quickly, and when he opened his eyes he looked so wild I was afraid he would not know me.

"I believe I die," he whispered. He spoke like it surprised him. "Well, better here than in the foul wards. My painting is not finished, though." Tears came to his eyes and overflowed the banks of them, not on account of the pains of death or the fear of Judgment Day, but on account of that poor unfinished canvas with its splotches of color.

Yet I was heartened to hear him speak so rational.

"Ye're more stronger by half than my father when *he* died of fever," I said to encourage him. "And yer mind is more sounder, too."

"How like you . . . to reproach me for not being ill enough."

"I beg yer pardon, sir, that an't my meaning."

"I know."

Then I persuaded him to let me brush his hair, for the tangles fretted him when they came upon his face. While I brushed I said to him, "I thought I was dying once—from this great frost, what was killing God's creatures all around me. But I did not wait for it, instead I took my feet and walked with them to the Golden Lion, and there ye was, waiting to meet me. We do not know the ways of the Lord."

"You comfort me, Kit. Yet . . . one must prepare. Did you not prepare when you thought death was near?"

"Yes, sir." I brung his hair gently to one side, and wrapped a ribbon round it. "I spoke the Lord's Prayer, and my Creed . . . well, a part of my Creed."

"I will do the same, but first . . . you must fetch me a scrivener. And then bring George and . . ." He could not seem to find the name of Petrus. "Bid them come," he said.

"If ye prepare for death, sir . . . have ye aught to say to yer brother?"

He did not answer me a moment, but lay with noisy breath. He seemed unable to recollect hisself, and I wondered if he remembered why he did not wish to see his brother.

At last he looked at me with surprise and said, "Has the scrivener come yet?"

So I knowed I must go now before his mind went.

Many people was yet about as I made my way through the dark streets, coughing the while. God be praised, the scrivener in Bow Street was at home, and went at once to my master. George and Petrus was both at the Bear. They heared my grave news and said they would go with me to Mrs. Larkham's house, but I said I had another errand, and bade them go alone. Then I set off for the Strand, what would bring me to Middle Temple Lane.

No brother, my master had said, and I was his servant. But I could not imagine that Nate would not care to see Joshua in his last moments of life, if they was indeed coming. I knowed if I was dying, I would wish myself with Christy.

At the Fowler home I asked for Joshua, but was took instead to his wife.

"What do you here?" she asked me, not unkindly. She sat at ease on a cane chair, with a linen garment in her lap and a needle in her hand, as though she helped her husband with his business.

"I have come to tell Mr. Joshua Fowler that my master is gravely ill."

I had ever saw that woman bright and babbling, but she was not so now. She laid her needlework quiet-like to one side and said, "Tell me."

I told my master's symptoms yet again, and what had been done for him. "But—he an't strong, Mistress Fowler, and he has called to see his friends, that he might say farewell."

Priscilla came into the room at that moment, and cried out, "Oh, madame!" For she had saw the grief and strain in Gertrude's face.

"Go, Priss," she said, speaking near to a whisper. "Bring my husband to me."

Priscilla hastened out, and Gertrude sat with her head bowed so I could not see her face. I sidled nearer to the fire to get the good of it. Above the mantel hung a portrait, and I saw that it was the one my master had done of his brother's wife. I looked long upon it, thinking of our conversation. I could see why he thought it good, for there was something lively and bright in it.

Priscilla runned back in. "He is coming," she said, and her mistress nodded.

Then she looked at me, and there was almost more kindness in her eyes than I could abear. I had not saw her since the day we had spoke of the pox, when she growed so cross with me, and I had tried not to think of her, either, not wanting to remember how cold she was when we parted. But now she had forgave me, and though my heart could not be light with my master so ill, I own it was eased somewhat.

Joshua came in, more hastier than I had ever saw him.

"My brother?" he asked when he saw me.

This time 'twas Gertrude who told of Nate's health, and when finished she said, "He has sent for his friends."

"And for a scrivener," I added.

Joshua turned a quick, sharp look upon me. "He makes his will?"

"I have told ye what I know, sir."

"Let me go to him, dearest," Gertrude said. "He will need a woman's tending."

"Nay, my sweet hen, you must not suffer any alarms *now.* Think of your little chick."

He put his hand upon her belly, and I saw that it did swell a little there. I willed Mrs. Fowler to send her maidservant to do what she could not, but my wishing was in vain.

Gertrude began to weep. "Then tell him . . . tell him I am heartily sorry to have tormented him as I did . . . tell him . . ."

"I will tell him what will give him ease," her husband said.

Joshua hired a coach at Temple Bar, and we thundered through the dark toward Covent Garden, which made me think of my own death more than Nate's, for to have a accident seemed likelier than not to have one.

"Thank God he was not so full of foolish pride as to die without sending for me," Joshua said.

"I came myself, sir."

"Without his command?"

"Against it, sir."

"And he remakes his will! You did well to come for me, boy, and I'll not forget it."

I wished to say that I did it for my master, and not for the brother he disliked, but stilled my tongue as a poor man must. *Be it better or be it worse, be ruled by him who holds the purse*, they say.

He went on, speaking to hisself maybe, or maybe he was praying. "May God soften my brother's intractable, impious heart."

I hoped he would not say such a thing before my master.

"You have come after all," Nate whispered when he saw his brother. George and Petrus moved back from the bed, that Joshua might approach. "Go," Nate said to them. "I have said my goodbyes, and must speak to my brother now." His voice was more stronger than when I left him, which eased me.

They went, and Joshua sat down on a stool what disappeared within the skirts of his coat. I kept my coat on as well, though the fire burned as hot as I could make it.

"Well, Brother," he said. "I am come to see you in your illness. What have you to say to me?"

"That you need not have troubled yourself, as you will see. My will is there, upon the table; nothing in it will distress you greatly. I have left the tools of my art to George, and the painting of the Frost Fair, too. Perhaps he will finish it one day. But the lion's share remains for you. Let it be enough, this once."

"What can you mean by such words!" Joshua was vexed. "It is for God to determine the limits of a man's prosperity. Would you have me be less diligent, or less earnest?"

"I would have you remember that I die," Nate said, and his voice sounded more weaker than before.

"Not yet, not yet, that, too, is in God's hands. I am glad if you have remembered your duty to your family. You have been sometimes so short with me, I thought you might forget it." He looked at the table where Nate had pointed, and I could tell he wished to pick the will up and read it, but would not allow hisself. "Take heart," he continued. "I made my will once from my sickbed, and am a well man. You may yet recover, and live to inherit my estate."

Nate gave a great sigh, and then put his hand upon his throat, as though the sigh had hurt him.

Joshua spoke again. "And yet, if it should be God's will . . . have you prepared, Brother, for the next world? Have you asked God's forgiveness for your sins?"

"Yes. For all that I could remember."

"Do not jest about such things, Brother."

"I do not jest, Brother."

"Gertrude asks your forgiveness. May I tell her you grant it?"

"My forgiveness! For which offense, I wonder? But it does not matter, all is forgiven."

"And you have forgiven others for their trespasses against you?"

"Yes, Joshua. I forgive Petrus for being a better painter than

I. I forgive fashionable men for caring more for portraiture than for landskips. I forgive the slippery thatch for laming me. I forgive Kit for bringing you here. I even forgive you, Brother."

To my surprise, Joshua picked up my master's hand, and his tears fell upon it. "I did not think to hurt you so," he said. "These things fall as they will."

"All things fall as they will, have you not noticed?"

"Gertrude wanted to come to you, but I did not permit it. She is carrying my child, Brother. If it is a son we will baptize him Nathaniel."

My master closed his eyes. "Ah . . . then she will love her Nate after all," he said.

"Nate—" Joshua began, then stopped hisself, and began again with the words of the twenty-third psalm. I joined with him, and we spoke it together, but my master did not rouse hisself from his sleep.

We was silent for a little, and all was still. I heared the watch call the hour in the street below: 'twas eleven of the clock.

Joshua asked for the Bible, and read from it aloud, words what was familiar and comforting to me. When we heared the watch call midnight he rose and said, "Come to me if there is a change, or send the girl. Stay, what is this?"

His foot, being near to the bed, had kicked my master's purse what had fell there when I brung him home. He stooped and picked it up.

"My brother's?"

"Yes, sir."

"I will take it with me," he said. " 'Tis not that I do not trust you, Kit, but 'twould be unkind to tempt you."

My face burned, but he did not see it. I was glad when he had went, and thought that for all Joshua's fashion and prosperity, his brother was the better master, after all.

My truckle bed was not took from neath my master's bed before I laid him down, and so I spent the night in a chair beside him. I slept but little, for I woke again and again to hear my master tossing and moaning, throwing his blankets off and later clutching for them when he shivered with cold. Each time I heared him I thanked God, for it meant he yet lived. I wiped his face a half-dozen times with a rag, and prayed that he would not be took yet, and wondered what would become of me if he died.

In the deep of the night I was woke not by a moan but by labored words what I could not make out.

"What is it, sir? Wait, I will light a candle."

I did so, and set it at a distance, that the smell of the tallow might not make my master yet more sicker.

"Hear me."

I leaned close to him, for his voice was hoarse and low.

"My brother . . ."

"Ye've a message for yer brother?"

"Nay, for you, Kit. My brother is . . . pious and proper but . . . he is grasping, do you understand me?"

"Yes, sir," I said.

"He thinks always of . . . prudence and . . . advancement . . . You admire him, I know . . . but . . . he is forever . . . grasping . . . grasping . . . I bid you . . ."

He paused long, and at last I spoke. "What, sir? What must I do?"

He began to shiver, so I got up from my stool and put my

blanket upon him, and then put more coal into the grate, though it burned well enough. When I came to the bed again he had forgot what he spoke of.

"Kit?"

"I am here, sir."

"I would have a servant with a brand in the thumb . . . if 'twas you."

He knowed! I could not speak, but hanged my head whilst he slipped once more into sleep.

Toward dawn he spoke again, in a loud, hoarse cry. "My leg! My leg! Will it mend, Doctor? Say I will not lose it."

I put a hand upon his arm, thinking how to answer him. When my dad was dying he cried for his dead mam, and my own mam let him think she was his, which made me wonder did I ought to pretend to be the surgeon.

"Don't trouble yerself, sir. Ye'll be a bit lame, is all," I said at last.

He quieted, but before long spoke again in much the same way. His sense had left him. I answered him as best I could, and sometimes he was satisfied, and sometimes he was not, but went on speaking in much distress, most often about his leg, or about poor Tom, who would never paint again.

Sophy knocked upon the door, and then came through the parlor and workshop to us that she might take away the chamber pot.

"We'll be needing more coal soon," I told her, keeping my voice low.

"How does he?" she whispered back at me.

"His sense has left him. Someone must tell the sexton . . ." I could not speak for a moment, my throat had swelled so. I swallowed and finished. "Tell the sexton to ring the passing bell, and bespeak . . . bespeak a grave for him."

"Poor man. He has always paid his rent on time, Mrs. Larkham says. Shall I sit with him while you go?"

But I did not answer her, and she saw in my face that I would not leave my master, and went sorrowfully away.

I heared the bell toll before she returned—nine slow strokes, to let the people know that a man of this parish was dying. I watched the blankets that lay upon his chest rise and fall and thought of Old Haywood of our village, who used to brag that the passing bell had been rang for him twice and yet he lived. Because a bell tolls does not mean a man must die.

Suddenly Nate's eyes opened wide and his face twisted in dismay. "Help me—help me, sir!" he cried out. He grasped my arm with his hand and pulled till he sat hisself up in bed, whilst I stared at him agape. I did not think he had such strength.

"Ah, that's better. That's better, Kit."

Tears came when I heared him call me by my name. "Shall I send for someone, sir?"

"Remember what I told you about my brother. I said it, didn't I?"

Then he let go my arm and fell back upon the bed with his eyes staring open, and I knowed that he was dead.

"Oh, sir," I cried, and wept as if he was my own dad.

15

I WAS YET weeping when I heared footsteps. I did not want Sophy to come into the bedchamber just now, so I went to take the coal from her at the door that opened from the parlor onto the stairs.

But she had not brung the coal. She had brung a shrunken old woman who wore a blanket wrapped round herself.

"Does he yet live?" Sophy asked.

"He is dead," I said, and broke into sobbing once more.

"Ah, Kit, I am sorry for it!"

She shed a few tears of her own, and dried them upon her apron, whilst I wiped mine upon my sleeve. I wondered that the old woman did not cry, for I supposed she must be some relation of Nate's that I knowed not.

"I have brung Mrs. Cogan, she is the searcher," Sophy said.

"The searcher? What has been lost?"

"You are from the countryside, I reckon," Mrs. Cogan said. "In London everyone who is buried in the parish churchyards must be registered in the Bills of Mortality, and the cause of death named. I will examine Mr. Fowler and search for the cause of his death."

For a moment I said nothing. Then I spoke to Sophy, saying, "Ye have forgot the coal." I said it so that my tongue would have work to do, that it might not say such things as, "'Twas not the pox," or, "Ye cannot see him."

"The coal!" she said, and started down the stairs again.

Mrs. Cogan came into the parlor, and I shut the door behind her, as I knowed not what else to do. She was so short of stature I might have tucked her under my arm, yet I feared her.

"We old crones have seen much dying in our lives, that is why we are chosen for this work," she said. "It won't take long. Where does he lie?"

"Ye need not see him," I said. "He died of fever."

"I must make an examination, except if a physician or an apothecary be by."

There was no fire in the parlor, and I began to shiver.

Mrs. Cogan looked at me very sharp, and made her own way to the bedchamber, and I followed behind.

"He died of fever," I said again. "His ears hurt him, and his throat, but 'twas the fever what killed him. The sweat runned from him and his skin was so hot it nearly burned me when I touched him."

She pulled the blankets away, and I snatched them from her and laid them upon him again.

"The cold cannot hurt him now, boy."

"I have been with him every hour, ask me anything you like."

"Very well. Why do you try to keep me from examining him?"

"He died of fever," I said, but I did not try to stop her again.

She took the blankets from the bed and lifted his nightshirt. "Ah!" she said when she saw the pink blotch upon him. "French pox. I thought as much, when you liked not for me to see him. A common story. Many try to hide it, and when they fail, why some try to pay me to name some other cause in the Bills!"

She smiled at me, a knowing smile, and I understood her, but was in despair, for Nate's brother had took his purse and I knowed not where he kept the rest of his money hid.

She had pulled my master's nightshirt down again, for which I was glad. Now she turned his head from side to side, and pressed upon the chest of the corpse, only to make a show for me, I thought.

I wanted to cry out that 'twas not the pox he died of, though he had it, but I reckoned she cared not for the truth, but only to enrich herself.

"How much did they offer?" I asked.

"Why do you trouble yourself so?" Mrs. Cogan asked me. "What is it to you if all the world knows how he died? He is not the first man to catch the Covent Garden gout."

I could not abear to hear those words from her, those words that my master so feared! I fell to my knees and pulled the truckle bed from neath my master's bedstead, and felt under the mattress for my knotted rag.

She took it from me and felt its weight, then shook it, to hear the coins clink. Her face was thoughtful-like.

"Have pity, madame! 'Tis every coin I have!"

She nodded, satisfied, now she knowed she had took my all.

"You must have been with your master many years, to be so devoted," she said.

"Nay. But he was good to me."

"You are a good lad," she said with a wink. "Take care that those who lay out the body are in on the secret." And she shuffled away.

So I saw that I must do all myself. Though 'twas more natural for a woman than for a man to prepare a corpse for burying, I knowed that I must do it and do it well, so they would not take the graveclothes from him and do it over again, and then see the blotch upon his belly.

I thought about what I must do. When the old squire died—the squire's father—he had a dole for the poor at his funeral, as is sometimes done for charity's sake, though not so often as it was in former times. We was gave each two penny loaves to eat or to take home, and I was most content. But I remembered now how the squire's shroud was not of wool, though the law says it must be, but of linen, and they said a fine was paid, that it might be so. Where might I find such a shroud?

I heared footsteps on the stairs again, and went through to the parlor, supposing Sophy had brung the coal. But she had not.

"I am to sit with the corpse, whilst you go to tell Mr. Joshua Fowler of his brother's death," she said.

"Ye'll freeze if ye do: the fire is low, for more coal is wanted."

"La! I forgot," she said.

"And when ye've fetched the coal, I suppose ye'll lay out the corpse. An't ye afeared to touch that cold, clammy skin?"

"Is it cold and clammy, then?" I saw from the look on her face that I had led her where I wanted. "I never did dress a corpse before. Perhaps Mr. Fowler may send his servant to do it."

"I tell ye what, Sophy. I'll do it myself, if ye but buy the graveclothes. Linen, not wool, for a man of medium stature, as fine as may be—have it charged to the estate of Nathaniel Fowler. Do ye know where such things can be bought?"

"Oh, certainly, there is a special shop for 'em where they are ready-made. As fine as may be? With lace, then?"

"Yes, of course with lace," I said.

"'Tis dreadful cold out."

She knowed I wanted something of her, and meant to make me pay for it. I had no more coin for bribery, so used what I had.

"But ye'll do it, won't ye, Sophy . . . for my sake? Here, wear my gloves, so yer hands won't grow too cold."

Whilst she was gone I went to the kitchen and, despite the scullery girl's scolding, took the water what had been brung from the spring that morning. I took also what dried herbs I could find what might bring a sweet scent to the winding sheet, for there was no flowers to be had in this frost. With the door barred I washed my master's body. 'Twas the first time it had been bathed with water since the frost came, though he was a cleanly man, and often used a dry brush to scrub hisself. Praise God his illness was a short one, and his beard had not growed.

When Sophy brung the graveclothes I dressed him finely, though 'twas not so easy a thing to do by myself. But at last I propped his back against a stool as though he sat, and pulled the shirt over his head, and by such means got it on him entirely, and scattered the herbs within. The shirt was nearly a foot longer than my master's body, that it might be tied in a tuft neath his feet with woollen thread, which I did do. The wrists and the slit down the chest was edged with lace. I put the cap upon his head and fastened the wide cloth band neath his chin, and wound the cravat round his neck. Last of all I pulled the gloves onto his hands. Putting lifeless fingers into the places made for them is not a easy task, and I wondered would it be easier when he growed stiff, but I did not dare to wait.

When all was complete he looked a fine picture—but he did not look like my master. 'Twas so easy to see he was not there, it made me want to seek him elsewhere, and for a moment I imagined I might find him at the Bear, or back at Thames-side, working upon his painting.

I heared steps on the stairs once more, but from the slowness of them and the creaking of wood I knowed it was Mrs. Larkham. I did not remember that she had ever came upstairs to us before; she did not like the climb, being so fat.

I opened the door to her as she stood panting before it.

"Why, you were to go!" she said when she saw me. "What do you here alone with Mr. Fowler's things? You have been in his purse, I warrant."

"Mr. Joshua Fowler has my master's purse. He took it last night," I said, and was now glad that he did.

She came within and looked round the parlor with suspicion,

then made her heavy way into the workshop and turned a squinty gaze on everything there.

"Where is Mr. Fowler's marble grindstone? Porphyry, it was. 'Twas here last time I came."

"It was took by his friend Tom."

"It never was, or he'd have called the constable. He was prideful of that stone, nearly bit me like a bee once when I touched it. If anyone took it, *you* are that one—took it off and pawned it once he was too sick to notice, most likely."

"No, Mrs. Larkham!" I said, much alarmed. "I've took nothing from Mr. Fowler but my wages, and some of those is owed me, too."

"Not likely, boy. Your trick is discovered, I say. Sophy!" She made her way back into the parlor and bellowed down the stairs. "Sophy, come here! We've a thief among us again!"

"No, Mrs. Larkham! Ask Sophy has she saw the grinding stone lately, she'll tell ye!" So I said, but my fear growed, for Sophy was not a maid to depend upon.

We waited for Sophy to finish her clattering climb up the stairs, and she had not yet bobbed her curtsy when Mrs. Larkham said, "Remember that beautiful grinding stone Mr. Fowler was so careful of?"

"Yes, Mrs. Larkham."

"It is gone now. You did not take it, did you?"

"No, madame, I never dared even to touch it!"

"When did you see it last? 'Twas here Thursday, was it not?"

"I'm not certain—" she began, but then she looked at her glaring mistress and said, "Why, yes, so it was!"

"Call the constable, Sophy. Go now, before he flies from us. This boy will be brought to justice!"

So again I runned. 'Twas all I could think of to do. I clattered down the stairs more faster than Sophy could do with the greatest will in the world, which likely she hadn't got, anyways. As I came into the street I saw Priscilla hastening along it, coming, I suppose, for word of my master. For a moment I stopped, wondering would I ever see her again. I longed to speak with her only for a minute, to say hers was the sweetest face I'd knowed since I came to London, and that I'd sorrow to see it no more.

But if Mrs. Larkham charged me with stealing my master's grinding stone, and Mrs. Dean with stealing her scarf—well, the neck verse could not save me twice. I must choose quick between hazards, and did. I set my back against every soul I knowed in the great city of London, and made my quiet way from Covent Garden.

16

I WENT NORTH and east, through Lincoln's Inn Fields to High Holborn and on toward the old City. At first I thought only of my master. I was whelmed with sorrow, that we would never make the journeys through green England together that he had spoke of with such zeal. I was filled also with shame, that I left him lying there with only Mrs. Larkham to watch him; I did never think to be so undutiful. But my fear of the hangman's noose overcame all.

At last I resolved to change my thoughts, lest in looking at past griefs I forget my present needs. For what now lay ahead for me? My late master did employ and befriend me, knowing nothing of me but what I said of myself. Who would do such a thing again? What hope was there for me, I wondered as I fled through London Town without a farthing, and the constables maybe looking out for me.

My second set of clothes was yet back in that room, and Sophy had my gloves, too. I kept my fists in balls and my hands hid in my pocket slits, but still, the cold did bite deep. I knowed I must beg or earn a few pence before the terrible chill of night came upon me, that I might buy myself a place to sleep in some crowded room.

How might I come by some coin? I knowed I could not get another place as a servant without a testimonial from my last master. What work could a boy get without one? I'd saw boys blacking shoes, but for that I must buy blacking; linkboys carried torches, but for that I must buy some rope, and some resin to stiffen it with; even boys what swept crossings must first buy themselves brooms.

Suddenly amid the clamorous London streets I heared a sound what made my heart ache, and followed it till I stood before the Smithfield pens. It was a terrible place, where cattle lowed and sheep bawled, for many butchers had their stalls nearby. There was a great noise of barking dogs, for they was baiting a cow before her slaughter, that her meat might be made tender from her fear. The kennels of the street runned with the blood of dying animals, and in other places the blood had froze solid. Everywhere was offal and entrails, and even in the cold the smell was noisome.

I never was special fond of beasts the way some are, and anyways these was so close to the spill of blood that they was restless and distressed. But for all that they made me think of home, and for a moment I longed for it.

A moment was all I had. A door opened in the street behind me, and a man hollered, "Henry! Henry! That package is ready to go to Mr. Cross."

"I'll take it, sir, if ye please," I said, bright as a daisy.

"You'd like to, I warrant, and pawn it, I suppose! Go on, you thieving boy, and stop trying to take work from those who need it more than you do."

I walked on, much aggrieved, for who could need work worser than me?

But I could not find any. I made my way through so many little streets they was like a rabbit's warren, and I asked work of every man I saw, and of some women, too. As the day drawed on, my hunger growed, for I'd ate but little since my master fell ill. Back in Essex I'd been many times more hungrier, but in London my belly growed accustomed to being filled, and that made the hunger harder to bear. At last I knocked on a door and asked the maidservant who answered it for the broken foods.

"Why, I have already given them to the char who cleans the stairs," the girl said. "But have you not heard? The King has decreed a collection be taken up for the poor, on account of the severe weather, and gave two thousand pounds himself, as an example. Isn't it fine? Go to your parish, lad, you'll be provided for."

I stopped, then, and calculated the number of days I had worked in the parish of St. Paul's, Covent Garden. But the sum fell short of forty, just as Nate Fowler foretold, though he did not guess the reason. That meant 'twas my parish in Essex that must provide for me, and I could not get there in this weather even if I would.

I went into the next street and knocked at a house there, and once more I asked for the broken foods. But that time the servant said, "Shame on you, begging, when you're dressed as fine as a working man! Go earn your bread and do not beg for it."

By then my stomach was clamorous, and the light was failing, and the day growed more colder. My fingers was stinging, and I wished mightily for my gloves, and for my hat. Then I remembered that a great market was said to be nearby, and resolved to go there, and feast upon the leavings of the stalls.

"Can ye tell me where the market is? I've lost my way, sir," I said to the next man I saw.

He looked me up and down and said, "Leadenhall or Cheapside?"

"Cheapside, sir," I said, for I must say one or the other.

He directed me in words so swift I hardly understood him, and then did say, "But you'd best make haste, or 'twill be closed. Candle time is nearly upon us." And he walked brisk away.

Instead of making haste, I looked after him, watching his walking stick rise and fall with his stride, and wished I had a stick that might help me go as well. I was so tired I feared to drop, and hungry, and the cold was painful to every uncovered part of me. My mind, what was so quick and clear most times, was slowed and bewildered.

Then I heared the market bell, what ends the selling of foods, and I made my way toward it, hoping I might glean what had been trod underfoot.

Indeed, the market was being took apart as I came there, but 'twas warmer than in the streets, and on the ground I saw cabbage stalks and spilled meal and cheese rinds, and other things that might make a meal. *Hungry dogs will eat dirty puddings,* they say. I nibbled at the best of what I found, and kept my eyes open for more.

Then I spied a apple what had rolled away, and my mouth

watered. I bent to scoop it up, and was gave a rude push what made me stagger.

"That's me livelihood, it is! Leave it be!" the woman said when I turned round to see her. She was a thin, hunched, ragged-dressed woman, fair-haired and red-cheeked, and her fingers was purple with chilblains.

"I'm hungry," I said, clutching the apple as I might a jewel. The skin was withered, it was smashed on one side, and I knowed it would be pulpy, but at that moment I wanted it more than rest or warmth.

"Hungry, in that coat! Not likely! Ye're wanting to sell them apples at the stocks, to be pelted at the prisoners, same as me."

I made no answer, but stood gaping till she saw my hunger was real.

"A farthing for it, then," she said, and put a hand out for it.

"My rag is empty," I said. I meant to say "purse," but was honest by accident.

"Faith, ye're not right in yer head! Is it Bedlam ye belong to?"

But even I'd heared of Bedlam, where the lunatics was kept, and her naming it brung me round.

"Poor and mad an't the same," I said. "I reckon I an't the first to find hisself penniless in London Town."

"Well, that apple will hold ye till ye pawn yer coat and boots," she said with a shrug, and turned away from me.

I gobbled it up, but it only made me more hungrier. I could think of nothing better to do than to wander through the streets. Maidservants was setting out the lanterns, and prentices was unhitching the shutters to fold them closed, and barring the shop doors.

One of the prentices was dressed more finer than Daniel; I nearly took him for his master when I saw him through the shop window. What a fine place it was, with leather chairs for customers to sit in, and looking glasses upon the wall. The prentice was handling crimson velvets and violet silks, putting them away in presses for the night, so I knowed his master was a mercer. If only I could have been such a prentice!

He saw me watching him and pulled the door open to speak. "Who's that lurking about? Go on, you're not wanted here."

"I an't lurking," I said. "I'm looking for work is all. Yer master need any messages carried?"

"Not my master, nor any master in Milk Street," he said.

"Why, is this Milk Street?" I asked, looking around.

"What does Milk Street mean to you?"

"Nothing, only I know someone . . . someone who knows . . ." For a moment I could not think of the name of the linendraper Dick Osborne had spoke of to me one day last December. What a long time it seemed now, since I sat with the peddler and his sister in his cottage, and drank barley beer whilst Christy teased the chickens. "Someone who knows Mr. Jackson," I finished at last. "An't his shop on this street?"

"Over against the Boar," he said, with a jerk of his head toward a tavern. "The shop's closed up tight as a tun, but there's a candle in the window of his home, there. You can call on him, I suppose, if you've aught to say to him."

I thought that over a minute. Would knowing Dick Osborne

be a help? Dick was trusted enough to be gave handkerchiefs on credit, but if he was still owing, it might be that Mr. Jackson would scowl at the mention of his name. At last I shook my head, and turned toward Cheapside.

"I thought not," the prentice said to my back.

The afternoon got blacker and icier each minute, and I could not think what to do. As much as I prized my coat, I did not know if it would keep me living through the night if I must sleep upon the streets. Ought I to pawn it, after all? And where must I go to do such a thing? I would not go to the woman whose shop was near St. Paul's! I wandered a little way along Cheapside again, and then went north into Wood Street, what was even more darker. At the sound of my footsteps a figure before me turned round to look me over, and at that moment a boy from behind me said, "You dropped your handkerchief, sir. Here it is."

Fear licked through me like a fire, and warmed my blood, for I had no handkerchief, and I saw that they was working together toward evil ends. I turned my back against the wall of a house and spoke loud as I could as they came toward me.

"Don't be a ninnyhammer," I yelled. "I an't some city spark what carries a handkerchief. Ye've both more coin on ye than I have, I warrant, for I've none at all." I took my hands from my pocket slits and showed my palms; they made patches of white in the dark.

They saw I wore no gloves, and made noises of disgust and disappointment, one to the other.

"An't no use shouting," the taller of them said, very surly. "The watch an't near. What the Devil do you here?"

"And how will you lodge, if you've no money?" the other asked.

"I know not," I said, before I thought.

They looked at each other. I could not see their faces through the black, but the tall one began to question me closely.

"Where stayed you last night?"

"With my master, but he died this morning."

"He must have owed you wages, did he not?"

"Perhaps he did . . . but his landlady would not let me stay."

"Would not let you stay! Does she carry a sword, that she ran you off so quickly?"

"Nay . . ."

There was a silence, and the shorter one said, "Perhaps she carried a threat, instead. Do the constables seek you?"

I made no answer.

"Come, we can be useful to each other, I believe," the short man said. "I am Peazy, and this is Peck. How are you called?"

I had not said a lie till then, even knowing I was with thieves. But though my name was shadowed and maybe ruined by now, I would not make them free of it. Instead I gave them the name of the man I hated most.

"I am called John Frith," I said.

"Well met, Frith. Here, I've some pie left from dinner, an't you hungry?" Peazy offered me a little bundle wrapped in paper. I meant not to take it, but my hand did not obey my thought, and in a moment the food was ate up, and after that there was nothing to do but walk along with them.

"We an't bad fellows, Peck and me," Peazy said as we made our way south. "We an't neither of us been to Newgate or Fleet."

"Come close once," Peck said, thoughtful-like.

"We work when we can, collecting coals Thames-side, mostly. They fall from the barges and wash up on the bank, see. That fills our bellies, and we sleep rough. When the weather an't bad we bulk it—sleep under the bulks."

Peazy pointed through the shadows at one of the wooden shelves that stuck out from the shuttered shops we passed by. By day they was loaded with merchandise, but they was cleared for the night.

"Keeps the rain off," he said.

"If the wind an't wrong," Peck said, but Peazy did not heed him.

"When it's colder we sleep in the ashes at the glass-yard—they's warm from the furnace—the annealing furnace, what cooks the glass. Lovely warm they are on most winter nights, but this an't most winters, is it? The Thames froze up, no mackerel to be had, and no cinders to be gathered, a body's got to have lodgings, that's all. We've a place to lay our heads, thirteen of us was there last night—"

"Seventeen," Peck said.

"Have ye a fire there?" I asked.

"With seventeen bodies we don't need one. But it an't free, understand? So we do what we must, that's all. No one much minds it, it's the way of things for such as us, an't it? You're in the same spot yourself, I reckon."

I could not deny it.

"You haven't much to say," Peck said in the same surly voice I had heared from him before.

"He an't so garrulous as you," Peazy told him. "Here's how you can help us, Frith. We an't bad fellows, as I say, but the thing is we're *known*. Our faces have been seen about. There an't no hue and cry after us, nothing like that, but the constables and the bailiffs, they keep a eye on us. What we need is a new face."

It seemed to me that Peck and Peazy was only being sensible. A man had to live, however he must. Though I had stole before, I never meant it to be a way of life. Now I saw it must be. All my dreams of betterment was done, but they was always fantastical, from the days I used to picture Mr. Dean setting me up in a shop. I saw that now.

"Have you been much on the ice?"

"Most every day," I said.

"That an't no good, then," Peazy said. "But if you've been every day on the ice, you've been little elsewhere. I know what we'll do. A delivery from the Oxford coach."

"We'll need bricks, then, and something to wrap 'em," Peck said.

"That's for you to find," Peazy told him.

Peck went off to search through the icy dunghills for what was needed, while Peazy explained to me what I must do. 'Twas simple enough. I was to walk into a tavern and proclaim: "The Oxford coach has got through!" And say I had a package for delivery, only I must demand three shillings for it.

"We'll go to the Cardinal's Cap, over near Cornhill," Peazy

said. "A little bit of a walk, but worth it, for the tavern keeper there is every kind of fool. Have you any questions?"

I had many: how I had came to this, and would I ever again see Essex, and what the folks at home would think of me if they knowed. But those was not questions for one such as Peazy.

I reckoned Peazy was the brains of the pair, but Peck had his gifts, and soon we was carrying a parcel made with things what had came out of rubbish heaps and looking like it had came instead from the Oxford coach. We walked all three together along Cheapside and into Poultry, and then Peck went into Cornhill and Peazy into Lombard, for Cardinal's Cap Alley ran right between 'em.

"You look the picture of it," Peazy said when we parted, with a encouraging smile.

I reckon if the weather was warmer I'd have stood outside the tavern thinking it all over and argufying with myself about what I was about to do and what it might mean for my future. But my hands was cold almost to lifeless, for I could not keep them under my arms or in my pocket slits whilst carrying a parcel of bricks. It was in hope of a little warmth that I went so quick into the Cardinal's Cap. I opened my mouth to holler, but took in some of the thick smoke of the place, and coughed instead. And whilst I was yet coughing I heard a voice say, "'Tis Kit Chidley, didn't I say so!"

And there was John Frith in his gold-and-black livery. Somehow I was not surprised—'twas almost like I knowed I would meet him when I walked through the tavern door. I reckon there are certain things God plans for us and in the end there is no running from them. If truth be told, 'twas almost a relief that the running was over at last.

"Good evening to ye, John," I said.

"I knowed 'twas you I saw on the ice! That was you, wasn't it?"

"'Twas me," I allowed.

"We knowed ye was in London, the innkeeper of the Golden Lion said so. Mr. Dean was angry as a hornet. He said ye stole a scarf, and wanted to send a hue and cry after ye. But Mrs. Dean said she made a gift of it to ye."

"A gift . . . ?"

"A gift of the scarf, man. Where is it, then? Ye could use it in this cold."

I was stupid with wonder. I was not a thief, after all. If I had knowed! Then I thought, What could have been different, though I knowed? It would not have kept my master alive.

"Where is it, I said?"

"Had to pawn it."

"Well, ye had yer use of it first, I reckon."

"What . . . what of Christy?"

"Naught of Christy."

"Did he stay with Mr. Dean?"

"How am I to know? We came to town three days after ye left yerself. Since Innocents' Day no one has come or gone, I think; there was a great snowfall that day in the countryside; that is what the squire heared. Maybe we will never go back! I like it well enough here. We are lodged in Holborn; where does yer master live? Ye've a master, I know, for ye're carrying parcels for him."

I looked down at the parcel of bricks and stones in my arms.

"I must go," I said.

"Come see me, when ye've time. Ask for the squire at the Chequer in Holborn, that is where he dines."

What a wonder it was to see him so friendly, him who had scorned me and Christy together more times than I could count. I reckoned he was lonely here in London, and glad to see a countryman. But I knowed I wouldn't be asking after him at the Chequer or anywheres else.

We bade each other farewell, and then I was out in the bitter cold again, with Peck waiting at one end of the alley for me and Peazy at the other.

"Why, ye've still got it," Peazy said when he saw me, ill pleased.

"I didn't dare. There was a lad in there knowed me and he was ready to tattle."

Peazy cursed. "And I thought you were a new face! We'll try again, that's all, we've got to, haven't we? Not at the Fleece, we've done it before, not at the Pope's Head, the taverner there has a quick wit."

Peck had joined us now, and we was walking together back the way we had came, along Poultry to Cheapside. I reckon all London streets is thick with taverns; I know those was, but I wasn't paying much mind. I'd no feeling in my hands, and couldn't be sure if they was still there or not. I told one of them to stretch out its fingers, and it did, and the parcel fell and hit Peck's foot.

"God's fish, watch yourself! Is he simple, Peazy?"

"Only cold, Peck. That's right, isn't it, John, you're cold?"

I made no answer; I'd forgot I was John to them.

"Well, pick it up, then, we're yet needing it," Peck said angrily.

"I'll just warm my hands a minute first," I said, and buried them neath my coat.

"We've not time for this." Peck was getting every moment more angrier.

"A pox, there's the watch," Peazy said.

"What matter? It's not yet curfew."

"You're an ass, Peck. We don't want him seen with us, do we? Duck into Foster Lane, Frith, and when you come to the Church of St. Zachary wait for us there. And take the parcel!"

I did not know Foster Lane from any other, but went where I was pointed with a haste and will I'd not yet showed, for to be catched doing roguish tricks now, when I had just learnt I was no thief, would be too cruel. Peck and Peazy went strolling on toward the watch, who held his lantern aloft to see their faces. At that moment the odor of livestock came to me on the air and I realized I was not so far from Smithfield. The moment they could not see me I dropped the parcel and runned, hastening on my weaving way through the streets till I was at the pens again.

The beasts was quiet now, it being natural for them to sleep by night. I could not see, for it was mortal dark, but I pictured the sheep massed together for warmth and wondered might I share it with them, and live till morning after all. Then instead of wondering I climbed over the fence and found my way to them.

Indeed, they was lovely warm, the heat rose from them. I plunged my frozen fingers into the greasy fleece of one, and though at first I felt nothing, after a little they began to sting, so I knowed they was warming.

"Mr. Radcliffe?"

Hearing a man's voice in the midst of those sheep startled me so that I stepped back, and the sheep I jostled said his baa, and then others, all around, like they meant to bring the law to me.

"Who . . . who comes here in the dark? Mr. Radcliffe says I am the only one who may sleep in the pens!"

'Twas not a young voice, but it had a child's fear in it. I kept mine gentle as I could when I made my answer.

"I've nowhere to lay my head tonight and am afraid to die of the cold. Might I stay with you just this once, if I am gone at first light?"

"Mr. Radcliffe says I am the only one who may sleep in the pens."

I could tell he was not angry nor resolved, only anxious.

"I will make it right with Mr. Radcliffe if he sees me, and tell him 'twas not yer fault. I am called Kit. What is your name?"

"Henry."

"Thank ye for sharing yer bedchamber with me, Henry."

But he did not see the joke.

"Mrs. Radcliffe says I am not to share, not ever. She gives me the broken foods. She says men will steal from me if I let them."

I said naught for a moment, for the knowledge of who he was—how he was—catched in my throat. After a little I said, "She's wise, Mrs. Radcliffe."

"And Mr. Radcliffe."

"Yes, Mr. Radcliffe as well. Is he yer master?"

"I carry his packages. He gives me tuppence. I'm strong. I porter for Mr. Cross, as well, and sometimes Mr. Burns."

"Ye're like my brother," I said, because I could not help myself.

"Ye've a brother?"

"Yes."

"Like me?"

"Yes."

"A idiot?"

"Not a idiot," I said. I reached through the darkness and found a bit of his arm, wrapped in rags upon rags. I stroked it a little, like I would a cat. "Only simple," I said.

We talked past the curfew bell, Henry and me. He knowed about the Frost Fair but had not saw it, for Mr. Radcliffe told him he must never go beyond the bounds of the parish. He heared my stories eagerly and made me tell him over and over again about the jugglers, though I had paid them little heed. He'd saw jugglers before and to him they was miraculous.

At last he yawned, and I told him he must sleep, if he meant to carry parcels next day. We held each other close for warmth, and the sheep pressed against us.

"I want to see the Frost Fair," Henry said. "Will you take me, Kit?"

"Ye'd best stay with Mr. Radcliffe, Henry, and not go losing yerself in London Town."

After that he slept, but I lay long awake, thinking first only that I was not a thief. The wonder of it wrapped round me like the blanket I wished I had. I was saved from the gallows and the brand on my thumb, saved from damnation itself, maybe, all on account of Mrs. Dean's kindness. What was I to her, that she let her favorite scarf be took away and said not a word against the taker? I felt more humbler than I ever did before from knowing I did not deserve the gift that I was gave—not the scarf itself, I mean to say, but the freedom she sent after it.

But I wanted to stay free, and for that I must find honest work—or get what was owed me. Mr. Joshua Fowler had the keeping of Nate's things, most likely. Had Nate writ anywhere what I was owed? Would Joshua believe me against the word of Mrs. Larkham, that I had not took the grindstone?

I huddled close to Henry, shivering. He made me think of Christy. I wished John Frith had gave me news of him. Where did he lie tonight, I wondered. Was he with my mother at the Curtis place? Was he boarded with some kinder family of the parish? Or did he yet live under Mr. Dean's stick? Whatever had passed with him, anyways he did not spend his frozen nights with the beasts, I reckoned, and comforted myself with that thought.

I didn't sleep, but drifted near to it a dozen times, and each time came back to full waking with fear, and checked the sky for light, wondering what I'd do with myself when at last it came. Should I go to my master's brother? There was danger there, maybe, but without my wages there was nothing for me but to throw in my lot with the Pecks and Peazys of the world. Then I had another thought: Was it certain that George Pearse would believe Mrs. Larkham over me? Why, Nate might have mentioned the theft of the grinding stone to his friend the very day it happened. I resolved to go to Mr. Pearse and ask him straight if my master had told him. It might be he and I could go together to Joshua Fowler.

When the dawn came I stirred myself, and the sheep I lay against stirred as well. I stood, which caused so much bleating that Henry roused and drawed his arm across his snotty nose.

"Will you bring your brother to meet me?" he asked.

"He an't in London, Henry. He's far away."

"Then come to visit me," he said.

"I can't promise. I know not what will next befall me. But I'll come if I can."

Then I climbed over the sheep and out of the pen and began trudging back to Covent Garden.

17

GEORGE PEARSE WAS not at the Bear, nor down the lane at the Rose. I wondered could he be at the theater, and went there, but I liked not to disturb him if he worked, so I just stood before it, staring at the white columns like I meant to paint them. 'Twas bitter cold now that I had no sheep to warm me, and when standing still I began to shiver, and my belly pained me so I would have held it, but that I had my balled fists within my coat. I stood there some minutes and then could not abear more, but before I stirred I heared my name called, and turned to see Mr. Pearse hastening toward the theater.

"Kit! We have wondered where you were! My God, lad, where did you sleep?"

For my coat was covered in dung and fleece.

"In the Smithfield pens, sir."

"Well, it has kept you alive, at any rate. You must go to Mr. Joshua Fowler, he looks for you."

"Do ye know why he wants to see me, sir?"

He clapped a hand to my shoulder. "Not about that foolish business of the grinding stone, that is done with. I told Mr. Fowler all about Tom."

"Thank ye, sir," I said, thinking: I need not have runned. Need not have passed those long, icy hours in streets that was strange to me, need not have ate what had been walked upon. But all that was past, and I must think of the future, for a servant must have a master.

"Have ye any need of me? I could carry yer messages for ye."

"Go to see Mr. Fowler first. I believe he has something for you."

That was welcome news, for it meant I would get the wages I was owed. But I did not think I could go as far as the next street without something in my belly.

"Yes, sir," I said to Mr. Pearse. "Only . . . if I could borrow enough to feed myself, first . . . I'm terrible hungry."

"Of course you are, I did not think! Here, this will get you breakfast, you need not repay me. Now go, I will see you at the funeral tomorrow, certainly, if we do not meet before that."

"Thank ye, sir," I said again, folding my fingers over the coin. 'Twas enough to feed me for three days, if I was careful with it, or to gorge myself once, which is what I meant to do.

I did not go to the cookshop in Fleet Street what had fed me so many cheap dinners, but to the one in Bow Street where I had fetched a meal for Tom the first night he spent with us. It had four spits turning, each with a different meat: beef, mutton, pork, and veal. I knowed not which was more delicious, the smell of the roasting or the warmth of it. I ordered a great quantity of beef and a smaller one of pork, both cooked well and with plenty of fat, and ate it with salt and mustard and two rolls—but only one bottle of beer. Not even the Christmas pie I had ate in Middle Temple Lane tasted so good.

I hoped 'twould be Priscilla opened the door, but 'twas Dorothy. She pinched her nose as she held the door open for me.

"Leave that coat on the peg," she said to me as I came in. "It smells like the barnyard."

I wished my linen was more cleaner, and that I'd had a wash before coming. But there was no unfroze water out of doors to wash with.

I opened my mouth to ask her if I might clean myself in the kitchen, but instead I heared myself say, "Where does he lie?"

"Mr. Nathaniel Fowler? Why, in his home," she said. "Priscilla is with him. But Mr. Fowler waits to see you."

I was sent to him in his countinghouse, where I found him dressed already in mourning clothes. When I came into the chamber he put down his quill and looked at me most gravely.

"Well, Kit, so here you are. How came you to disappear from my brother's bedside? I did not expect it of you."

"Mrs. Larkham said she would call the constable, for she believed I had took my master's grinding stone."

"And did you take the stone?"

"No, sir."

"Then why did you run?"

"I was not sure of being believed, sir. But then I remembered that my master might have spoke to his friends when the stone was stole, and I hoped that one of them could prove me innocent."

"As Mr. Pearse has done."

"Yes, sir."

"And you are the one who laid out my brother?"

"I did, sir."

"'Twas well done, lad."

I was not expecting praise, and it eased me, and also let me know they had not took off Nate's graveclothes and learnt his secret; which gave me yet greater relief. The way he said it made me recall that he had lost his brother, and I was ashamed that I had not told him my sorrow, and had thought only of myself.

"I'm sorry for yer grief, sir, and I share it. He was kind to me."

He studied me, and I felt myself grow wary, though I could not say why. After a little he said, "I have some money for you, Kit. You knew that, of course, or you would not have come."

"Yes I would, sir. Anyways, I would come to the funeral, and say a proper prayer over my master. But 'tis true there is money owing me, and it's only right that I should have what is mine, is it not?"

"Of course," he said, very sharp. "No one seeks to take from you anything that is yours."

I saw that I'd displeased him, but I did not beg his pardon, for I could not see how I erred in what I said.

"For what are you owed?" he asked me.

"My wages since Epiphany, sir. Three crowns come Lady Day, but I have worked less than a third of that."

He nodded, now much pleased. "You are an honest lad, I see. I will pay you a full crown, just on that account."

"Thank ye, sir."

He took up his purse, and counted the money out upon the table.

"There, does that suffice?"

"It does, sir."

"You are expecting nothing more?"

"No, sir. Unless ye've brung my things from Mrs. Larkham's room."

"Had you things there? We must be sure that they are not counted as part of my brother's inventory."

I waited, but he did not offer me the coins what was on the table, and I growed anxious that he meant to keep them from me, after all.

"What will you do, Kit, now that you have no master?"

"I hope to be entrusted with messages, sir, by Mr. Pearse and Mr. de Lange, and perhaps by others they know, and with good fortune to be a servant again, when I have proved myself."

"I see. And that is your greatest wish, to be a servant? You do not think of bettering yourself?"

"I have thought much of it, sir. I would learn a trade, if I could. But I've not the means to pay a premium."

He nodded once, twice, and his eyes gleamed. "You do have the means, Kit."

"Sir?"

"My brother, Nate, greatly valued your service to him, and

remembered you in the making of his will. He has left you ten pounds."

Ten pounds! I hardly believed it. How could he have done so much for me, when I was impertinent, and argufied with him, and in my thoughts judged him severely, and admired his brother more? Ten pounds. That was enough for anything—enough to buy boots for Christy, and gloves besides. Why, I could buy him a coat of many colors, if I liked! I wanted to laugh out loud at the absurdity of fortune, how it turned of a sudden from best to worst and to best again.

"'Tis enough to pay the premium in some trades. You might be a cooper, or perhaps a cutler. In the cloth trades the premiums are more, I'm afraid. Daniel paid a hundred pounds. Still . . . because my brother esteemed you so, it might be done, if you would agree to serve eight years, instead of seven. Your labor would be quite valuable by then, for you would have mastered all the skills that make up the craft of tailoring, and that way I would make good the loss of having taken you on for so little."

I stared at him with amazement and doubt. How was it that he was so generous, when his brother said he was grasping? And, too, though I'd dreamed of such a life, I knowed I had not the qualities a tailor looked for in a prentice—the elegant ways and genteel speech and education. "I cannot read, sir," I told him as I tried to understand this puzzle. "That is, I can spell out the sounds, if the printing is plain, and your brother taught me to recognize many words. But I cannot read script, or Roman, and I cannot write at all."

"Your honesty is worth more than education," he said. "But we need not speak of it yet. We will await the proving of the will, in any case, and such decisions must not be taken in haste, or without prayer. There are many ways the money can be spent, if you are content to remain as you are."

But he knowed I was not.

He gave me then the coins he had put upon the table, but said I might bide with his family in Middle Temple Lane, for a time, if I liked, so long as I helped Francis with his tasks, and sometimes Priscilla with hers.

"Stay till Ash Wednesday, that is more than two weeks," he said. "Have a look at the household, and at the art of tailoring, and I will have a look at you, and in the meanwhile we will both ask God for counsel."

I thanked him and said that I would.

"I ask only this, Kit. Say nothing during this time to anyone in my household of the money you have been left—'twill only stir up gossip and envy. Do you promise?"

I made the promise, though unhappily, for who does not wish to boast of good fortune and a rise in life?

Nate's funeral was on Monday. It was strange to me, for the corpse had been put in a coffin with several inches of bran neath him, and when it was carried he made no sound of moving about, because of the bran he lay upon. A grave had been dug in the churchyard, with much difficulty. The sexton had to break the ground with a chisel, and was paid extra for the digging, Francis said. We had no sprigs of rosemary to throw upon the coffin, for it had all been killed by the frost. And though he was not a nobleman and owned no land, a stone was to be put upon the spot he lay with his name upon it, that he might be easily found. However, it was not there yet.

There was no sermon, for in his will Nate had said there must not be, to save the cost of having it preached. The will even named the amount that should be spent on the whole of the funeral, which was very small for London, Francis said. There was only one glass of mulled wine for each guest who came back to Mrs. Larkham's house after, and two biscuits. They none of them stayed long. And when we left I took my clothes what was there, most especially my gloves.

18

HOW MANY TIMES I had wished to be a part of Mr. Joshua Fowler's household, and now that it was so, I was not disappointed. For the first time in my life I lodged with other boys, and their society added such great pleasure to my days that I now looked back upon everything that went before as a gray and lonely time. We was always fooling and jostling one with another, fighting over a football bladder, or if one was not near, over a glove; it did not matter. Ralph liked most to fight, and did most often triumph; he was stout and strong. Humphrey liked it least, but he liked everything least. He was of a sour temperament, and complained often of weariness, or pain in his shoulders, or aching eyes, and he envied boys what was learning other trades.

"Why, what would you wish?" I asked him once. "There are few tradesmen who can turn a greater profit, surely." I said this less to argufy with him than to hear his reply, for I did ponder my future, and wondered what trades lay open to me.

"So said my father, and thus he apprenticed me here, though I begged he would set me to learning printing and engraving. I have no aptitude for this foppish work."

I thought much of that. Not of being a printer, there was nothing more duller than that, to my mind. What I loved was ells of wool and yards of satin ribbon and handfuls of buttons. Even as a child the things from Dick Osborne's pack was my favorite toys. What craft could be more better for me than tailoring?

We all of us but Francis slept together in a garret chamber at the top of the house, and the female servants was in the room next to us. Sometimes we heared their talking and giggling through the wall, and called back at them. Francis slept on the ground floor, where the workshop and the kitchen was, to see that burglars did not enter in the night. He missed the great fun we had together.

Daniel was our leader, though he joined in our play but rarely. Humphrey said he feared to ruin his fine clothes, but I reckoned his haughtiness was earned, and admired him with all my heart. He felt it, and growed less icy with me.

"I wish he was so affable with *me*," Francis said to me once, as we went together to the woollen draper's, to pick up some cloth Mr. Fowler had ordered. "He is always finding fault."

"It is your tongue he finds fault with," I said, for Francis was ever talking, and sometimes made oaths. "You must master it if you would become the sort of tailor Mr. Fowler is."

"I will never be that sort, I have not the gift for it. Daniel does; he and Mr. Fowler will sit over meat for an hour discussing the cut of a man's breeches while the rest of us perish from boredom."

I wished that I might be present at such a conversation, for I was very noticing of clothing, both men's and women's, and thought I might say a useful thing, and so prove my worth. But I did not sit at table with the others, being only a servant.

Mr. Fowler had said to think on what was best to do with the money I was left, so I did, and I prayed as well. Though heaping presents upon Christy was my first thought, I soon saw 'twould be imprudent only to buy pleasures or even useful things that would so soon be wore out again. Was there other ways I might be of use to my twin? I might send him something every quarter day, but that would not make the money grow. I thought of the parable of the talents, in the Gospels, and how men was chided for spending and even for saving, when they ought to have used their coin to make more. Such was God's will. I knowed of no way to make my ten pounds grow but to use it as a premium, that I might someday have a trade and become a prosperous man. Then I could buy all manner of things for Christy.

Then a thought came to me, and I wished it didn't. The thought was this: If I was to go home I could prentice myself to someone in our village, or anyways in Braintree, and the premium would be much less. With the money what was not needed for a premium I could make things easier for Christy, and even for Mam.

The moment that thought came to me I started argufying with it, saying what was true, that a Braintree smith could never rise so high as a London tailor; and what was false, that Christy would not want me to ruin my chances for his sake. When I saw that I lied to myself I growed angry. What should Christy's wishes matter, anyways, and why *should* I throw away all the good things what had came to me only because he was too simple to walk where I walked?

And neath all my argufying was a seed of shame on account of Mrs. Dean, for if I went home I must look her in the face, which I could not abear to do.

In the end I resolved I would consider the matter another day. But there are some tomorrows that never come, and I did not trouble myself again about my brother before Ash Wednesday dawned.

Joshua Fowler had bade me have a look at his household, and of all who was a part of it I liked most to look at Priscilla. To my joy, I was gave many chances to do so. Mrs. Fowler was with child, and her husband liked not for her to go to market each morning, so I was sent with Priscilla instead, to carry home part of what we bought there. Sometimes we bought from the butchers near to Smithfield, and whenever we was sent there I kept a eye out for Henry, but I never saw him, so I reckoned he was kept busy portering. But most often we went to the Clare Market, what was near to us. I had never saw so much food laid out in one place, not even at the Chelmsford Market, which served so many towns and villages. But Priscilla said the Leadenhall Market was far greater, and anyways, the offerings was scant now because of the frost.

"When will it end, I wonder," she sighed one morning.

"Daniel has wagered Ralph that 'twill end before Ash Wednesday," I answered her.

She laughed. "Mr. and Mrs. Fowler have the same wager. But that is forever, I hope it ends before that."

And she spoke of the ruination the frost had brung, of the deer that perished in the parks all through England.

"But there will be plenty of venison when it has aged," I said.

She laughed then, and said a man as filled with hope as me could never be kept down. "But the frost has been hard to your family, has it not? Mr. Fowler told my mistress that your own brother died of the cold."

"My brother Michael, yes. He was but three years old."

"Do you miss your family greatly?"

A picture of Christy came into my head, which vexed me. But I knowed now how to make such thoughts go.

"Not enough to wish to return," I said to Priscilla. "There was no prospects for me there. But—they do come 'cross my mind, at times. And yerself, have ye family ye miss?"

She looked so saddened by my question that I was surprised when she said, "No, not greatly. I see my parents every month; they live not far from here."

"And have ye brothers and sisters?" I asked.

"I had a brother who went to the West Indies. I had but few years then, and do not remember him well."

Was that the loss that made her look so sad, I wondered, and felt she had not told me all.

And next day I learned my guess was true. We was in the market together but had parted ways; I looked over the roots, and she sought barley that was not musty. Then I came back to her, but before I reached her I heared a woman cry, "Priss!" And she kissed Priscilla upon the cheek.

In the time I'd knowed her I'd saw Priscilla dreamy and sad and saucy and vexed, but never scared before that moment. She drawed away from the young woman and spoke to her in a low voice, and the woman turned her back to me and hastened away.

Priscilla saw me see, and a coldness came upon her face that bade
me not ask questions.

But I was troubled, and could not master my feelings.

"What is it, Priss?" 'Twas the first time I called her so,
though all the household did it. "What is wrong?"

"The choices grow every day more meager," she said. She
did not look at me, but at a woman brushing away the straw that
kept her basket of apples from the cold. Of a sudden tears
coursed down her cheeks.

"Let me help," I said, and took her basket, though 'twas light.
"Who was that woman, why does she trouble you so? There an't
no need to fear me, Priss, I am your friend."

"If you are my friend, say nothing of this at home."

That made me grave, though I promised I would not. We finished our shopping and started back, but I was urgent with my
desire to know Priscilla's secret, and at last I bade her again to
tell me.

"'Twill be hard enough for you to hold your tongue as it is,"
she said. "If you knowed the rest, you would tell it to all the
world."

"I am no gossip!"

"What secret have you ever kept?"

I thought of Nate's pox, but could not speak of it, for the
sake of his honor.

"I will share a secret of mine with you," I told her. "If you
promise that you will not tell it, and that you will tell me yours
when I have finished."

"Truly, Kit?"

She stopped walking. Our way led through a alley what went

between two buildings, only wide enough for the two of us to walk side by side. A chimney was built against one wall that did lessen the coldness there, and we sometimes lingered a moment in that alley, for the relief of it.

"Truly," I said.

"What is your secret, then?"

"I have a brother who is my twin. He has my very face—but he is simple."

She spoke nothing, but began to walk again, and I walked beside her. I wondered was she thinking, *That makes clear why this one is so slow* or *Why is he fussed about such a thing as that, what can't be helped?* Or something in between.

"What is his name?" she asked at last.

"Christopher—like mine. He is called Christy, though."

"Tell me of him."

So I spoke a little of his childish ways, and of all his many smiles, and the way he trusted me so and followed me everywhere, and how sore my heart was to have left him. Whilst I spoke she made sweet buzzings of sympathy that did ease my grief, and I was grateful to her.

"My sister is called Mary," she said after I had done.

I looked at her without understanding, wondering if she told me of a sister who was simple or mad.

"I am shamed to own her, even as you are shamed to own your brother. 'Twas her you saw in the market. She is a nightwalker."

A nightwalker! I'd vowed to myself that whatever she spoke I would treat it gently, but I had not thought of so bad a thing. I checked the first words I thought to say, and the next, as well, whilst we walked on.

"You fault me because I yet speak with her," she said in a low voice. "But I love her, even as you love your brother."

I wanted to console her, as she did me. I remembered I was not spotless myself, though I was lucky. Still, for a woman to lose her chastity—was there a greater wrong?

"How came she to fall?" I asked her at last.

"A servant takes her chances. I have found an honest master whose passions are well governed, but Mary did not. Her master would have her, and did, in spite of her pleading. He said he would turn her out with a bad testimonial if she did not submit to him. He got her with child, and though the child was born before its time, and died, she lost her good name, and any chance of honest work."

"What a great sorrow to you."

"Now we are friends, and will not speak again of brothers and sisters," she said.

We clasped hands on it, and I was glad not to have to speak of her sister again, or of Christy, either.

Though we lived so close to the Thames I seldom saw the Frost Fair now. I told myself I did not mind it; that a working lad should keep busy, and not idle on the ice. But at night my dreams was filled with play: snowballs and football and men sliding on skates, and the dizzy, whirling sledge.

On Candlemas, which falls the second day of February, a

whole ox was roasted upon the ice, in front of Whitehall Palace. By afternoon the lovely scent of it came drifting down the river to Middle Temple Lane. Mr. Fowler was in good humor, for that morning he had delivered to a goldsmith a wedding suit of figured silk, and had been well paid and well praised. When we heared that slices of that ox was being sold on sticks for sixpence, he said his prentices need not work the rest of the day, and myself as well, and Mrs. Fowler freed Priscilla, too, for a few hours. So we all of us went together down the stairs to the Thames and onto the ice.

I had enough left over from what Mr. Pearse had gave me to buy myself a taste of the ox, and I bought one for Priscilla as well.

"Come, we'll join the football," Ralph said.

But Daniel wanted to sit at the Bottle of Hay, which was a blanket tavern, and Humphrey and Francis wanted to see a puppet play.

"And yerself?" I asked Priscilla. "What will ye?"

"It matters not," she said. "'Tis all so merry!"

So I began to look for the whirling sledge, though I didn't tell her so. We wandered by the ropedancers, and the man who walked on stilts, and the drum boat. We saw Ralph tumbling to the ice, and spent a few minutes at the puppet play. Priss would have stayed longer there, but I pulled her away. Still I did not find the whirling sledge. At last I asked a man at a chocolate house about it, and he said the men who pulled it had went home for the day, which disappointed me bitterly.

"'Twill be candle time soon," Priscilla said. "We had better go."

We had not fell all that time, but near to the stairs I slipped, and as she had my arm she fell, too, fell against me. I did not contrive it, but was grateful for it, and resolved to find a way to enjoy the whirling sledge with her again before the thaw should come.

"I am sick to death of cabbages and turnips," Priscilla said on Monday as we left the market. "We might be having peas by now, without this frost. If it does not thaw soon we shall all starve."

"Ye know nothing of starving, do not speak of it," I said, glancing at the spoiled grain and carrot tops what had collected at the edge of the footpath. "Anyways, the thaw will come soon enough. We ought to enjoy the Frost Fair while it lasts."

"I have had enough of games upon the ice."

"Have ye? I have not. I could ride that whirling sledge a dozen times more."

She looked at me quickly, and found me showing her with my eyes just how my words was meant. Then she cast her eyes down into her basket and her cheeks growed a little pink, but she did not look angry.

"That would be a foolish way to spend what little you have," she said.

"I've more than ye guess, though. I was left something by my late master. But I will not spend it all on amusements. I mean to be a prentice, like Daniel."

I'd thought much before I spoke, for I'd promised my master—which words now meant the brother who lived, and not the one who died—I'd say nothing. Yet it was my secret to tell, and I knowed that any girl would look with more favor on a lad with a inheritance than on one without.

But she showed no surprise.

"I know, Kit. Mr. Fowler tells all to his wife, and she tells all to me. But are you sure you wish to sign articles with him? Are there not other trades that will suit you better?"

I thought I knowed her meaning. "You do not wish me to stay."

"Nay, Kit, not that! But Mr. Fowler—swear that you will not go to him, if I tell you?"

I so vowed.

"He thinks you will run away if the work is hard enough, and he means to make it hard, once you have signed. He says you have run before and will again, and he will have your ten pounds. Don't let him take them, Kit!"

So that was it! I ought to have knowed he did not mean to make me a prentice for so little. The more I thought of it, the more my ire was roused, but it was anger filled with power, a kind of exaltation, such as holy words can bring on Easter Sunday.

"Priss, see, 'twill work to my advantage. I *won't* run, he cannot make me! And in the end I will have gained what I never could anywhere else for so small a sum."

She smiled. "You are more sure of yourself than any man I know, save Daniel."

She compared me to Daniel!

"I'm grateful to ye, Priss—that ye're so concerned for my future. I hope it means—I hope ye'll be pleased that I stay."

"Of course I am pleased."

She squeezed my arm, and my blood rolled and leaped as tumblers do. Did it mean she cared for me? Did she care for me as I cared for her?

I did almost fly about London's streets that day. I was sent for coal, and with a message from Mr. Fowler to a attorney at the Middle Temple, and with Francis to the lace-man. And all the while I whistled, or if I did not whistle I sang. I felt like a bright bird with a pretty song what is followed about by the she-birds, like the sort of bird what seizes on his chances.

Next morning when Priscilla and me went to market we was merry together, jeering at the cookmaid who had burnt the tarts, and laughing over the boil Humphrey had got upon his neck. While we shopped I urged her to make haste, till she looked nettled, but I did not trouble myself about that.

As we passed through our alley I paused my step. "Look at the time we have saved with our hurry," I said. "We've time for a ride on the sledge, if ye like."

But she looked discomfited, and did not answer like I planned.

"The food will fly from our baskets if we whirl about that way."

I had not thought of that. "Why, I will cover them with my coat," I said, for I could think of nothing else.

"You cannot, it is too cold."

We had turned to face each other, which left Priscilla with her back to the wall. I set my basket down and reached for hers, and she did let it go, which I took the meaning of. I set it, too, upon the ground. I had not thought of this, but only of the sledge, yet I knowed what to do.

"You warm me," I said, and leaned toward her, and with a hand I pushed back the hood that kept her face from the icy air. And then I did kiss her lips, which was pretty and soft, though they was chapped.

She did not stop me, but when I drawed back she said, "You must not, Kit."

I did not believe her, though, for when I kissed her again she took my kiss willingly. We kissed again, and again, and our hot breaths growed more quicker. I tried to touch her breast, but she was wrapped in so many clothes I could not find it.

"Kit, stop."

I did not like to stop. Though I had felt lusty many times, I had never felt so strong a wanting as I did that moment.

"We must go now, Kit. You know we must."

I heared the fear in her voice, and it gave me heart, for I knowed 'twas her own desire she feared. I stepped back and picked up my basket, and hers as well, for I needed the weight of them to calm myself. What I knowed was not that we must go, but that it must happen again between us, kisses and more, till my wanting was satisfied—and her wanting, too.

I was gentle with her as we walked, the way Mr. Fowler was of his breeding wife. Priscilla took my help, but kept her eyes cast down, so I was left to wonder was I wrong in my guesses. When we got home we took our baskets to the kitchen and put them upon the table for the scullery maid to empty. 'Twas our habit to stand a minute before the kitchen fire, to warm ourselves, but when I took my place there Priscilla spoke, saying, "I must go upstairs, and see if my mistress wants me."

Before I could be discouraged she let her eyes meet mine at last, and I read there such a look as did make my heart leap. I fed my hope with that look and went about my duties with zeal, though at times my hands shook with a excitement I knowed was not wholesome.

All that day I felt the coming of something, of some *change*, though I was not sure it would be the change I longed for. As to that, I was under the command of a force more stronger than anything I had knowed before, and there was no fight in me. I was like a ship that rides the tide, and cannot do otherwise, and I was glad of it, glad to jubilation.

That night I dreamed I wore skates, and slid upon the Thames, and the ice flew like shattered glass neath my feet. Of a sudden I saw that the blade of my skate had cut through some blue flowers what had growed through the ice. I was greatly dismayed, and gathered up the bright, dead things and held them in my gloved hands. "You had best be careful, Kit," Joshua Fowler said to me. "The frost holds your treasure."

I woke confused, as though I'd forgot where I slept, or did not know the time of day. I lay a minute troubled, and then I knowed that the world had changed itself while I slept. The thaw had begun; I heared it in the dripping world from outside the garret window, and felt it in the softening of the air. I almost cried out against that softening, though I had many times wished, as all

England had wished, for a end to our strange weather. Yet that weather had changed my fortunes: while it held I did prosper, and know such merriment as I had never knowed before. While it held I had took my first kiss. I thought of Priscilla, lying on the other side of the wall I slept so near. Would everything come undone? How could it? Yet I feared that it might, that the world would discover somehow that Christopher Chidley was never meant to be a prentice, or kiss a clever girl.

The Thames was still froze the next morning, but all the booths was hastily took down, and coaches made much money taking away piles of goods and hundredweights of blankets, while the rain poured down upon them.

It took a week for the river to thaw. For several days it would freeze by morning, but warm later in the afternoon. At low water, people went upon the ice, but it was much sunk, and at high tide the ice was overflowed by water. On the eighth day of February it rained again all day, yet still the Thames was hard. Soon after, though, the ice began to break, and to float upon the river, great flakes of it, what sometimes split the timber of the boats what had been lying catched within it all those weeks. By the twelfth the ice was gone, and the river open to traffic once more.

"I never saw so many boats," I said to Priscilla as we left the house to go to market that morning, and I could not keep the wonder from my voice.

'Twas Shrove Tuesday. Daniel's banquet was to be that night, and next day I would sign articles with Mr. Fowler, and become a prentice as I'd so long dreamed of doing. I was restless and bestirred, and Priscilla's nearness to me as we walked was both bliss and torment.

"There will be great fun, now the ice is gone," Priscilla said.

"There was great fun whilst the ice held."

She laughed. "The Thames will offer different merriments now."

"So says Ralph. He says that he and Francis do shoot through the arches of London Bridge in little boats, that the water surges through in a torrent."

"That is dangerous sport. But my mistress and I will go by water to the pleasure gardens at Vauxhall, when the cherry trees blossom there. 'Tis lovely to walk among the groves and be quite hid from view."

Her words roused me, and made me resolve to find my way to the pleasure gardens, and take Priscilla with me.

But the cherry trees was a long ways from their flowering, and on the way home from market, as we went through our little alley, I said to her, "We are hid from view here, Priss."

Then we set down our baskets, as had become our custom, and she stood with her back to the wall whilst I gave her long, sweet kisses, and sometimes did seek her pap, though 'twas yet well covered in layers of wool.

"Stop, Kit," she said at last, as she always did.

But I did not want to stop; I could not abear to stop.

"Don't ye care for me, Priss? Ye said once ye'd do anything for one ye loved."

"Anything lawful, I meant. Anyway, we are too young to speak of such things. Tomorrow you will sign articles with Mr. Fowler, will you not? And you will be bound not to marry for all the eight years you work for him. And if you are prudent, you will not marry for a long while after that, till you have become independent and can support a family."

I was not interested in any of those words, just then: not *marry* nor *years* nor *prudent* nor *independent* nor *family*.

"I cannot wait, Priss," I whispered to her, and she took my kiss again, and whilst I kissed her I slipped the glove from my right hand, and did reach for the buttons of her cloak, which at first she did not feel through the thickness of her clothes.

But when she saw what I did she spoke sharply to me, and hit my hand away from her. I stopped, as she bade me, but I was angry that she would not yield to me a little. I knowed that I could not go day upon day with morning kisses what stirred me where they shouldn't but stopped so far short of glory.

19

DANIEL'S BANQUET WAS far more grander than anything I had ever saw before. He rented a hall for it in the old City, and asked twenty-three lads, one for each of his years. They was all prentices, or very lately so, save me. Mostly they was from the cloth trades, and was prenticed, if not to tailors, then to haberdashers or lace-men or woollen drapers or mercers. The prentice who had shooed me away from Milk Street the night Nathaniel Fowler died sat to my right, but he did not remember me. He was called Jeffrey. There was no masters there, and no women.

The dishes was brung from the cookshop in a great procession, with a drum and fife leading the way. There was many courses: fresh mackerel, now that the thaw had come, and eel pie, and venison. And there was much wine. We drank healths all the night long: the King's, the Queen's, the Lord Mayor's, Mr. Fowler's, his wife's.

"Charlotte's!" someone cried, and there was much laughter as we raised our tankards.

"Who is Charlotte?" I asked of my neighbors, but they shook their heads at me.

So I asked no more questions, but listened eagerly whilst they spoke of their shops and of how the trade was changing, with some making only military wear, and others only graveclothes, and now there was salesmen who sold clothing that was not made to a man's measure, but was put together by women who knowed nothing of the proper way to make a suit. Daniel was not to have his own shop, but to be a journeyman in a larger shop, where full twenty such men worked for wages. Up and down the table boys shook their heads, and said all this change would bring no good to such as them.

And then they spoke of a scandalous pamphlet one had read, called "The Nightwalker of Bloomsbury." Langly Curtis had printed it, and was to be tried soon for doing so. I had never heared conversation of this sort before, and wished that I might always have such company.

I reckon that was how it started, about the brothels; anyways, it began at the head of the table, near to Daniel. The first of it I heared was the bang of a fist upon the table as a lad cried, "Yes, let us! 'Tis the night for it!"

"What, what?" we cried from our end.

"Let us go to Chiswell Street, and rid this town of a brothel or two," another boy said.

"We cannot tear down a brothel with but twenty-three hands," said the lace-man's prentice.

"More will join on the way," Daniel said.

We knowed then that he favored the plan, and meant it to happen.

I had heared of riots on Shrove Tuesday, and the tearing down of brothels, but I never thought to be a part of such a effort. But I was, and eagerly so. I was angry at all whores for what had befell my late master, and at all women because Priscilla made me lust for her but gave me no relief. And I was excited to see whores in their rooms, perhaps undressed.

We rose from our littered banquet table and pressed out the door. When first I took my feet I swayed a little, and Jeffrey laughed and grabbed at me to keep me straight, and asked did I never have wine before, but I made no answer. We rushed out the door and through the streets, filled with power and righteousness. Several of the lads carried torches, and there was much shouting about the evil of strumpets, how poxy they was and how vile, and how they did tempt and corrupt our best men. But what made me hate them most—them and all the rest of womankind beside—was how they catched us in their nets of wanting.

"Join us!" Daniel shouted as he strode at the head of us through Old Jewry Street toward the Moorfields. "Join us, and we will rid this town of its verminous whores!"

A few did join us, but not many, and 'twas resolved at last we would not try to tear the building down, but would only smash the mirrors and rip the bed hangings, and throw the whores naked into the street, perhaps.

"There!" Daniel said, pointing at a building across the way. And then, with a roar, *"Now!"*

Like a tide we surged across the street and into the building, and at once there was screams, and warnings shouted out, and men came flying from within the chambers, pulling their coats round 'em and holding their swords high. We did let them by, and then went where they had been whilst the women screamed curses at us. Ralph throwed hisself at looking glasses and nests of drawers, and Jeffrey used his sword to slash at draperies and the fine clothes what sprang forth from the presses. Daniel liked best to take the struggling women by the arms and wrestle them into the street. They was none of them naked, but mostly in shifts, though ye could see their breasts dance neath the thin cloth.

I runned from room to room, but found most of the great work done, and of course I had no sword, so must content myself with breaking things of the smaller sort: I dropped a clock from a window, and smashed a squat green wine bottle, and turned a cushion what had been made of rags back to rags again. I throwed the contents of a earthenware chamber pot upon a bed, and then hurled it down to shatter on the floor. Was we finished? The lads was leaving again; I heared them in the street, but felt unsatisfied to have wrecked so little. I saw a ladder what led above to a garret, and climbed up, but as my head reached the hole someone began to kick at me. I catched her round the ankle with my hand and she fell, and then I came quickly into the tiny chamber there. There was no looking glass to be broke, nor bed-stead, only a pallet on the floor. But there was a press what stood open with a flame-red petticoat within, and I reached for it.

"Don't, I beg ye!" she cried out as she gained her feet. "We can make a bargain, can't we?"

"I don't bargain with poxy whores," I said, but stayed my hand, for suddenly I remembered Priscilla's sister, and wondered was this girl brung to be a whore by causes what was beyond her own making, as Mary was.

She put her hand upon my arm and squeezed it tight. "Why,

there's things we can do without bringing on the pox, lad, if ye've a mind, and no charge to ye, so long as ye leave be my things."

I could not keep my eyes from her swelling paps. The neck of her shift was so low that the dirty frill of lace around it only just covered her teats. My hands was sweating in their gloves, and I made a move with one hand to take the glove from the other. Then I thought: This is the very reason they are so evil—they tempt good men to fall! Almost I had took my pleasure with her, which no righteous man should do. My hatred growed, and I knowed I must do what I had came for. I seized the petticoat with both gloved hands.

Her hand fell from my arm, and she turned away. "I wish I'd never came to London," she said.

She had came to London, same as me, hoping for betterment, and finding sin instead. I dropped the petticoat and started down the ladder. Ladders are more slower than other ways to leave a place, and there was time for me to see the whore's face fill with delight that I had spared her petticoat.

"Come back when ye can!" she called after me. "Come back and bring yer wages!"

My friends was not in the street when I came into it, but I could hear them not far off. I did not follow them, though, for they was whooping with triumph, and I was crazed with shame and need. I found a dark and empty lane and made as though I pissed against the wall, but instead I gave myself relief. Then I went to a tavern and drank more wine, and again more. I was filled with shame at what I had done and what I had not. One kind of man would have took his pleasure, and another would have tore the petticoat. But what manly man would do nothing at all?

I drank till I was turned out, and staggered through the streets, falling and resting awhile from time to time, and then puking. At last I found my way to Mrs. Larkham's, and hammered at the door to be let in. But the door was not opened for me, so I cast myself across the steps, and slept till first light came next morning.

Dorothy, the scullery maid at Mr. Fowler's house, opened the door to me when I came there. I thanked God 'twas only she. "You've took your pleasures this Shrove Tuesday," she said, looking at my clothing. "Have you aught to wear while those things is cleaned?"

I told her I had, and she bade me change my clothing before going to Mr. Fowler, who wished to see me.

So things was that way took out of my hands, or so I supposed, for I did not doubt my master would send from his household the boy who stayed out all night and came home smelling of drink. Almost I was glad of it. I was ashamed to see Daniel again, because I had took pity on the whore and spared her petticoat, and afraid to see Priscilla, because she tempted me so.

I was wearing my second-best things, what I had worn to feed the livestock at Mr. Dean's, when I went in to see Mr. Fowler in his countinghouse. They wanted cleaning, but anyways they was not covered with vomit.

"So, I heard that you had come," Mr. Fowler said, and he spoke as jolly as I had ever saw him, which made me stare. "The constable did not get you after all, hey? That is what we guessed when Daniel did not find you."

"No, sir, 'twas not the constable," I said, wondering did Daniel tell him where we went, and what we did together.

He saw my fear and said, "Do not trouble yourself, Kit. If the authorities cannot keep London free from the scourge of these filthy women, 'tis only right that the citizenry should do its part, though they act outside the law. It is a good night's work. Why did you not come back with the others?"

"I was too drunk, sir, to find my way home." I spoke it clearly, and waited for the worst.

"To be drunk on Shrove Tuesday is no great sin. Ash Wednesday is the very day to repent of it, and to pledge that you will keep sober the rest of the year. I know that you are not a drunkard, Kit. But perhaps there are other things I know not. Though I have watched you closely, I have not known you long. One thing I do know, however, is that you are honest. That I prize most highly, for it means you will answer me honestly when I ask you this: If I knew as much of you as you do of yourself, would I find reason to tell you today that you cannot be my apprentice?"

I wondered why he cared about my wrongdoing, when he only meant for me to stay a short while with him and then to run off and leave him with my ten pounds. But I reckoned any man's morality is a kind of patchwork of the Scriptures he's understood and the ones he has not. How God wished me to answer him I could not tell, for my head ached, my tongue was furred, and my clothes was my second-best. I had not yet prayed, and lacked the strength to do God's will had I knowed it. Even of worldly matters I had not thought clearly, being so sure, the day before, that my future lay here in Middle Temple Lane, and as certain, since rising this morning, that it did not.

"You are thinking long, Kit," Mr. Fowler said. "Have you something you would tell me?"

"Nothing, sir. I am not used to wine, though, and it still muddles my head."

That satisfied him, and he showed me the contract we must both sign, and told me the contents of it. "I am to provide you with meat, drink, lodging, and apparel. Because your premium is so small I will wait till the clothes you have brought show more wear before we outfit you anew, that is fair, is it not?"

"Yes, sir," I said, though I was disappointed. I had not thought to be dressed like Daniel, but hoped to wear at least clothes of the sort that Francis did.

"And you will have a little pocket money, as well. As for your part, you must keep my secrets, and undertake not to damage my goods. You shall not play at cards or dice, nor commit fornication, nor contract matrimony, throughout this eight-year period. You shall not haunt playhouses or taverns, nor absent yourself unlawfully from my service. All apprentices must so promise, when they sign articles. Are you ready to make such a promise, Kit?"

"Yes, sir."

He called into the workshop for Francis, that he might witness the signing of the contract.

Mr. Fowler signed it first and blowed upon it to dry the ink. At last he turned it round for me, that I might make my mark with the quill he gave to me. I knowed how to draw the cross, but feared to drip ink upon the page; however, it fell upon the blotter instead. Then Francis signed as witness, so that it could be proved I was the one who made that mark; he could write his full name with great ease.

"There, it is done!" Mr. Fowler said with great satisfaction. "You are an apprentice now."

And for the first time I understood it. I was a prentice! After so many fantastical dreams of it I was truly a prentice, and in one of the finest trades. Perhaps God smiled on me because I had not touched the whore, after all, and if I withstood all female enticements—even Priscilla's—He would stay by me, and see that my good fortune was not took from me.

Lent is the time to leave yer sin behind, and I did so eagerly. I looked no more at the women of the streets, nor hardly at Priscilla, if I could help it. When next we went together to market, I asked could we go home a different way, as I'd a errand in the Strand. She agreed, and we did not go through our kissing alley. The next day we went through it, but I did not stop, and I reckon she knowed I would not, for she seemed not surprised, and made no remark upon it. We was quiet with each other now, and did not banter, though she took many glances at me, like she had a question but would not ask it.

Now that I was a prentice, Francis and me changed places. I slept in the kitchen, and was glad enough not to have Priss on the other side of a wall from me. Anyways, my duties gave me something to think on besides matters of the flesh. As the newest prentice I did the more heavier household chores, such as carrying the coal from the cellar to the chambers above, and blacking the shoes; I swept out the workshop, and was sometimes made to help Dorothy scrub the kitchen. But I was not disheartened, and worked with zeal, thinking always: He cannot make me run.

And not all duties was unpleasant, for I was sent also to the shops where Mr. Fowler had his accounts: to the lace-man to buy gold lace to use for the trimming of a suit, and to the haberdasher to buy ribbons and laces. I idled a little there, looking at silk buttons and black thread, and thinking of all the ware I'd saw in Dick Osborne's pack through the years. Tailors bought such things wholesale, just as packmen did. But Francis said Mr. Fowler charged a large sum for every button he put on a new coat sold to a judge or a merchant, and I knowed Dick Osborne could charge a country housewife only a little for the same buttons carried in his pack, for she had but little to spend.

I was not yet put to sewing, but Francis told me I ought not be eager to learn it, for now that he sat hunched and cross-legged all the day, he wished he was carrying coal again.

I reckoned he was right, for I had always liked to be out of doors, though the gloomy London streets was not so fair as the countryside that was my home. The smoke had growed less after the thaw, but 'twas still plentiful, and I did not stop my coughing. The skies was still gray more often than they was blue, and everyone walked about in coats and cloaks. The new grasses did not grow, nor the bright flowers bloom.

The roads have opened, though, I thought. The squire had gone home again, most likely, and John Frith had told it at the tavern that he had saw me in London Town, and Christy thought of me, and wondered why I did not come to him.

But I could not give room to such thoughts if I was to get the best of Joshua Fowler.

One morning the sun did shine, and Priscilla came out without her cloak, wearing only a short cape wrapped round her shoulders. She had on a blue gown, with the overskirt tied up in the back so it would not drag. It had been Mrs. Fowler's gown first, of course, and 'twas the color of the mistress's eyes, and not the maid's. All the same, she looked fair, and I could not keep my eyes from her, which she saw. When I took off my gloves to touch the beans at market, I did not put them on again, but cast them upon the cheese that lay in my basket, from which I learned what I meant to do when we reached our lane that day. And I did not even think of what God had done for me by making me a prentice, or of my resolve to keep myself from the snares of females.

When we walked through our alley I slowed my step and she did the same. Then we set our baskets down and I took many kisses, and put my hand at last upon her blouse, where her bosom rose neath it, and she did not stop me, though her stays kept the best part from me.

"Do ye like it, Priss?" I whispered, but she made no answer. "Meet me in the kitchen tonight, when the household sleeps," I said, for my stones ached, and I felt I would die without relief.

"I cannot. You know I cannot."

Then I stepped back, and would kiss her no more, though she was took aback, and tried to pull me to her again.

We was silent walking home, till at last she said, "Say you are not angry with me, Kit."

"I an't angry with ye. Only we can't always do so much and no more, and leave me a sound man, that is all."

She pondered that a moment, and said at last, "Then there will be no more kisses between us. But we are still friends, Kit, are we not?"

I felt near to crying when she said there would be no more kissing, and wished I'd not said what I did, though 'twas true, or anyways, so it seemed.

"Tell me we are friends," she coaxed when I made no answer.

"Not today," I said roughly. "But in time."

That night I lay long awake, thinking not of Priscilla, but of the whore I turned away from the night of Daniel's banquet. What would it cost, to have her do the things I longed to do with Priscilla, that she would not let me? But I did not want the whore as I did Priscilla.

I dreamed that night of a road what had two forks. I was lost, and stood before them, frightened, for I knowed if I took the wrong turning I would not reach my home before nightfall. "Take the middle path," said Nate. He stood beside me, and carried a great peddler's pack upon his back. I was distressed, for I knowed 'twas me ought to be abearing the burdens. "There is no middle way," I said, and then I woke.

'Twas still darkest night. I lay wondering why I waked, and then I heared footfalls coming down the stairs. I cast off my blanket and rose just as she entered. She was in her shift, with only a shawl around her shoulders; she held her candle in one hand, and a tankard in the other. But what made me catch my breath was the dark, beautiful hair what streamed loose down her back.

"Here I am, Priss," I whispered from behind her.

She started and turned.

"Ye've come after all," I said.

"Mrs. Fowler's head pains her, and I took her a remedy to give her ease and help her to sleep. You did not wake when I came for it. Now I bring the remains to the stillroom; that is all, I vow. Say that you believe me, Kit."

"I believe ye," I said, wondering if I did. "Does she wait for ye?"

"Nay, she sleeps now."

I followed her into the stillroom. There was no fire there, but a little light from the kitchen fire flickered in the stoppered bottles what was lined up along the table.

"What's in all these bottles?" I asked.

"Remedies, or what goes into them. Mrs. Fowler keeps a very good cupboard."

She reached up to put the tankard on a shelf, and as she did the loose sleeve of her shift fell down her arm. I had never saw her arm uncovered before, and my hunger growed.

"I wish there was a remedy to relieve *my* suffering," I said. "Only you can do it, Priss."

"Stop it, Kit."

She went back into the kitchen, and I followed her.

"Ye must pity me, Priss. Don't ye, only a little?"

She paused by the fire.

"Let me have just one kiss, then. A kiss farewell, because there are to be no more kisses."

She did not say yea or nay, so I took a kiss, and at the same time put my hand to her hair, where it lay warm and live upon her head, and she did not stop me. I petted the silky skein of it and took another kiss. Then my hands stole neath her shawl and this time they could not miss her breasts what swung so free neath her shift. Still she did not say yea or nay, but her breath catched. For a long while we did only that: the kissing and the touching of her breasts. But then I growed more bolder.

"Let me touch yer thing, Priss, please. I warmed my hands by the fire."

"No, Kit! We must stop, please stop."

But she did not push my hands away. I did not try words again, for I saw now she was strong with words, and would never say yes to what she should not. Only I let my hand slide over the sweet, soft roundness of her belly, and into the fork between her legs, pushing my hand against the cloth of her shift, and left it there a long while, turning it this way and that, and I saw it roused her. I thought I would die if she did not touch my prick in return, but I knowed she would not do it if I asked. At last I took her hand with my own and put it upon my prick, that she might feel it through my nightshirt. And when she seized it I loved her so I was filled with passion, and I knowed that my seed would soon rush through me, which made me dare quickly to pull her shift up and to grope neath it with my hand. I felt her coney softness and the parting there, and slid my finger within. I had touched a woman's thing at last.

And then my seed came, and I groaned despite myself.

Priscilla drawed her hand away in dismay when she saw what it had done for me, and at the same moment I let her go, and the shift what had been held up by my hand fell down again.

"God save me—save me!" She was whispering and crying at once, which sounded most strange. She clutched her shawl right around her, like I might try to touch her again. "What did we do? My name will be ruined, I'll be driven from the house!"

For a moment I cared not for her terror; I was so spent and sated. But as she cried, her fear did infect me.

"Hush, Priss, ye'll rouse the house! Why did ye let me do it, then, if ye felt so?"

"I bade you to stop! You know I did not want to do it! You know I did not!"

We was both angry now, hissing like geese at one another.

"I did not wish it either, what man does wish to sin? It is women who put these lustful thoughts into our heads, wenches like you! If there was no women, no men would burn with lust. 'Twas Eve who tempted Adam, you know, and not the other way round."

"You are as much a simpleton as your brother," she said.

A great rage growed in me, that she took the secret I had shared with her and used it against me, and that she put Christy and me together the same way that Mam used to do.

"And ye're as great a whore as yer sister." I had spoke from my rage, but the moment I said the words I hated myself for them. "I'm sorry, Priss—I don't mean it. It an't true. But—if ye tempt a man that way, why something comes of it, that's all."

"*I* tempted *you*! I think not."

I made no answer, but wondered was it possible for a female to be the tempted one after all.

Then she said, "I suppose you'll be telling my master."

"Think ye I'm eager for Mr. Fowler to know how I've sinned? I'd lose my place, and my ten pounds with it."

"Then you'll tell his apprentices, and he will learn it late or soon. Men tell, that is the way of it."

"Don't speak so, Priss. We've showed we can keep each other's secrets, have we not?"

"Do you vow you'll never speak of it to any living soul of any land, no matter what may pass, no matter if I am struck down by a coach in the street tomorrow?"

I did not answer quickly, for I knowed I would sometime, among men, want to brag that I had had my fingers within a girl's coney, and though I did not speak her name, if I was not careful it might be guessed.

But she began to cry again.

"Don't cry, Priss. I so vow, before God. And do ye likewise vow to me?"

"I so vow, before God. Yet the threat to you is not so great, there are many courses open to a man. But I—if it should become known what we have done, I will find no place in all of London, and will have no peace from men who wish to do to me what *you* have done."

I hated that she spoke so of my doing something *to* her, as if I'd harmed her with the hand what had been the first to touch her there, when she wanted me to do it.

"I'm sorry to have brung pain upon ye. I care for ye, and thought ye cared for me." I spoke without looking at her. "Anyways, we can't undo what we have done. We won't speak of it and, please God, we'll be forgave it."

I turned away from her, and she catched at me and turned me back. "I forgive you, Kit, if you will forgive me for my harsh words. I am afraid, that is all, but I vow I do care for you, the same as you care for me."

And then I kissed her again, and she took my kiss, and would have took another, I think, but I did not offer one. Then we parted, only before she left, she wiped up what was spilt before the fire, whilst tears rolled down her cheeks.

My heart ached, though my stones did not, and I was much troubled as I wondered what would become of us. Though she made me vow not to tell of it, she did not make me vow never to kiss her again, and I could not see what lay ahead, except a kind of circle: repentance what led to amendment, and then our resolve weakening when we was near to one another, and a few kisses, and then more, and then a meeting by the kitchen fire followed by tears and vows and repentance again. I thought of what I'd said to her about women leading men into sin. So I'd been told all my life long, and wasn't it in the Bible, just as I'd said to Priss? But 'twas me that took her hand and put it where I would have it, and me that wondered now if she loved me enough to let me put my thing in hers, another time. And wasn't her sister Mary led into sin by her master? I thought suddenly of my dream, and remembered the whole of what Nate Fowler had said to me on that morning when we'd spoke of carnality. *'Tis a part of our nature, Kit, and has been since we left Eden. Some fight it, some glory in it, and some tread a middle path, though seldom without a misstep.* Maybe that was the way of it, after all, not women leading men or men leading women, but all of us having these carnal natures what brung us so much pleasure and so much sorrow, and each of us being left to manage those natures as best we could, some fighting and some glorying and some treading a middle path. *Though seldom without misstep.* Priss and me had misstepped, I reckoned, but I knowed not how to set our feet upon the path again.

We was quiet with each other as we went to market next morning, and did not go through our alley when we made our way home.

"We will never walk that way again," Priss said.

"Never?" I asked. "What if a great pig was to chase us, and 'twas our only escape?"

She laughed. "We will go there only when chased by great pigs."

"Or if the frost comes again, why then 'tis much warmer to go through that alley."

She looked with pleasure about her. The sun shined and the blossoming trees had finally began to bud. "There will be no more frost this year."

"But when it comes . . . next year, perhaps . . ."

"Very well, when the frost comes."

"Or if we was to see some haughty person we wished to avoid, we might step in there one day."

"Stop it, Kit."

She was not smiling now, and I did rue my running tongue, yet could not curb it. "Do not say 'never' to me, Priss."

She said nothing, and looked into her basket as if she counted the oranges there.

But at evening prayer that night, I learned that she answered me not with words, but with deeds.

Mr. Fowler began with the forty-second psalm: *As the hart panteth after the water brooks, so panteth my soul after thee, O God,* but whilst I listened I did not pant for God, but for Priscilla. To turn my thoughts I wondered would I someday lead my own household in evening prayer. That made me think of Priscilla again, now my bride, and of the marriage bed. When I found where my attention had wandered I became resolute, and brung it back to Mr. Fowler's voice in time to hear him say: "We pray especially tonight for Mrs. Ashton, Priscilla's mother, who is gravely ill, and for Priscilla's safe journey home tomorrow. We thank you for her service with us, and pray that we have been helpful in forming that good character which her parents have a right to expect, now that she goes home to them. We praise you that you have by such happy chance arranged to bring, on the same day, Mrs. Fowler's sister, Mrs. Wrayburn, to our household, to live with us till my wife should be brought to childbed . . ."

I jerked up my head and looked straight at Priss, but her head was bowed and her eyes was closed.

When prayers was done I followed her from the room, and stayed her with a hand upon her arm. I knowed that I was reckless, but I cared not.

"Yer mother an't ill," I said angrily.

"She's ailing," Priss said, not looking at me.

"She an't ailing more than last week."

"What do you want of me, Kit? One of us must go, 'tis the only hope for us, and you are bound by contract. I will stay at home awhile, and then take the testimonial Mrs. Fowler has writ for me and find another place."

"Why must one of us go?" I said.

She shook her head at me. "My mistress waits for me."

Anyways, I knowed the answer, though it angered and grieved me. Priscilla was not content, as I was, to fall and repent and fall again. It made me feel she did not care for me as I did for her; I resented that her reason was more stronger than her passion, and mine was not.

She must have saw my pain, for she whispered to me, "I do not dare, Kit. I cannot trust myself."

Then my anger went, and I felt tears prick my eyes. "Say ye're not angry with me, Priss."

"I am not angry with you, Kit."

Say ye don't regret what we shared, I would have added, but I knowed that she did, for now she must lose her place, and leave the family she enjoyed so much this past year, and worry would I keep my vow. I felt bad that all the woe had came to Priss, and to me only the pain of losing her. I vowed I would be more careful of my carnal nature from now on, and keep myself from misstep if only God would help me. All the same, I could not regret what we did, for 'twas more sweeter than any moment that had came before it in my life.

20

I'D WONDERED WOULD all my good fortune melt with the ice, and in the days after Priscilla left I thought it had. I reckon a man is the stronger for having a woman by he wishes to win, for he will be staunch whilst she is watching. Without Priss I wondered for the first time could I serve eight years under a master who did not want me, or would my will be broke, after all. And for the first time it seemed not so wonderful to be a prentice in dirty London Town, though I'd spent so many hours longing for it when I was home in Essex. The very thought frightened me back into resolve, for I knowed that to rise a man must strive, and to strive he must want the thing he strives for, must want it exceedingly, mightily. So I cast myself back into fantastical thoughts of what might come to me when I'd served my term: of investments that prospered, of being elected alderman, of Mr. Dean coming to London and seeing me wave from the Merchant-Taylors' float upon the Thames in the Lord Mayor's Show.

But that was not yet, and though spring drawed near, my

days was gray and sullen, filled mainly with household chores and with the worser ones at that. I no more went to market, for when Mrs. Wrayburn went to Clare Market she went with Dorothy, the scullery maid; else she went alone. But Mrs. Wrayburn could not abear the smell at Smithfield, so one morning I was sent with Dorothy to one of the butchers there.

"Look at that pork, it is measled, I know," Dorothy said.

I looked as I was bade, and saw that the fat of the meat was indeed riddled as though with hailshot; full of worms, it was. "Beef, then?"

"The last we had from here was tough, I think he does not bait it before it is slaughtered."

"Then what will ye?"

I did not look at her as I spoke, but beyond her at the sheep pens where I'd spent the night with Henry. A man stood by, and I guessed he was the master Henry had told me of. I hastened toward him.

"Mr. Radcliffe, sir?"

"Who are you, boy, and how do you come to know my name?"

"Henry told it to me, sir. I have not saw him for some time, and I am wondering how he does."

"I am sorry to tell you that Henry died on the last day of January, poor fellow. His leg was frozen, and then turned black, and he could not be saved."

I could not speak, even in courtesy, only made my bow, and he went away.

"What is it, Kit?" Dorothy asked me when she saw my face.

I only shook my head, and used my hand to show we should

go on and find what we looked for. But she did not mind me, and asked if I had heared ill news.

"There was a man I knowed died of the frost," I said to her.

I did not tell her more. I did not speak of my sorrow, nor of my fear, which was more greater. For if a simpleton in London Town could die of the cold, how much easier might a simpleton in Essex do it? Of course, Christy had not slept in the open air. Anyways, I hoped he had not. But who there had saw to it that he did not? Who was it made sure, while winter lasted, that he did not go outside without his hands wrapped in rags? Who checked his hands and feet for black spots in the cold morning?

That night I dreamed that I looked for Henry at Smithfield but could not find him. I pushed my way through the clamorous sheep, seeking a spot where Henry might be lying asleep. At last I saw him, and rejoiced.

"Wake up, Christy," I said, for now 'twas Christy lying there.

He opened his eyes and said, "Joseph! I do like yer coat of many colors!"

I looked at myself and found I was wearing a coat so rich and warm no one had saw anything like it before. Silks and velvets of every hue, both deep and pale, and with the softest fur round the collar and the cuffs. "Why, this should be yours, Christy," I said.

"No, Kit, I'm going now, I won't need it."

Then I heared a voice from far off, what said, *He has a claim on me*.

I woke with sweat on my brow, feeling frightened and horrid. Was it God who spoke at the end? Did he take Christy to heaven? Was it a vision of my brother's death, and if so, had it passed, or was it yet to come?

I had to know, so I resolved I would send to Dick Osborne, who could read and write, and ask him how my brother did. Only I could not have him send the answer to Middle Temple Lane, for if it came to Mr. Fowler's household there would be many questions, and offers to read it, and I could not abear so many noses in my secret business. What if Mr. Fowler, when he learned of Christy, thought I should go home to him and stay a poor man all my life, when what I wanted was to stay in London and prosper? I thought all that morning where I might have a answer sent instead, and near to dinnertime, when I found myself in Cheapside on a errand for my master, I remembered Mr. Jackson, the linendraper.

I found his shop in Milk Street, and thanks be to God, he was behind the counter as I entered.

"Mr. Jackson, sir?"

"Yes, boy, what is it?" He looked at me in a friendly way.

"I am a friend to Dick Osborne," I said, and watched him carefully to see if a scowl crossed his face, but none did.

"Are you indeed? I am expecting him around the first week of April, that is when the packmen begin their traveling. Unless you have come to tell me differently?"

"No, sir. I came to ask ye, if I send a letter to Dick, can he send his answer to your shop?"

If he asked the reason I meant to say I would be changing lodgings soon, but he did not, only smiled and said surely, and told me to pass his greetings on to Dick.

A week passed before I was again doing errands and had time enough to do business of my own in the midst of them. I had been thinking all those days of what I must say, so when I came to the man who sat at a coffeehouse in Long Acre and wrote letters for others at the rate of a penny a page, I knowed exactly the words I wanted to use. I went to Covent Garden, not because it was more closer than other such places, but because I thought I could not be saw there by anyone from Mr. Fowler's household. I stood a moment outside the coffeehouse, thinking how I'd dreamed of sending home fine news of myself, how I was a prentice in one of the finest trades there is, and would make my fortune someday, perhaps; or if not, anyways I would earn my bread more regular than any Chidleys ever did before. But Mr. Fowler gave me only a little pocket money, and I could not afford more than a page.

This is what I told the man to write:

To Richard Osborne, Packman
Dick,

It is me, Kit Chidley, who writes to ye. I have come to London Town, I am well and have work. I hope no one has took it ill and that no harm has come from my leaving so sudden. I dislike to trouble ye but as ye are so kind a man and can read and make your letters I will ask ye to send word of my family, in particular if my brother Christy be well. I will call for your letter at Mr. Jackson's in Milk Street, the linendraper what sold ye the handkerchiefs. He sends his greetings.

Yer obedient servant,
Christopher Chidley

I paid the man and went out into the street, and as I did so I saw a young man dressed very fine, and at his side a woman dressed just as fine. I say "woman," for I'd lived very near to this place, and knowed she was no maid. The man saluted her on her cheek, and she went within, and he strolled toward me. Then I saw 'twas Daniel.

I was much took aback. Daniel, who was so pious, who hated whores so much he spat upon them, and throwed them into the streets! I knowed not what to say, and only gaped at him as he drawed nigh.

"Why, Kit, what do you here? No, do not tell me, I can guess." He winked.

My blood did turn so hot 'twas painful in me. I was angry and proud, both at once, that he thought I took a man's pleasure with a whore.

"That woman—" I said.

"Ah, Charlotte. She is very different to these common whores who are shared by a sea of mankind, you know. They are all very well for lads like you. But someone like myself must have a port to which only his ship comes. It does much for my reputation among men of fashion, you know, that I can afford to keep a woman in Covent Garden, and to dress her as I do, since I am not yet settled enough to marry."

"Does your new master know?" I asked before I could stop myself.

"Oh, certainly. He does not mind if I spend my dinnertime this way; he is a man of fashion himself. Not every tailor is as pious as Mr. Fowler, you know. But take heart, I am discreet, and will never say I saw you here."

I gestured with the paper I held, as though it could explain to him what my mouth seemed unable to utter, but he went on his way, and at last my feet moved again, and I went on mine.

I had been too long abroad, and now hastened back to Middle Temple Lane, but thought the while of Daniel, not liking to condemn the man I had admired so long. We have all carnal natures, and must struggle with 'em, I thought, remembering the words of my late master. But Daniel had spoke nothing of carnality, much less of love. He had spoke only of his reputation among other men, and somehow, I could not feel toward him as I had felt before.

I did not find a chance to take my letter to the post office for many days, but on a Wednesday in the second week of March I was sent with a message to a man in Threadneedle Street, what was near to Lombard Street, where the post office was. There I paid tuppence, and asked the clerk how long it would take to go.

"Why, the post travels a hundred and twenty miles in a day!" he told me. "But it will not go out to Essex again till tomorrow, today we dispatch only to Kent and the Downs."

I could have wished the post went a little more slower, for I dreaded as much as I longed to hear what had passed with Christy.

'Twas now a full month since I'd signed articles, and I had been taught nothing of the craft of tailoring. Mr. Fowler was no longer friendly with me, and I knowed he was wishing I would run, that he might take on a new prentice who would bring him a handsome premium. He could not do so whilst I stayed without plac-

ing me above the new prentice and teaching me the trade, and if
he did that I would never run. So I was gave drudgery to do from
dawn till night. I was more under the charge of Mrs. Fowler than
of my master, or else under the charge of Mrs. Wrayburn, as Mrs.
Fowler kept more and more to her chamber. I drawed ale and carried ashes and made beds, as though I was a maid, but I did not
carp or question, for the youngest prentice may be asked to do
most anything. Still, I had not been taught so much as to thread a
needle (though I knowed that much already), and that did trouble
me a little. I wondered would I have to take my master to law to
make him honor our contract. I knowed not how that was done,
nor if it cost much money.

Business growed brisk, for though it was Lent many had be-
spoke suits, so's to show new finery on Easter Day. Francis now
was more swifter with his needle, and could not be spared for errands, so one day I was sent again into the streets, to the mercer
whose shop was in Milk Street, that I might bring home more of
a certain pale silk being used for the lining of a suit. And when I
was done in the mercer's shop, I stepped across to Mr. Jackson's
in the hope that I might learn what had passed with my brother.

"I remember you," Mr. Jackson said when he saw me. He
was well pleased with hisself for that remembering, like it was a
great feat. "You are Dick Osborne's friend. He will be here very
soon, I daresay, and take some handkerchiefs of me, and some
holland, and sell it in Suffolk and Norfolk. I wish I had someone
to sell my ware up Shropshire way, and into Wales. Ah, well, perhaps next year."

"Has a letter come for me, Mr. Jackson?" I asked, wondering
if he had forgot the reason I came to him.

"Ah, yes, a letter." He put a pair of spectacles upon his nose, then reached neath the counter and drawed out a handful of papers, and sorted carefully through, till he found what he looked for. Then he scowled at me through the lenses. "Can you read, boy?"

"Not well, sir, but I can find someone who will do it for me."

"As you are a friend of Dick's, I will read it to you myself, if you so choose."

I thought a moment about that, but did not see why he might not know my secrets as well as anyone, for I need not see him again, if I did not like. So I thanked him, and listened to what he read.

Dear Kit,

Yer letter has brung us great joy. We knowed from the innkeeper of the Golden Lion that ye did not die of the frost, and from John Frith that ye're in London Town. But it an't the same as hearing from ye that ye are well. Christy was most especially joyful, and asked many times when would ye come for him. He did not understand when I said ye will not.

I am sorry to say to ye that Christy an't well. He lives now with the Edwards family, and they are gave something by the parish for his keep. But this punishing winter has been severe on everyone, and they spend mostly on their own children. I reckon that is natural, but yer brother has growed most thin and is ever hungry. He moans and begs of everyone he sees. We are none of us sure he will live through another winter. He misses ye most sorely, and cries often. But he an't much beat, so that's a mercy.

I am happy to tell ye that yer mam does well. She still has her

place with the Curtis family, and is well treated there. Tabitha and I
keep well.

Leave a message at Mr. Jackson's as to where I might find ye,
and God willing, we will see each other soon.

Yer obedient servant,
Richard Osborne, Packman

Mr. Jackson took his spectacles off and looked at me. "That is mostly good news, but for what is said of Christy," he said, encouraging-like. "He is your brother?"

"Yes, sir."

I'd readied myself for word of his death, but this news was worser; it gave me a ache of remorse all through. 'Twas easy to picture him took to heaven and delighting in God's love and mercy, but to know he was moaning and begging, and waiting for me to come for him, and not likely to live through the next winter—that was another matter. He an't beat much, I said to myself, and told myself, too, that I could not do much for him if I went back.

"What shall I say to Dick, then, when he comes, of where to find you?" Mr. Jackson asked.

But I could not bring myself to speak of Middle Temple Lane, could not abear to have Dick come to me there, reeking of my village and my past and my brother, so I said that I would let him know another day, and hastened back to the Fowler house.

21

ALL DAY I could feel obstinancy in my own clenched muscles. I an't going back, I told myself again and again, and told myself, too, that the Lord would not have gave me so many good turns of fortune if fortune was not meant for me. Surely God didn't want me walking all the way back to the village and begging my bread along the way? What could I do for Christy when I got there, anyways, with myself as poor as a rat, and him as poor as cheese?

That night I did not even say my prayers, for fear of having 'em answered. But a few hours later I woke in the dark kitchen from a dream of cattle lowing to be fed, and for a moment thought I was at Mr. Dean's. When I recalled where I was, and all that had passed between that time and this, instead of relief I felt heartbroke, and I wept. And though I recalled nothing more of my dream, it did not take a Joseph to know the meaning of it, and what I must now do.

The moment my morning chores was done I found my master in his countinghouse and asked if I might speak with him. He said he would hear me, looking pleased but cautious. I knowed what he was hoping, and I meant to give him what he hoped for.

"There's something I ought to have told ye before I signed our contract, sir," I said to him. "I have a brother—a twin—who is simple, and cannot care for hisself. And I've lately heared that the family he lives with an't caring well for him either. 'Tis my duty to go to him, sir. He has a claim on me."

Mr. Fowler frowned, but I knowed he was playacting. "Yes," he said. "You certainly ought to have told me. Do you mean to go to him only for a while, or are you done with your apprenticeship?"

It was hard to speak it, and with my speech cast away my chances forever, but there was no help for it.

"I cannot see how I might ever return, sir. I should have saw that he would always need me. I deceived myself. I wanted so much to be yer prentice, sir."

"Then you do not complain of your treatment here, or suggest that I have not met my obligations?"

"No, sir."

"You make no objection, then, if I keep the premium you have paid me?"

"No, sir."

"How will you return to Essex?"

"I'll walk, sir, and beg upon my way."

"You have come all this way to London, and worked hard whilst here, and yet you return with your purse empty. That is a lesson, Kit, that only those undertakings that have been blessed by the Lord do prosper."

"Yes, sir." I wondered if he spoke true, and if all the things I supposed was favors from the Lord was really the snares of the world after all.

"I am glad that you have seen your Christian duty, Kit, though you have seen it late. You may stay through Easter Sunday, and receive Holy Communion with us before you begin your journey, and I will give you a sixpence for the road."

"Thank ye, sir."

I'd hoped for more—a shilling at least—but I ought to have knowed that a grasping man like Joshua Fowler would never give so much.

Holy Week passed slow for me. Now that I had no future in London, I was wanting to be gone, and had little interest in hauling ashes and blacking shoes, though I did those things as well as I had ever done, for that is my character. Also we was made to pray a great deal, which suited me ill. My heart was stony with ingratitude, for I felt like God had gave me a taste of gooseberry tart and then made me watch other boys eat it.

Mr. Fowler prayed as well, of course. He was made for praying, that man, and could not get enough of it.

On Good Friday we did not work past noon, but we was hours at church. The sermon was well preached, by a man who knowed to speak above the barking and spitting into kerchiefs. He told us of the many lessons we was taught by Christ dying in such a loathsome way, crucified on the cross like a thief, with nails drove into His hands and feet, which Reverend James said are the most sensitive parts of the body. I remembered how my feet pained me when I walked so far in the snow, and wondered was it true. So I lost a little of the sermon, and when I listened again he was speaking of charity, and cried shame upon those grasping men who was unwilling to part with a little of their wealth for the relief of their poor brothers, when Christ had parted with all His wealth and His life, too, only for our sake. I looked toward Mr. Fowler, who had took my legacy from me, but I could tell nothing from his face. Then Reverend James went on to say how could we fail to forgive others, when Christ had died for those same others, which did shame me, for I had not forgave Mr. Dean nor Mr. Joshua Fowler for what they had done to me and mine, and I vowed to mend my ways.

At last we left, wearied by pain and prayer, and made our way along Middle Temple Lane. Mr. Fowler was usually lively at such times; he liked to praise the sermon and tell us the main points over again, like we was too dull to understand them without help. But today he was slow and thoughtful, and I couldn't help hoping that he was troubled.

We was at Temple Bar when we was hailed by a attorney who knowed Mr. Fowler well. He spoke with great excitement, saying, "Did you hear? What a great pity it is! Six of the poor were crushed to death at the Surgeon's Entrance to Whitehall this day. The King has not touched the Evil for many weeks, you know, and tickets were to be given out this day, for those who wished to have the King's hands laid upon them come Easter Day, and so be healed of their scrofula. But there was such a crowd that they began to rush, and some were crushed, poor souls, such a great pity! Ah, well, please God they have gone where they will have no more suffering."

We all exclaimed at the horror of it, and Mr. Fowler most of all. "God's hand is in this," he said. He looked grave and uneasy. "It is a lesson to remind us that we must not be ever seeking for the things we have not, but must accept what is allotted to us according to God's plan."

I opened my eyes wide when he said that. For who was more greedy than he? Or was it only the poor who must be happy with what they had, be it ever so little?

But the graspingness of Mr. Joshua Fowler was not for me to mind. God had unclenched my own grasping fingers at last, and I needed no crowing sermons to remind me of it.

Mr. Fowler prayed all that weekend, I never knowed a man to pray so much, and several times he spoke of Christian charity, sounding much troubled, till at last I thought perhaps 'twas hisself he meant to mend, more than the rest of us. Once I catched him looking at me, and I wondered was he thinking to give me a shilling for my journey after all, or even a crown! But then I recalled that I'd had many fancies of such things in the past, and I turned my thoughts to Christy, where they went easily now, and without that piercing heat they had gave me for so many weeks.

On Easter Sunday all the world dressed in their best things, many of 'em made by Mr. Fowler, or in his shop. Even Francis was in a new waistcoat with gold diamonds upon a black ground, and I felt envy like a cramp within me, for I wore the same clothes Mr. Dean had gave me, what had suffered much. But again I thought of Christy, and of the look on his face he would have when I came to him, and I was easy once more.

That evening, a little before prayers, I was sent to see Mr. Fowler in the parlor. I supposed he would say goodbye and give me the sixpence he'd promised, or more, if he'd been moved by God to greater charity. But he surprised me, as humankind can do from time to time.

"Are you still resolved to go, Kit?" he asked me with a earnest look. "If you stay, I will begin to teach you the mysteries of my craft—I'll begin tomorrow. And I will have new apparel for you made at once. We can call Francis to witness my pledge, if you doubt me."

"Don't tempt me, sir!" I cried out. "It an't Christian!"

"There, there, you need not stay if your duty lies elsewhere. You are willing to give up much to go to your brother."

"You would—if you'd a brother like him."

I'd been keeping my eyes on the ground, proper-like, but when he did not speak for a moment I looked up, and saw him wiping his eyes with his handkerchief.

"I beg yer pardon, sir," I said, for I'd not meant to remind him of his own brother so lately dead.

"Kit," he said, in a weary way, "I have prayed much about the matter of your premium, and I am going to return it to you."

I gasped, like I'd been hit from behind. "Thank ye, sir!" I said as quick as I found voice.

"It is not your fault that you are kept from honoring your contract, and my outlay on your behalf has been but small. In such cases it is usual for the master to return all or most of the premium to his former prentice."

"I see, sir."

What I saw was that he'd meant to cheat me, and that he

dared to tell me so. It did not make me like him, though he turned my fortunes yet again. How many more times would they turn, before my life was done?

"I hope you will be wise with the money, Kit. 'Twould be easy to spend it on frivolities and passing pleasures."

"No, sir, I'll be a packman, sir, and walk through all of England, and my brother shall come with me."

"A packman! Can you not do better than that?"

"No, sir. That is the best that I can do."

Mr. Fowler gave me back all of the inheritance I had from his brother, less a little so that I might stay one more week whilst I prepared for my new employment. I bought a great sheet of canvas to hold the things that I would sell, and then began to fill it. From Mr. Jackson I got fine handkerchiefs and many ells of cloth: blue linen, holland, hempen cloth, and a little calico. I paid only a part of the cost, and was told I might pay him the rest next spring, when I had sold them; that was his usual way of doing business with peddlers. Other things I bought outright: haberdashery, of course; ballads and chapbooks; and many woodcuts of country scenes, which seemed more fairer to me now than they once did, though I had saw so many fine pictures since.

One thing I bought that was not new. 'Twas a coat, greatly worn, which I bought of a secondhand clothes dealer in Rosemary Lane.

"Why did you buy such a ragged thing?" Francis asked me. "You could sew a better one yourself, though you have learnt nothing yet."

I had come into the shop, with Mr. Fowler's permission, to pick up scraps of cloth before they was swept up and throwed away, and to patch the coat with them. I'd offered to pay for the thread I used, and first he said yes, that was fair, but then he said no, I might have it freely, as it amounted to so little. So I saw that he yet wrestled with his grasping nature.

"I wanted a coat with many patches," I said to Francis.

He laughed at me, and laughed yet more when instead of using cloth of the same sad color as the coat, I used swatches of bright red and blue and yellow, that drawed the eye, and made a show of the age and poverty of the garment.

"No man will put that upon his back," Francis said.

"Yes," I answered him. "One man will."

22

'TWAS THE FIRST week of April that I set out for home. My leave-takings was nothing to make my heart sore, both Nate and Priss having gone before me, in their different ways. I did linger a little when I spoke farewell to Mrs. Fowler, and at last asked, if she should see Priscilla again, that she might pass on my humble respects and gratitude for her maidservant's kindness.

She smiled upon me with great pity. "I know you fancied her, but Priss is not one to lose her heart, though the young men were as thick as freckles on a Scotsman. Ah, well, you were not well paired, you know. May God bring you a willing helpmeet of your own standing, in His good time."

That made me glad enough to be quit of Middle Temple Lane.

I went next to the churchyard of St. Paul's in Covent Garden, to stand a few moments before Nate Fowler's stone. I told him I would go to the Malvern Hills that he had spoke of, after all, and see the orchards of Herefordshire. Though I would not paint them, I would look long upon them—upon the trees themselves—and make the looking last in my memory, if God so willed.

The last man I saw in London was Mr. Jackson. Dick had not yet come there, so I left a message for him: only that he might know I was now a packman, too, but would not sell on his routes.

"And tell him I take Christy with me," I said.

"That is the brother who is unwell?" Mr. Jackson said. "He will hinder you in your walking, I fear."

"Christy's a great walker, sir. Once he's fed regular again he'll be fine."

It took me five days to reach our village. I longed to make haste but could not, for I had not yet learnt to bear the great bundle on my back. I had a tall staff in one hand, what helped to balance me, for I was bent far forward and bore the weight more on one side than the other. After only a hour my shoulders ached, and my neck also, and I could hardly abear the heaviness that pressed upon me. After a day my skin was rubbed raw where the canvas touched me, and I had to fish cloth from my pack and wear it like a scarf around my neck. So I walked slowly and rested often as I made my way back to Essex.

I looked mostly at the ground before my feet as I went, and missed little by doing so, for the road from London was a ugly one in its first miles, only dunghills and limekilns, and acrid smoke what filled the air. But at last I left London and its smoke behind, and then I was amazed, for I'd forgot what air and trees and grasses was like when not befouled by smuts. I took air deep

within and did not cough: 'twas like a miracle. And the quiet—
the quiet did amaze, too, all still save the birds, and how they
sang!

I sang as well, sometimes, when I had breath enough. I'd
learnt the verses of the ballads what I carried with me, that I
might make a show of 'em. "'I am a peddler, here's my pack, /
now you that are at leisure, / come take a view, see what you
lack, / I have great choice of treasure . . .'" I sang. And I sang a
song what told of the changing fortunes of Dick Whittington,
how he began as a poor boy but did rise in life. Like me.

On the fifth day I set out on the road between Chelmsford
and our village, what I had walked through such bitter cold. Now
'twas blooming and hopeful, though the spring was not so boun-
tiful as in other years, for many plants was killed by the frost.
Still, the clefts in trees what was split in the frost had growed together again, which seemed a promising sign.

Late that morning I spied Mr. Dean's house in the distance. I
was glad it came first, before the tavern, and the Curtis place, and
the cottage where Christy now lived with the Edwards family.
For speaking my piece to Mrs. Dean was like giving a tuppence to
the waterman at the Old Barge House Stairs; I could not pass till
I did it.

Betty answered the door, and saw my pack but not my face.
"I'll call the mistress," she said, and left me by the door till 'twas
opened again by Mrs. Dean.

"So, what d'ye bring today?" she asked, wiping her hands on
her soiled apron. "I'm needing inkle, and fringe. Have ye combs,
by chance? They need not be ivory, horn will do."

"It's Kit Chidley, Mrs. Dean."

"Kit! Is it you? I never thought to see ye in these parts again." She stared at me, more wary than friendly.

"I've come to thank ye, that ye did not set the law upon me."

"Hush." She looked behind her, and I wondered was her husband there.

"I wish I could have brung it back to ye—yer scarf, I mean. I tried—"

"I hope ye got the good of it, anyways," Mrs. Dean said, being too kind a woman to make me tell the story of my wrongs.

"It saved my life. That I can never repay, but I wish ye would take anything from my pack that ye like, please."

"Why, ye never will prosper if ye give yer wares away, Kit," she said, and she looked more friendlier than before.

"Only to you, Mrs. Dean."

Then she let me open my great sheet of canvas, and looked upon all the things within, till at last she took a few yards of inkle and two combs of horn. She did not like to take even so much, I think, but did it that I might feel eased of my debt.

Gathering my ware together again was not so easy as I thought it would be, for I was not yet practiced in doing so. But at last I managed it. As I heaved my pack onto my back once more, I heared Mr. Dean's voice.

"I hope you have not spent too much on frippery," he said to his wife.

"Kit Chidley has become a packman," she answered him.

"A packman! I knew no good would come of that boy!"

And then the door was closed, and I was alone upon the road.

∾

Now my step was light, and soon I came to the tavern what Mr. Lowry kept. I went inside, and again my pack was looked at and my face was not; even Kate Haddon did not know me, which tickled me.

"Why, it's me, Kit Chidley," I told her. "I'm a packman now. My brother and I will be taking our meals here for a few days, and today we'll be wanting twice the dinner ye're thinking of serving us, so don't be mean with the ladle, Kate." And I winked at her.

"Why, I can see ye'll be needing yer victuals, for ye've grown, I do believe," she said, and looked on me most favorable.

I thought to myself that 'twas not my height that made the difference, but the pack on my back, and a air of knowing things I'd not knowed before.

"Ye was to London, I hear," she said.

"Yes, ye'll not credit me when I tell ye what I saw there. Ye've heared of the Frost Fair?"

"Ye saw the Frost Fair!"

"Saw it every day! I ate of a ox what was roasted on the ice!"

There was two or three other men there, and Robert Fryer hanging behind, and all of 'em was agog.

Then I took my pack off and sat telling stories a little while, till the smells of dinner made my stomach growl, and I knowed I must go for Christy.

I thought I'd steadied myself, that I was ready to see him changed, but it may be such readiness an't possible when it's a matter of kin. As I came near to the cottage where the Edwards family lived I saw a woman working in the vegetables, and two children playing near to her with sticks, and a frail man in tattered clothes I supposed was Mr. Edwards. I watched him as he brung a handful of dirt to his nose for a hungry sniff. But 'twas not Mr. Edwards. 'Twas Christy.

"Christy!"

It burst out of me in a hoarse whisper, not near loud enough to be heared by anyone I looked at. But his head came up anyways, and he saw me, and knowed me right away.

"Kit! Kit! I knowed ye would come! Mr. Osborne said ye would not, but he was wrong, and I am right!"

What a fool he was, a bony fool wrapped in rags, grinning and triumphant. I was never more gladder to see anyone in all my life.

"Have ye brung me something, Kit? Have ye brung me something to eat?"

"Ye may start with this, Christy," I said, handing him a hunk of barley bread and some yellow cheese I'd brung along. "But I'm taking ye to the tavern for dinner—ye'll have a whole pie to yerself, if ye like. Only ye must not be sick after, for we are packmen now, and in a few days we must begin our walk round England. Ye're still a good walker, an't ye, Christy?"

He was like a dog what has never been hit, all eagerness and joy, gobbling his food, and promising me what a great walker he was, and wondering where we would sleep, and crowing that he'd knowed I would come back for him, after all.

"It snowed on Innocents' Day, Kit, it snowed and snowed and snowed, and the roads was blocked and the firewood was all used up! The carters brung coals, that we might not freeze, but the roads was blocked, so they took their carts upon the ice of the river! Did ye ever hear of such a thing, Kit?"

"I brung ye something," I told him when his food was ate up, and he at last growed more calmer. "Ye'll need a coat for our travels."

I dug into my pack and got it—the coat with all its bright patches.

He knowed at once what it was.

"It's my coat of many colors, Kit! Look—here is blue. Here is red. Here is green."

And so on. I had to help him find the violet, his favorite color. There was just one swatch of it, and it was small, but I'd sewed it so it would lie upon his heart.

"I am Joseph, Kit! I'm Joseph, and ye're Reuben, the kind brother."

"Yes, Christy," I told him. "I am Reuben, after all."

AUTHOR'S NOTE

Many people believe that the winter of 1683–1684 was the coldest that inhabited England has known. In some parts of the kingdom the ground froze a full meter down. The sea froze for "many leagues," both off the Dover coast and on the opposite side of the English Channel. The River Thames froze where it wound through London, thereby supporting the traffic of coaches, the makeshift shops, the entertainments, and the throngs of Londoners who came to see the wonder of it all. The description and chronology of the Great Frost and the particulars of the Frost Fair described in *The Brothers Story* are based closely on accounts written by seventeenth-century observers, including John Evelyn and Narcissus Luttrell; I also drew on papers presented to the Royal Society in the months following the phenomenon. Special events such as the roasting of the ox are part of the historical record.

In order to construct Kit's voice and the speech of the other characters in the book, I studied books on Essex dialect and on the history of Cockney; I borrowed not only vocabulary but several colorful figures of speech from these sources, especially from Ned Ward's *The London Spy*, the first number of which was published in 1698. The simile "a face like a turd full of cherry-stones" came from a pamphlet called "The Whore's Rhetorick," which was reprinted several times during the period; no doubt Nate had read it.

I took a liberty by including the verses used in Kit's reading lessons. Though graffiti existed in seventeenth-century London (and earlier), few examples were recorded before the publication in 1731 of *The Merry-Thought: Or, the Glass-Window and Boghouse Miscellany*, from which all the rhymed graffiti in my story is taken. Of course it's perfectly possible that some of these verses do date back to 1684; many are probably more recent.

Writing *The Brothers Story* took me into many corners of history that were new to me. Fortunately, historical research has gotten easier—and more exciting—over the last few years, as libraries from all over the world have put the books and records of the past online. From the conveniently close University of California at Berkeley, I was able to access original seventeenth-century sources: *The English Physicians Dayly Practice* by Nicholas Culpeper, *Bills of Mortality* by John Graunt, *The Art of Painting* by John Smith, and *The Experimental History of Cold* by the early chemist Robert Boyle, among others.

Many people helped with the creation of this novel. Thanks are due to Kay Frydenborg, Ellen Hopkins, Tracy Hurley, Amy McQuade, and Ed Spicer for helping an urban Californian envision farm animals in cold climes; to Susan Hart Lindquist and Larry Holben for reading the book in manuscript and giving useful feedback; and to Wesley Adams, Karla Reganold, and Elaine Chubb at FSG for excellent editing. Much of *The Brothers Story* was written in the mountains of northern California; I owe a great debt of gratitude to Karen Ramey and family for their generosity in letting me use their house at Lake Almanor as a writing retreat.

A final word: I am the mother of a developmentally disabled son, and this novel in some sense grew out of that experience. I'm certainly familiar with the conflict Kit has between his love for his vulnerable brother and his desire to make something of his own gifts. But Christy is not modeled on my son. Christy is a fictional creation and is uniquely himself—as are we all, whatever our abilities.